THE TERRACOTTA DOG

Andrea Camilleri is one of Italy's most famous contemporary writers. His Montalbano series has been adapted for Italian television and translated into nine languages. He lives in Rome.

Stephen Sartarelli is an award-winning translator. He is also the author of three books of poetry, most recently *The Open Vault*. He lives in France.

D0802304

Also by Andrea Camilleri

THE SHAPE OF WATER

THE SNACK THIEF

THE VOICE OF THE VIOLIN

EXCURSION TO TINDARI

THE SCENT OF THE NIGHT

ROUNDING THE MARK

THE PATIENCE OF THE SPIDER

THE PAPER MOON

AUGUST HEAT

THE WINGS OF THE SPHINX

THE TRACK OF SAND

THE POTTER'S FIELD

ANDREA CAMILLERI

THE TERRACOTTA DOG

Translated by Stephen Sartarelli

PICADOR

First published 2002 by Viking Penguin,
a member of Penguin Putnam Inc., New York

First published in Great Britain 2004 by Picador

First published in paperback 2004 by Picador
an imprint of Pan Macmillan, a division of Macmillan Publishers Limited
Pan Macmillan, 20 New Wharf Road, London N1 9RR
Basingstoke and Oxford
Associated companies throughout the world
www.panmacmillan.com

ISBN 978-1-4472-3508-8

Originally published in Italian as *Il cane di terracotta* by Sellerio editore, Palermo.

1 3 5 7 9 8 6 4 2

A CIP catalogue record for this book is available from
the British Library.

Typeset by Intype Libra Ltd
Printed and bound by CPI Group (UK) Ltd, Croydon, CR0 4YY

Visit **www.picador.com** to read more about all our books and to buy
them. You will also find features, author interviews and news of any author
events, and you can sign up for e-newsletters so that you're always first to hear
about our new releases.

THE TERRACOTTA DOG

ONE

To judge from the entrance the dawn was making, it promised to be a very iffy day – that is, blasts of angry sunlight one minute, fits of freezing rain the next, all of it seasoned with sudden gusts of wind – one of those days when someone who is sensitive to abrupt shifts in weather and suffers them in his blood and brain is likely to change opinion and direction continuously, like those sheets of tin, cut in the shape of banners and roosters, that spin every which way on rooftops with each new puff of wind.

Inspector Salvo Montalbano had always belonged to this unhappy category of humanity. It was something passed on to him by his mother, a sickly woman who used to shut herself up in her bedroom, in the dark, whenever she had a headache, and when this happened one could make no noise about the house and had to tread lightly. His father, on the other hand, on stormy seas and smooth, always maintained an even keel, always the same unchanging state of mind, rain or shine.

This time, too, the inspector did not fail to live up to

his inborn nature. No sooner had he stopped his car at the ten-kilometre marker along the Vigàta–Fela highway, as he had been told to do, than he felt like putting it back in gear and returning to town, bagging the whole operation. He managed to control himself, brought the car closer to the edge of the road, opened the glove compartment, and reached for the pistol he normally did not carry on his person. His hand, however, remained poised in mid-air: immobile, spellbound, he stared at the weapon.

Good God! It's real! he thought.

The previous evening, a few hours before Gegè Gullotta called to set up the whole mess – Gegè being a small-time dealer of soft drugs and the manager of an open-air bordello known as 'the Pasture' – the inspector had been reading a detective novel by a writer from Barcelona who greatly intrigued him and had the same surname as he, though hispanicized: Montalbán. One sentence in particular had struck him: 'The pistol slept, looking like a cold lizard.' He withdrew his hand with a slight feeling of disgust and closed the glove compartment, leaving the lizard to its slumber. After all, if the whole business that was about to unfold turned out to be a trap, an ambush, he could carry all the pistols he wanted, and still they would fill him with holes with their Kalashnikovs however and whenever they so desired, thank you and good night. He could only hope that Gegè, remembering the years they'd spent together on the same bench in elementary school and the friendship they'd carried over into adulthood, had not decided, out of self-interest, to sell him like pork at the market, feeding him any old bullshit just to lead him to the slaughter. No, not just any old bullshit: this business, if for real, could be really big, make a lot of noise.

He sighed deeply and began to make his way slowly, step by step, up a narrow, rocky path between broad expanses of vineyard. The vines bore table grapes, with round, firm seeds, the kind called, who knows why, 'Italian grapes', the only kind that would take in this soil. As for trying to grow vines for making wine, you were better off sparing yourself the labour and expense.

The two-storey cottage, one room on top of another, was at the summit of the hill, half hidden by four large Saracen olive trees that nearly surrounded it. It was just as Gegè had described it. Faded, shuttered windows and door, a huge caper bush in front, with some smaller shrubs of touch-me-not – the small, wild cucumber that squirts seeds into the air if you touch it with the tip of a stick – a collapsed wicker chair turned upside down, an old zinc bucket eaten up by rust and now useless. Grass had over-grown everything else. It all conspired to give the impression that the place had been uninhabited for years, but this appearance was deceptive, and experience had made Mon-talbano too savvy to be fooled. In fact, he was convinced somebody was eyeing him from inside the cottage, trying to guess his intentions from the moves he would make. He stopped three steps away from the front of the house, took off his jacket, and hung it from a branch of the olive tree so they could see he wasn't armed. Then he called out without raising his voice much, like a friend come to visit a friend.

'Hey! Anybody home?'

No answer, not a sound. Montalbano pulled a lighter and a packet of cigarettes from his trouser pocket, put a cigarette in his mouth, and lit it, turning round halfway to shelter himself from the wind. That way whoever was inside the house could examine him from behind, having already examined him from the front. He took two puffs, then went to the door and knocked with his fist, hard enough to hurt his knuckles on the crusts of paint on the wood.

'Is there anyone here?' he asked again.

He was ready for anything, except the calm, ironic voice that surprised him from behind.

'Sure there is. Over here.'

*

It had all started with a phone call.

'Hello? Hello? Montalbano! Salvuzzo! It's me, Gegè.'

'I know it's you. Calm down. How are you, my little honey-eyed orange blossom?'

'I'm fine.'

'Working the mouth hard these days? Been perfecting your blow-job techniques?'

'Come on, Salvù, don't start with your usual faggot stuff. You know damn well that I don't work myself. I only make other mouths work for me.'

'But aren't you the instructor? Aren't you the one who

teaches your multicoloured assortment of whores how to hold their lips and how hard to suck?'

'Salvù, even if what you're saying was true, they'd be the ones teaching me. They come to me at age ten already well trained, and at fifteen they're top-of-the-line professionals. I've got a little Albanian fourteen-year-old—'

'You trying to sell me your merchandise now?'

'Listen, I got no time to fuck around. I have something I'm supposed to give you, a package.'

'At this hour? Can't you get it to me tomorrow morning?'

'I won't be in town tomorrow.'

'Do you know what's in the package?'

'Of course. *Mostaccioli* with mulled wine, the way you like 'em. My sister Mariannina made them just for you.'

'How's Mariannina doing with her eyes?'

'Much better. They work miracles in Barcelona.'

'They also write good books in Barcelona.'

'What's that?'

'Never mind. Just talking to myself. Where do you want to meet?'

'The usual place, in an hour.'

＊

The usual place was the little beach of Puntasecca, a short tongue of sand beneath a white marl hill, almost inaccessible by land, or rather, accessible only to Montalbano and Gegè, who back in grade school had discovered a trail that

1

was difficult enough on foot and downright foolhardy to attempt by car. Puntasecca was only a few kilometres from Montalbano's little house by the sea just outside of Vigàta, and that was why he took his time. But the moment he opened the door to go to his rendezvous, the telephone rang.

'Hi, darling. It's me, right on time. How did things go today?'

'Business as usual. And you?'

'Ditto. Listen, Salvo, I've been thinking long and hard about what—'

'Livia, sorry to interrupt, but I haven't got much time. Actually I don't have any time at all. You caught me just as I was going out of the door.'

'All right then, goodnight.'

Livia hung up and Montalbano was left standing with the receiver in his hand. Then he remembered that the night before, he had told her to call him at midnight on the dot, because they would certainly have as much time as they wanted to talk at that hour. He couldn't decide whether to call Livia back right then or when he returned, after his meeting with Gegè. With a pang of remorse, he put the receiver down and went out.

*

When he arrived a few minutes late, Gegè was already waiting for him, pacing back and forth the length of his car. They exchanged an embrace and kissed; it had been a while since they'd seen each other.

'Let's go sit in my car,' said the inspector, 'it's a little chilly tonight.'

'They put me up to this,' Gegè broke in as soon as he sat down.

'Who did?'

'Some people I can't say no to. You know, Salvù, like every businessman, I gotta pay my dues so I can work in peace and keep the Pasture, or they'd put me out to pasture in a hurry. Every month the good Lord sends our way, somebody comes by to collect.'

'For whom? Can you tell me?'

'For Tano the Greek.'

Montalbano shuddered, but didn't let his friend notice. Gaetano 'the Greek' Bennici had never so much as seen Greece, not even through a telescope, and knew as much about things Hellenic as a cast-iron pipe, but he came by his nickname owing to a certain vice thought in the popular imagination to be greatly appreciated in the vicinity of the Acropolis. He had three certain murders under his belt, and in his circles held a position one step below the top bosses. But he was not known to operate in or around Vigàta; it was the Cuffaro and Sinagra families who competed for that territory. Tano belonged to another parish.

'So what's Tano the Greek's business in these parts?'

'What kind of stupid question is that? What kind of fucking cop are you? Don't you know that for Tano the Greek there's no such thing as "these parts" and "those parts" when it comes to women? He was given control and a piece of every whore on the island.'

'I didn't know. Go on.'

'Around eight o'clock this evening the usual guy came by to collect; today was the appointed day for paying dues. He took the money, but then, instead of leaving, he opens his car door and tells me to get in.'

'So what'd you do?'

'I got scared and broke out in a cold sweat. What could I do? I got in, and we drove off. To make a long story short, he took the road for Fela, and stopped after barely half an hour's drive . . .'

'Did you ask him where you were going?'

'Of course.'

'And what did he say?'

'Nothing, as if I hadn't spoken. After half an hour, he makes me get out in some deserted spot without a soul around, and gestures to me to follow some dirt road. There wasn't even a dog around. At a certain point, and I have no idea where he popped out from, Tano the Greek suddenly appears in front of me. I nearly had a stroke, my knees turned to butter. Don't get me wrong, I'm no coward, but the guy's killed five people.'

'Five?'

'Why, how many do you think he's killed?'

'Three.'

'No way. It's five, I guarantee it.'

'Okay, go on.'

'I got to thinking. Since I always pay on time, I figured

Tano wanted to raise the price. Business is good, I got no complaints, and they know it. But I was wrong, it wasn't about money.'

'What did he want?'

'Without even saying hello, he asked me if I knew you.'

Montalbano thought he hadn't heard right.

'If you knew who?'

'You, Salvù, you.'

'And what did you tell him?'

'Well, I was shitting my pants, so I said, yeah, I knew you, but just casually, by sight — you know, hello, how ya doin'. And he looked at me, you gotta believe me, with a pair of eyes that looked like a statue's eyes, motionless, dead, then he leaned his head back and gave this little laugh and asked me if I wanted to know how many hairs I had on my arse 'cause he could tell me within two. What he meant was that he knew everything about me from the cradle to the grave, and I hope that won't be too soon. And so I just looked at the ground and didn't open my mouth. That's when he told me he wanted to see you.'

'When and where?'

'Tonight, at dawn. I'll tell you where in a second.'

'Do you know what he wants from me?'

'I don't know and I don't want to know. He said to rest assured you could trust him like a brother.'

Like a brother. Those words, instead of reassuring Montalbano, sent a shiver down his spine. It was well known that foremost among Tano's three — or five — murder victims was his older brother Nicolino, whom he first strangled and then, in accordance with some mysterious semiological rule, meticulously flayed. The inspector started thinking dark thoughts, which became even darker, if that was possible, at the words that Gegè, putting his hand on his shoulder, then whispered in his ear.

'Be careful, Salvù, the guy's an evil beast.'

*

He was driving slowly back home when the headlights of Gegè's car behind him started flashing repeatedly. He pulled over and Gegè, pulling up, leaned all the way across the seat towards the window on the side closest to Montalbano and handed him a package.

'I forgot the *mostaccioli*.'

'Thanks. I thought it was just an excuse.'

'What do you think I am? Somebody who says something and means something else?'

He accelerated away, offended.

*

The inspector spent the kind of night one tells the doctor about. His first thought was to phone the commissioner, wake him up, and fill him in, to protect himself in the event the affair took any unexpected turns. But Tano the Greek had been explicit, according to Gegè: Montalbano must not say anything to anyone and must come to the appointment alone. This was not, however, a game of cops and robbers: his duty was his duty. That is, he must inform his superiors and plan, down to the smallest details, how to surround and capture the criminal, perhaps with the help of considerable reinforcements. Tano had been a fugitive for nearly ten years, and he, Montalbano, was supposed to go and visit him as if he were some pal just back from America? There was no getting around it, the commissioner must by all means be informed of the matter. He dialed the number of his superior's home in Montelusa, the provincial capital.

'Is that you, love?' murmured the voice of Livia from Boccadasse, Genoa.

Montalbano remained speechless for a moment. Apparently his instinct was leading him away from speaking to the commissioner, making him dial the wrong number.

'Sorry about before. I had just received an unexpected phone call and had to go out.'

'Never mind, Salvo, I know what your work is like. Actually, I'm sorry I got upset. I was just feeling disappointed.'

Montalbano looked at his watch: he had at least three hours before he was supposed to meet Tano.

'If you want, we could talk now.'

'Now? Look, Salvo, it's not to get back at you, but I'd rather not. I took a sleeping pill and can barely keep my eyes open.'

'All right, all right. Till tomorrow, then. I love you, Livia.'

Livia's tone of voice suddenly changed, becoming more awake and agitated.

'Huh? What's wrong? Eh, what's wrong, Salvo?'

'Nothing's wrong. What could be wrong?'

'Oh, no you don't, you're hiding something. Are you about to do something dangerous? Don't make me worry, Salvo.'

'Where do you get such ideas?'

'Tell me the truth, Salvo.'

'I'm not doing anything dangerous.'

'I don't believe you.'

'Why not, for Christ's sake?'

'Because you said "I love you", and since I've known you, you've said it only three times. I've counted them, and every time it was for something out of the ordinary.'

The only hope was to cut the conversation short; with Livia, one could easily end up talking till morning.

'Ciao, my love. Sleep well. Don't be silly. I have to go out again.'

*

So how was he going to pass the time now? He took a shower, read a few pages of the book by Montalbán, understood little, shuffled from one room to the other, straightening a picture, re-reading a letter, a bill, a note, touching everything that came within his reach. He took another shower and shaved, managing to cut himself right on the chin. He turned on the television and immediately shut it off. It made him feel nauseated. Finally, it was time. As he was on his way out, he decided he needed a *mostacciolo*.

With sincere astonishment, he saw that the box on the table had been opened and not a single pastry was left in the cardboard tray. He had eaten them all, too nervous to notice. And what was worse, he hadn't even enjoyed them.

TWO

Montalbano turned around slowly, as if to offset the dull, sudden anger he felt at having let himself be caught unawares from behind like a beginner. For all that he'd been on his guard, he hadn't heard the slightest sound.

One to nothing in your favour, bastard! he thought.

Though he'd never seen him in person, he recognized him at once: as compared with the mugshots from a few years back, Tano had grown his moustache and beard, but the eyes remained the same, expressionless, 'like a statue's', as Gegè had accurately described them.

Tano the Greek gave a short bow, and there wasn't the slightest hint of provocation or mockery in the gesture. Montalbano automatically returned the greeting. Tano threw his head back and laughed.

'We're like two Japanese warriors, the kind with swords and breastplates. What do you call them?'

'Samurai.'

Tano opened his arms, as if wanting to embrace the man standing before him.

'What a pleasure to meet the famous Inspector Montalbano, personally in person.'

Montalbano decided to dispense with the ceremonies and get straight to the point, just to put the encounter on the right footing.

'I'm not sure how much pleasure you'll get from meeting me, sir.'

'Well, you've already given me one.'

'Explain.'

'You called me "sir". That's no small thing. No cop, not a single one — and I've met a lot — has ever called me "sir".'

'You realize, I hope, that I'm a representative of the law, while you are a dangerous fugitive charged with several murders. And here we are, face to face.'

'I'm unarmed. How about you?'

'Me too.'

Tano threw his head back again and gave a full-throated laugh.

'I'm never wrong about people, never!'

'Unarmed or not, I have to arrest you just the same.'

'And I am here, Inspector, to let you arrest me. That's why I wanted to see you.'

He was sincere, no doubt about it. But it was this very sincerity that put Montalbano on his guard, since he couldn't tell where Tano wanted to go with this.

'You could have come to police headquarters and turned yourself in. Here or in Vigàta, it's the same thing.'

'Ah, no, dear Inspector, it is not the same thing. You

surprise me, you who know how to read and write. The words are not the same. I am letting myself be arrested, I am not turning myself in. Go and get your jacket and we'll talk inside. I'll open the door in the meantime.'

Montalbano took his jacket from the olive tree, draped it over his arm, and entered the house behind Tano. It was completely dark inside. The Greek lit an oil lamp and gestured to the inspector to sit down in one of two chairs beside a small table. In the room there was a cot with only a bare mattress, no pillow or sheets, and a glass-fronted cupboard with bottles, glasses, biscuits, plates, packets of pasta, jars of tomato sauce and assorted tin cans. There was also a wood-burning stove with pots and pans hanging over it. But the inspector's eyes came to rest on a far more dangerous animal than the lizard sleeping in the glove compartment of his car: this was a veritable poisonous snake, a machine gun sleeping on its feet, propped against the wall beside the cot.

'I've got some good wine,' said Tano, like a true host.

'All right. Thanks,' replied Montalbano.

What with the cold, the night, the tension, and the two-plus pounds of *mostaccioli* he had wolfed down, he felt he could use some wine.

The Greek poured and then raised his glass.

'To your health.'

The inspector raised his own and returned the toast.

'To yours.'

The wine was something special; it went down beautifully, and on its way gave comfort and heat.

'This is truly good,' Montalbano complimented him.

'Another glass?'

To avoid the temptation, the inspector gruffly pushed the glass away.

'Let's talk.'

'Let's. As I was saying, I decided to let myself be arrested—'

'Why?'

Montalbano's question, fired point-blank, left the other momentarily confused. After a pause, Tano collected himself.

'I need medical care. I'm sick.'

'May I say something? Since you think you know me well, you probably also know that I'm not someone you can fuck with.'

'I'm sure of it.'

'Then why not show me some respect and stop feeding me bullshit?'

'You don't believe I'm sick?'

'I do. But don't try to make me swallow this bullshit that you need to be arrested to get medical help. I'll explain, if you like. You spent a month and a half at Our Lady of Lourdes Clinic in Palermo, then three months at the Gethsemane Clinic of Trapani, where Dr Amerigo Guarnera even operated on you. And although things today are a little different from a few years ago, if you want, you can find plenty of hospitals willing to look the other way and say nothing to the police if you stay there. So it's not because you're sick that you want to be arrested.'

'What if I told you that times are changing and that the wheel is turning fast?'

'That would be a little more convincing.'

'You see, when I was a little kid, my father – who was a man of honour when the word "honour" still meant something – my father, rest his soul, used to tell me that the cart that men of honour travelled on needed a lot of grease to make the wheels turn, to make them go fast. When my father's generation passed on and it was my turn to climb aboard the cart, some of our men said: "Why should we keep on buying the grease we need from the politicians, mayors, bankers and the rest of their kind? Let's make it ourselves! We'll make our own grease!" Great! Bravo! Everyone agreed. Sure, there was still the guy who stole his friend's horse, the guy who blocked the road for some associate of his, the guy who would start shooting blindly at some other gang's cart, horse, and horseman ... But these were all things we could settle among ourselves. The carts multiplied in number, there were more and more roads to travel. Then some genius had a big idea, he asked himself: "What's it mean that we're still travelling by cart? We're too slow," he explained, "we're getting screwed, left behind, everybody else is travelling by car, you can't stop progress!" Great! Bravo! And so everybody ran and traded in their cart for a car and got a driver's licence. Some of them, though, didn't pass the driving-school test and went out, or were pushed out. Then we didn't even have the time to get comfortable with our new cars before the younger guys, the ones who'd been riding in cars since they were born and who'd studied law or economics in the States or Germany, told us our cars were too slow. Now you were supposed to hop in a racing car, a Ferrari, a Maserati equipped with radiophone and fax, so you could take off like a flash of lightning. These kids are new, brand-new, they talk to cellphones instead of people, they don't even know you, don't know who you used to be and if they do, they don't give a fuck. Half the time they don't even know each other, they just talk over the computer. To cut it short, these kids don't ever look anyone in the eye. As soon as they see you in trouble with a slow car, they run you off the road without a second thought and you end up in the ditch with a broken neck.'

'And you don't know how to drive a Ferrari.'

'Exactly. That's why, before I end up dead in a ditch, it's better for me to step aside.'

'But you don't seem to me the type who steps aside of his own choosing.'

'It's my own choosing, Inspector, all my own, I assure you. Of course, there are ways to make someone act freely of his own choosing. Once a friend of mine who was educated and read a lot told me a story which I'm going to repeat to you exactly the way he told it, something he read in a German book. A man says to his friend: "Want to bet my cat will eat hot mustard, the kind that's so hot it makes a hole in your stomach?" "But cats don't like mustard," says his friend. "Well, I can make my cat eat it anyway," says the man. "Do you make him eat it with your fist or with a stick?" asks the friend. "No sirree," says the man, "he eats it freely, of his own choosing." So they make the bet, the man takes a nice spoonful of mustard, the kind that makes your stomach burn just to look at it, picks up the cat and wham! shoves it right up the animal's ass. Poor cat, feeling his asshole burn like that, he starts licking it. And so, licking it up little by little, he eats all the mustard, of his own choosing. And that, my friend, says it all.'

'I see what you mean. Now let's go back to where we started.'

'I was saying I want to be arrested, but I'm going to need some theatricals to save face.'

'I don't understand.'

'Let me explain.'

He explained at great length, drinking a glass of wine from time to time. In the end Montalbano was satisfied with Tano's reasons. But could he trust him? That was the question. In his youth, Montalbano had a great passion for card-playing, which he had luckily grown out of; for this reason he now sensed that Tano was playing him straight, with unmarked cards. He had no choice but to put his faith in this intuition and hope he was not mistaken. And so they meticulously, painstakingly worked out the details of the arrest to ensure that nothing could go wrong. When they had finished talking, the sun was already high in the sky. Before leaving the house and letting the performance begin, the inspector gave Tano a long look, eye to eye.

'Tell me the truth.'

'At your command, Inspector.'

'Why did you choose me?'

'Because you, as you are showing me even now, are someone who understands things.'

*

As he raced headlong down the little path between the vineyards, Montalbano remembered that Agatino Catarella would now be on duty at the station, and that therefore the phone conversation he was about to engage in promised at the very least to be problematic, if not the source of unfortunate and even dangerous misunderstandings. This Catarella was frankly hopeless. Slow to think and slow to act, he had been hired by the police because he was a distant relative of the formerly all-powerful Chamber Deputy Cusumano, who, after spending a summer cooling off in Ucciardone prison, had managed to re-establish solid enough connections with the new people in power to win himself a large slice of the cake, the very same cake that from time to time was miraculously renewed by merely sticking in a few new candied fruits or putting new candles in the place of the ones already melted.

With Catarella, things would get most muddled when-ever he got it in his head — which happened often — to speak in what he called Talian.

One day he had shown up with a troubled look.

'Chief, could you by any chance be able to give me the name of one of those doctors called specialists?'

'Specialist in what, Cat?'

'Gonorrhea.'

Montalbano had looked at him open-mouthed.

'Gonorrhea? You? When did you get that?'

'As I remember, I got it first when I was still a li'l thing, not yet six or seven years old.'

'What the hell are you saying, Cat? Are you sure you mean gonorrhea?'

'Absolutely. Had it all my life, on and off. It's here and gone, here and gone. Gonorrhea.'

✻

In the car, on his way to a telephone booth that was supposed to be near the Torresanta crossroads (supposed to be, that is, unless the receiver had been torn off, the entire telephone had been stolen, or the booth itself had disappeared), Montalbano decided not to call even his second-in-command, Mimì Augello, because he was the type – he couldn't help it – who before anything else would inform the newsmen and then pretend to be surprised when they showed up at the scene. That left only Fazio and Tortorella, the two sergeants or whatever the hell they were called nowadays. He chose Fazio, since Tortorella had been shot in the belly not long before and hadn't yet fully recovered, feeling pain now and then in the wound.

The booth was miraculously still there, the phone miraculously worked, and Fazio picked up before the second ring had finished.

'Fazio, are you already awake at this hour?'

'Sure am, Chief. Less than a minute ago I got a call from Catarella.'

'What did he want?'

'He was speaking Talian so I couldn't make much sense of it. But if I had to guess, I'd say that last night somebody cleaned out Carmelo Ingrassia's supermarket, the great big one just outside of town. They used a large truck or tractor-trailer at the very least.'

'Wasn't there a night watchman?'

'There was, but nobody can find him.'

'Were you on your way there now?'

'Yes.'

'Forget it. Phone Tortorella immediately and tell him to fill Augello in. Let those two take care of it. Tell them you can't go, make up whatever bullshit you can think of, say you fell out of bed and hit your head. No: tell them the carabinieri came and arrested you. Better yet, call them and tell them to notify the carabinieri – it's small potatoes, after all, just some shitty little robbery, and they're always happy when we bring them into our cases. Now listen, here's what I want you to do: notify Tortorella, Augello, and the carabinieri about the theft, then round up Gallo, Galluzzo – Jesus Christ, I feel like I'm running a chicken farm here – and Germanà, and bring them all where I tell you to go. And arm yourselves with sub-machine guns.'

'Shit!'

'Shit is right. This is a big deal and we have to handle it carefully. No one is to whisper even half a word about this, especially Galluzzo with his newsman brother-in-law. And tell that chickenhead Gallo not to drive like he's at Monza. No sirens, no flashing lights. When you splash and muddy the waters, the fish escapes. Now pay attention and I'll explain where you're to meet me.'

*

They arrived very quietly, not half an hour after the phone call, looking like a routine patrol. Getting out of the car, they went up to Montalbano, who signalled them to follow him. They met back up behind a half-ruined house, so they could not be seen from the main road.

'There's a machine gun in the car for you,' said Fazio.

'Stick it up your arse. Now listen: if we play our cards right, we just might bring Tano the Greek home with us.'

Montalbano palpably felt that his men had ceased to breathe for a moment.

'Tano the Greek is around here?' Fazio wondered aloud, being the first to recover.

'I got a good look at him, and it's him. He's grown a moustache and a beard, but you can still recognize him.'

'How did you find him?'

'Never mind, Fazio, I'll explain everything later. Tano's in a little house at the top of that hill. You can't see it from here. There are olive trees all around it. It's a two-room house, one room on top of the other. It's got a door and a window in front; there's another window to the top room, but that's in back. Is that clear? Did you take that all in? Tano's only way out is through the front, unless he decides in desperation to throw himself out of the rear window, though he'd risk breaking his legs. So here's what we'll do: Fazio and Gallo go in the back; me, Germanà, and Galluzzo will break in the door and go inside.'

Fazio looked doubtful.

'What's wrong? Don't you agree?'

'Wouldn't it be better to surround the house and tell him to surrender? It's five against one, he'd never get away.'

'How do you know there's nobody inside the house with Tano?'

Fazio shut up.

'Listen to me,' said Montalbano, concluding his brief war council, 'it's better if we bring him an Easter egg with a surprise inside.'

THREE

Montalbano calculated that Fazio and Gallo must have been in position behind the cottage for at least five minutes. As for him, sprawled belly down on the grass, pistol in hand, with a rock pushing irksomely straight into the pit of his stomach, he felt profoundly ridiculous, like a character in a gangster film, and therefore could not wait to give the signal to raise the curtain. He looked at Galluzzo, who was beside him — Germanà was farther away, to the right — and asked him in a whisper, 'Are you ready?'

'Yessir,' answered the policeman, who was a visible bundle of nerves and sweating. Montalbano felt sorry for him, but couldn't very well come out and tell him that it was all a put-on — of dubious outcome, it was true, but still humbug.

'Go!' he ordered him.

As though launched by a tightly compressed spring and almost not touching the ground, in three bounds Galluzzo reached the house and flattened himself against the wall to the left of the door. He seemed to have done so without effort, though Montalbano could see his chest heaving up and down, breathless. Galluzzo got a firm grip on his sub-machine gun and gestured to the inspector that he was ready for phase two. Montalbano then looked over at Germanà, who seemed not only serene, but actually relaxed.

'I'm going now,' he said to him without a sound, exaggeratedly moving his lips and forming the syllables.

'I'll cover you,' Germanà answered back in the same manner, gesturing with his head towards the machine gun in his hands.

Montalbano's first leap forward was one for the books, or at the very least a training manual: a decisive, balanced ascent from the ground, worthy of a high-jump specialist, a weightless, aerial suspension, and a clean, dignified landing that would have amazed a ballerina. Galluzzo and Germanà, who were watching him from different perspectives, took equal delight in their chief's bodily grace. The start of the second leap was even better calibrated than the first, but something happened in mid-air that caused Montalbano, from his upright posture, to tilt suddenly sideways like the tower of Pisa, then plunge earthward in what looked truly like a clown's routine. After tottering with arms outstretched in search of a non-existent handle to grab onto, he crashed heavily to one side. Instinctively, Galluzzo made a move as if to help him, but stopped himself in time, plastering himself back against the wall. Germanà also stood up a moment, but quickly got back down.

A good thing this was all a sham, the inspector thought. Otherwise Tano could have cut them down like ninepins then and there. Muttering some of the pithiest curses in his vast repertoire, Montalbano began to crawl around in search of the pistol that had slipped from his hand during the fall. At last he spotted it under a touch-me-not bush, but as soon as he stuck his arm in there to retrieve it, all the little cucumbers burst and sprayed his face with seeds. With a certain melancholy rage the inspector realized he'd been demoted from gangster-film hero to a character in an Abbott and Costello movie. No longer in the mood to play the athlete or dancer, he covered the last few yards between him and the house with a few quick steps, merely hunching forward a little.

Montalbano and Galluzzo looked one another in the eye without speaking and agreed on the plan. They positioned themselves three steps from the door, which did not look very resistant, took a deep breath and flung themselves against it with their full weight. The door turned out to be made of tissue paper, or almost – a swat of the hand would have sufficed to push it open – and thus they both found themselves hurtling inside. The inspector managed by some miracle to come to a stop, whereas Galluzzo, carried forward by the violence of his thrust, flew all the way across the room and slammed his face against the wall, crushing his nose and ending up choking on the blood that started to gush violently forth. By the dim light of the oil lamp that Tano had left burning, the inspector was able to appreciate the Greek's consummate acting skills. Pretending to have been surprised awake, he leapt to his feet cursing and hurled himself towards the Kalashnikov, which was now leaning against the table and therefore far from the cot. Montalbano was ready to recite his lines as the foil, as they say in the theatre.

'Stop in the name of the law! Stop or I'll shoot!' he shouted at the top of his lungs, then fired four shots into the ceiling. Tano froze, hands raised. Convinced that someone must be hiding upstairs, Galluzzo fired a burst from his machine gun at the wooden staircase. Outside, Fazio and Gallo, upon hearing all the shooting, opened fire on the little window to discourage anyone from trying that route. With everyone inside the cottage still deaf from the roar of the gunshots, Germanà burst in with the final flourish.

'Don't anybody move or I'll shoot!'

He barely had time to finish uttering his threat when he was bumped from behind by Fazio and Gallo and pushed directly between Montalbano and Galluzzo, who, having set down his weapon, was dabbing his nose with a handkerchief he had taken out of his pocket, the blood having already dripped onto his shirt, tie and jacket. At the sight of him, Gallo became agitated.

'Did he shoot you? The bastard shot you, didn't he?' he yelled in rage, turning towards Tano, who was still standing as patient as a saint in the middle of the room, hands raised, waiting for the forces of order to put some order to the great confusion they were creating.

'No, he didn't shoot me. I ran into the wall,' Galluzzo managed to say with some difficulty. Tano avoided their eyes, looking down at his shoes.

He thinks it's funny, thought Montalbano, then he brusquely ordered Galluzzo, 'Handcuff him.'

'Is it him?' asked Fazio in a soft voice.

'Sure it's him. Don't you recognize him?' said Montalbano.

'What do we do now?'

'Put him in the car and take him to police headquarters in Montelusa. On the way, ring up the commissioner and explain everything. Make sure nobody sees or recognizes the prisoner. The arrest, for the moment, has to remain top secret. Now go.'

'What about you?'

'I'm going to have a look around, search the house. You never know.'

Fazio and the officers, holding the handcuffed Tano between them, started moving towards the door, with Germanà holding the prisoner's Kalishnikov in his hand. Only then did Tano the Greek raise his head and look momentarily at Montalbano. The inspector noticed that the statue-like gaze was gone; now those eyes were animated, almost smiling.

When the group of five had vanished from sight at the bottom of the path, Montalbano went back inside the cottage to begin his search. In fact, he opened the cupboard, grabbed the bottle of wine, which was still half full, and went and sat in the shade of an olive tree, to drink it down in peace. The capture of a dangerous fugitive had been brought to a successful conclusion.

✻

As soon as he saw Montalbano come into the office, Mimì Augello, looking possessed by the devil, put him through the meat grinder.

'Where the hell have you been?! Where've you been hiding? What happened to everybody else? What the fuck is going on here, anyway?'

He must have been really angry to speak so frankly. In the three years they had been working together, the inspector had never heard his assistant use obscenities. Actually, no: the time some arsehole shot Tortorella in the stomach, Augello had reacted the same way.

'Mimì, what's got into you?'

'What's got into me? I got scared, that's what!'

'Scared? Of what?'

'At least six people have phoned here. Their stories all differed as to the details, but they were all in agreement as to the substance: a gunfight with dead and wounded. One of them even called it a bloodbath. You weren't at home. Fazio and the others had gone out with the car without saying a word to anyone . . . So I just put two and two together. Was I wrong?'

'No, you weren't wrong. But you shouldn't blame me, you should blame the telephone. It's the telephone's fault.'

'What's the telephone got to do with it?'

'It's got everything to do with it! Nowadays you've got telephones even in the most godforsaken country haylofts. So what do people do, when there's a phone within reach? They phone. And they say things. True things, imagined things, possible things, impossible things, dreamed-up things like in that Eduardo de Filippo comedy, what's it called, oh yes, *The Voices Inside* — they inflate things and deflate things but never give you their name and surname. They dial emergency numbers where anyone can say the craziest bullshit in the world without ever assuming any responsibility for it! And meanwhile the Mafia experts get all excited because they think *omertà* is on the decline in Sicily! No more complicity! No more fear! Hah! I'll tell you what's on the decline: my arse is on the decline, and meanwhile the phone bill is on the rise.'

'Montalbano! Stop confusing me with your chatter! Were there any dead and wounded or not?'

'Of course not. There was no gunfight. We just fired a few shots into the air, Galluzzo smashed his nose all by himself, and the guy surrendered.'

'What guy?'

'A fugitive.'

'Yeah, but who?'

Catarella arrived breathless and spared him the embarrassment of answering.

'Chief, that would be his honour the commissioner on the phone.'

'I'll tell you later,' said Montalbano, fleeing into his office.

*

'My dear friend, I want to give you my most heartfelt congratulations.'

'Thank you.'

'You really hit the bullseye this time.'

'We got lucky.'

'Apparently the man in question is even more important than he himself let on.'

'Where is he now?'

'On his way to Palermo. The Anti-Mafia Commission insisted; they wouldn't take no for an answer. Your men weren't even allowed to stop in Montelusa; they had to drive on. I sent along an escort car with four of my men to keep them company.'

'So you didn't speak with Fazio?'

'I didn't have the time or the chance. I know almost nothing about this case. So, actually, I'd appreciate it if you could pass by my office this afternoon and fill me in on the details.'

Ay, there's the hitch, thought Montalbano, remembering a nineteenth-century translation of Hamlet's monologue. But he merely asked, 'At what time?'

'Let's say around five. Ah, also, Palermo wants absolute secrecy about the operation, at least for now.'

'If it was only up to me . . .'

'I wasn't referring to you, since I know you well and can say that compared to you, even fish are a talkative species. Listen, by the way . . .'

There was a pause. The commissioner had broken off and Montalbano didn't feel like saying anything: a troubling alarm bell had gone off in his head at the sound of that laudatory 'I know you well.'

'Listen, Montalbano,' the commissioner hesitantly started over, and with that hesitation the alarm began to ring more loudly.

'Yes, Commissioner?'

'I'm afraid that this time there's no way I can prevent your promotion to assistant commissioner.'

'*Madunnuzza biniditta!* Why not?'

'Don't be silly, Montalbano.'

'Well, I'm sorry, but why should I be promoted?'

'What a question! Because of what you did this morning.'

Montalbano felt simultaneously hot and cold: he had sweat on his forehead and chills down his spine. The prospect terrorized him.

'I didn't do anything different from what my colleagues do every day, Commissioner.'

'I don't doubt it. But this particular arrest, when it comes to be known, will cause quite a stir.'

'So there's no hope?'

'Come on, don't be childish.'

The inspector felt like a tuna caught in the net, the chamber of death. He began to feel short of breath, mouth opening and closing on emptiness. Then he tried a desperate suggestion:

'Couldn't we blame Fazio?'

'Blame?'

'I'm sorry, I meant couldn't we give him the credit?'

'See you later, Montalbano.'

*

Augello, who was lurking behind the door, made a questioning face.

'What'd the commissioner say?'

'We spoke about the situation.'

'Oh, right! You should see the look on your face!'

'What look?'

'Like you've been to a funeral.'

'I had trouble digesting what I ate last night.'

'Anything interesting?'

'Three pounds of *mostaccioli*.'

Augello looked at him in dismay. Montalbano, sensing that he was about to ask him the name of the arrested fugitive, used the opportunity to change the subject and put him on another track.

'Did you guys ever find the night watchman?'

'The one in the supermarket? Yeah, I found him myself. The thieves bashed him in the head, then bound and gagged him and threw him in a great big freezer.'

'Is he dead?'

'No, but I don't think he's feeling very alive either. When we pulled him out, he looked like a giant frozen stockfish.'

'Any idea which way they went?'

'I've got half an idea myself and the carabinieri lieutenant has another. But one thing is certain: to haul all that stuff, they had to use a heavy truck. And there must have been a team of at least six people to load it, under the command of some professional.'

'Listen, Mimì, I have to run home and change my clothes. I'll be right back.'

✻

Near Marinella he noticed that the reserve light for the gas tank was flashing. He stopped at the same filling station where there'd been a drive-by shooting a while back, when he'd had to bring in the attendant to get him to talk. Upon seeing the inspector, the attendant, who bore him no grudge, greeted him in his usual high-pitched voice, which made Montalbano shudder. After filling the tank, the attendant counted the money and eyed the inspector.

'What's wrong? Didn't I give you enough?'

'No sir. There's enough money here, all right. I just wanted to tell you something.'

'Let's have it,' Montalbano said impatiently. If the guy went on talking, even a little, his nerves would give out.

'Look at that truck over there.'

And he pointed at a large tractor-trailer parked in the lot behind the filling station, tarps pulled down tight to hide the cargo.

'It was already here early this morning,' he continued, 'when I opened up. Now it's been four hours and still nobody's come to get it.'

'Did you look to see if anyone's sleeping in the cab?'

'Yessir, I looked, there's nobody. And another weird

thing: the keys are still in the ignition. The first soul to come along could start it up and drive it away.'

'Show me,' said Montalbano, suddenly interested.

FOUR

A tiny man with rat-tail moustaches, an unpleasant smile, gold-framed glasses, brown shoes, brown socks, brown suit, brown shirt, brown tie, a veritable nightmare in brown, Carmelo Ingrassia, owner of the supermarket, pressed the crease in his trousers with his fingers, right leg crossed over the left, and repeated his succinct interpretation of events for the third time.

'It was a joke, Inspector, a practical joke that somebody, I guess, wanted to play on me.'

Montalbano was lost in contemplation of the ballpoint pen he held in his hand. Concentrating his attention on the cap, he removed it, examined it inside and out as though he had never seen so strange a gizmo, blew into it as if to cleanse it of some invisible speck of dust, looked at it again, remained unsatisfied, blew into it again, put it down on the desk, unscrewed the pen's metal tip, thought about this for a moment, set it down alongside the cap, carefully considered the piece remaining in his hand, lined this up near the other two pieces, and sighed deeply. This allowed him to calm down and check the impulse – which for a second had nearly overwhelmed him – to get up, go over to Ingrassia, punch him in the face, and ask, 'Now tell me truthfully: in your opinion, am I joking or am I serious?'

Tortorella, who was present for the interview and knew his chief's reactions well, visibly relaxed.

'Let me try and understand,' said Montalbano, in full control of himself.

'What's to understand, Inspector? It's all clear as day. The stolen goods were all in the truck that you found. Not one toothpick was missing, not a single lollipop. So, if they didn't do it to rob me, they must have done it as a joke, for fun.'

'You'll have to be patient with me, Mr Ingrassia, I'm a little slow in the head. So: eight days ago, from a depot in Catania – that is, on the other side of the island – two people steal a truck with a trailer belonging to the Sferlazza company. At that moment the truck is empty. For eight days they keep this truck out of sight, hiding it somewhere between Catania and Vigàta, since it wasn't seen in circulation. Logically speaking, therefore, the only reason that truck was stolen and hidden was to take it out of circulation, when the time was right, to play a joke on you. Let me continue. Last night the truck rematerializes and around one a.m., when there's almost nobody on the streets, it stops in front of your supermarket. The night watchman thinks it's there to bring in new stocks, even at that odd hour. We don't know exactly how things went, the watchman still can't talk, but we do know that they put him out of commission, took his keys, and went inside. One of the thieves stripped the watchman and put on his uniform. This, I must say, was a brilliant move. The next brilliant move was that the others turned on the lights and got down to work in plain sight, taking no precautions – in broad daylight, one might say, if it wasn't night. Ingenious, no doubt about it. Because a stranger passing through the neighbourhood, noticing the watchman in uniform overseeing a few people loading a truck, would never dream that he was actually witnessing a robbery. This is the reconstruction of events offered by my colleague Augello; it was confirmed by the testimony of Cavaliere Misuraca, who was on his way home at the time.'

At the mention of that name, Ingrassia, who had seemed to be losing interest as the inspector went on, sat up in his chair as if stung by a wasp.

'Misuraca?!'

'Yes, the one who used to work at the Records Office.'

'But he's a Fascist!'

'I don't see what the cavaliere's political beliefs have to do with the case we're discussing.'

'They have everything to do with it! Because when I used to be involved in politics, he was my enemy.'

'You're no longer involved in politics?'

'What's to be involved in any more! With that handful of Milanese judges who've decided to ruin politics, commerce and industry, all at the same time!'

'Listen, the cavaliere merely gave a testimonial establishing the modus operandi of the thieves.'

'I don't give a shit what the cavaliere was establishing. He's an old geezer who can't even remember when he turned eighty. He's so senile he's liable to see a cat and say it's an elephant. What was he doing out at that time of the night anyway?'

'I don't know, I'll ask him. Shall we get back to the subject?'

'Fine.'

'Once it was loaded, at your supermarket, after at least two hours of labour, the truck leaves. It drives three or four miles, turns around, parks in the lot behind the filling station, and remains there until I find it. And, in your opinion, someone went through this whole elaborate set-up, committed half a dozen crimes, risking years in jail, just so he, or you, could have a good laugh?'

'Inspector, we could stay here all day arguing, but I swear to you that I can't imagine how it could have been anything but a joke.'

*

In the refrigerator Montalbano found a plate of cold pasta with tomatoes, basil, and black *passuluna* olives that gave off an aroma to wake the dead, and a second course of fresh anchovies with onions and vinegar. Montalbano was in the habit of trusting entirely in the simple but zestful culinary imagination of Adelina, the housekeeper who came once a day to see to his needs, a mother of two irremediably delinquent sons, one of whom was still in jail, put there by Montalbano. And this day, too, she did not disappoint him. Every time he was about to open the oven or fridge, he still felt the same trepidation he used to feel as a little boy when, on the second of November, he would look for the wicker basket in which the dead had left their gifts during the night – a celebration now lost, obliterated by the banality of presents under the Christmas tree, obliterated like the memory of the dead themselves. The only ones who did not forget their dead, and who indeed tenaciously kept their memory burning, were the mafiosi; but the presents they sent in remembrance were certainly not little tin trains or marzipan fruits.

Surprise, in short, was an indispensable spice in Adelina's dishes.

He took his two courses, a bottle of wine, and some bread to the table, turned on the television, and sat down to dinner. He loved to eat alone, relishing every bite in silence. This was yet another bond that tied him to Livia, who never opened her mouth when she ate. It occurred to him that in matters of taste he was closer to Maigret than to Pepe Carvalho, the protagonist of Montalbán's novels, who stuffed himself with dishes that would have set a shark's belly on fire.

On the national television stations, an ill wind of malaise was blowing. The governing majority found itself split over a law that would deny early prison release to those who had eaten up half the country; the magistrates who had laid bare the dirty secrets of political corruption were resigning in protest; and there was a faint breeze of revolt animating the interviews with people in the street.

He switched to the first of the two local TV stations. TeleVigàta was pro-government by congenital faith, whether the government was red, black, or sky blue. The news reporter made no mention of the capture of Tano the Greek, stating only that a few conscientious citizens had alerted the Vigàta police of a lively but mysterious shoot-out at dawn in the rural area known as 'the Walnut', and that investigators, after arriving promptly at the scene, had found nothing unusual. The newscaster for the Free Channel, Nicolò Zito, who did not hide his Communist sympathies, likewise failed to mention Tano's arrest. Which seemed to indicate that the news, fortunately, had not leaked out. But then, out of the blue, Zito started talking about the bizarre robbery at the Ingrassia supermarket and the inexplicable rediscovery of the truck with all the stolen merchandise. The common opinion, reported Zito, was that the vehicle must have been abandoned following an argument between the robbers over how to divide up the loot. Zito, however, did not agree. In his opinion, things had gone differently; the real explanation was surely far more complicated.

'And so I appeal directly to you, Inspector Montalbano. Is it not true that there must be more to this story than meets the eye?' the newsman asked, closing his report.

Hearing himself personally addressed and seeing Zito's eyes looking out at him from the screen as he was eating,

Montalbano let the wine he was drinking go down the wrong way and started coughing and cursing.

After finishing his meal, he put on his bathing suit and dived into the sea. It was freezing cold, but the swim brought him back to life.

*

'Now tell me exactly how it all happened,' said the commissioner.

After admitting the inspector into his office, he had stood up and gone right over to him, embracing him warmly.

One thing about Montalbano was that he was incapable of deceiving or stringing along people he knew were honest or who inspired his admiration. With crooks and people he didn't like, he could spin out the flimflam with the straightest of faces and was capable of swearing he'd seen the moon trimmed in lace. The fact that he not only admired his superior, but had actually at times spoken to him as to a father, now put him, after the other's command, in a state of agitation: he blushed, began to sweat, kept squirming in his chair as if he were under cross-examination. The commissioner noticed his uneasiness but attributed it to the discomfort that Montalbano genuinely felt whenever he had to talk about a particularly successful operation. The commissioner had not forgotten that at the last press conference, in front of the TV cameras, the inspector had expressed himself – if you could call it that – in long, painful stammerings at times devoid of common meaning, eyes bulging, pupils dancing as if he were drunk.

'I'd like some advice, before I begin.'

'At your service.'

'What should I write in the report?'

'What kind of question is that? Have you never written a report before? In reports you write down what happened,' the commissioner replied curtly, a bit astonished. And since Montalbano hadn't yet made up his mind to speak, he continued. 'In other words, you say you were able to take advantage of a chance encounter and turn it into a successful police operation, skilfully, courageously, it's true, but—'

'Look, I just wanted to say—'

'Let me finish. I can't help but notice that you took a big risk, and exposed your men to grave danger – you should have asked for substantial reinforcements, taken due precaution. Luckily, it all went well. But it was a gamble. That's what I'm trying to tell you, in all sincerity. Now let's hear your side.'

Montalbano studied the fingers on his left hand as if they had just sprouted spontaneously and he didn't know what they were there for.

'What's wrong?' the commissioner asked.

'What's wrong is that it's all untrue!' Montalbano burst out. 'There wasn't any chance encounter. I went to talk with Tano because he had asked to see me. And at that meeting we made an agreement.'

The commissioner ran his hand over his eyes.

'An agreement?'

'Yes, on everything.'

And while he was at it, he told him the whole story, from Gegè's phone call to the farce of the arrest.

'Is there anything else?' the commissioner asked when it was over.

'Yes. Things being what they are, in no way do I deserve to be promoted to assistant commissioner. If I were promoted, it would be for a lie, a deception.'

'Let me be the judge of that,' the commissioner said brusquely.

He got up, put his hands behind his back, and stood there thinking a moment. Then he made up his mind and turned around.

'Here's what we'll do. Write me two reports.'

'Two?' said Montalbano, mindful of the effort it normally cost him to apply ink to paper.

'Don't argue. The fake report I'll leave lying around for the inevitable mole who will make sure to leak it to the press or to the Mafia. The real one I'll put in the safe.'

He smiled.

'And as for this promotion business, which seems to be what terrifies you most, come to my house on Friday evening and we'll talk it over a little more calmly. My wife has invented a fabulous new sauce for sea bream.'

✻

Cavaliere Gerlando Misuraca, who carried his eighty-four years belligerently, was true to form, going immediately on the offensive as soon as the inspector said, 'Hello?'

'Who is that imbecile who transferred my call?'

'Why, what did he do?'

'He couldn't understand my surname! He couldn't get it into that thick head of his! "Bizugaga", he called me!' He paused warily, then changed his tone. 'Can you assure me, on your word of honour, that he's just some poor bastard who doesn't know any better?'

Realizing that it was Catarella who had answered the phone, Montalbano could reply with conviction.

'I can assure you. But why, may I ask, do you need my assurance?'

'Because if he meant to make fun of me or what I represent, I'll be down there at the station in five minutes and will give him such a thrashing, by God, he won't be able to walk!'

And just what did Cavaliere Misuraca represent? Montalbano wondered while the other continued to threaten to do terrible things. Nothing, absolutely nothing from a, so to speak, official point of view. A municipal employee long since retired, he did not hold nor had he ever held any public office, being merely a card-carrying member of his party. A man of unassailable honesty, he lived a life of dignified quasi-poverty. Even in the days of Mussolini, he had refused to seek personal gain, having always been a 'faithful follower', as one used to say back then. In return, from 1935 onwards, he had fought in every war and been in the thick of the worst battles. He hadn't missed a single one, and indeed seemed to have a gift for being everywhere at once, from Guadalajara, Spain, to Bir el Gobi in North

Africa by way of Axum, Ethiopia. Followed by imprisonment, his refusal to cooperate, and an even harsher imprisonment as a result, on nothing but bread and water. He therefore represented, Montalbano concluded, the historical memory of what were, of course, historic mistakes, but he had lived them with a naive faith and paid for them with his own skin: among several serious injuries, one had left him lame in his left leg.

'Tell me,' Montalbano had mischievously asked him one day face to face, 'if you'd been able, would you have gone to fight at Salò, alongside the Germans and the *repubblichini*?' In his way, the inspector was sort of fond of the old Fascist. How could he not be? In that circus of corrupters and corrupted, extortionists and grafters, bribe-takers, liars, thieves and perjurers – turning up each day in new combinations – Montalbano had begun to feel a kind of affection for people he knew to be incurably honest.

At this question, the old man had seemed to deflate from within, the wrinkles on his face multiplying as his eyes began to fog over. Montalbano then understood that Misuraca had asked himself the same question a thousand times and had never been able to come up with an answer. So he did not insist.

'Hello? Are you still there?' Misuraca's peevish voice asked.

'At your service, Cavaliere.'

'I just remembered something. Which is why I didn't mention it when I gave my testimony.'

'I have no reason to doubt you, Cavaliere. I'm all ears.'

'A strange thing happened to me when I was almost in front of the supermarket, but at the time I didn't pay it much mind. I was nervous and upset because these days there are certain bastards about who—'

'Please come to the point, Cavaliere.'

If one let him speak, Misuraca was capable of taking his story back to the foundation of the first Fascist militias.

'Actually, I can't tell you over the phone. I need to see you in person. It's something really big, if I saw right.'

The old man was considered someone who always told things straight, without overstating or understating the case.

'Is it about the robbery at the supermarket?'

'Of course.'

'Have you already discussed it with anybody?'

'Nobody.'

'Don't forget: not a word to anyone.'

'Are you trying to insult me? Silent as the grave, I am. I'll be at your office early tomorrow morning.'

'Just out of curiosity, Cavaliere, what were you doing, alone and upset, in your car at that hour of the night? You know, after a certain age, one must be careful.'

'I was on my way back from Montelusa, from a meeting of the local party leaders. I'm not one of them, of course, but I wanted to be present. Nobody shuts his door on Gerlando Misuraca. Someone has to save our party's honour. They can't continue to govern alongside those bastard sons of bastard politicians and agree to an ordinance allowing all the sons of bitches who devoured our country out of jail! You must understand, Inspector—'

'Did the meeting end late?'

'It went on till one o'clock in the morning. I wanted to continue, but everyone else was against it. They were all falling asleep. They've got no balls, those people.'

'And how long did it take you to get back to Vigàta?'

'Half an hour. I drive slowly. But as I was saying—'

'Excuse me, Cavaliere, I'm wanted on another line,' Montalbano cut him off. 'See you tomorrow.'

FIVE

'Worse than criminals! Worse than murderers! That's how those dirty sons of bitches treated us! Who do they think they are? The fuckers!'

There was no calming down Fazio, who had just returned from Palermo. Germanà, Gallo and Galluzzo served as his psalmodizing chorus, wildly gesticulating to convey the exceptional nature of the event.

'Total insanity! Total insanity!'

'Simmer down, boys. Let's proceed in an orderly fashion,' Montalbano ordered, imposing his authority.

Then, noticing that Galluzzo's shirt and jacket no longer bore traces of the blood from his crushed nose, the inspector asked him, 'Did you go home and change before coming here?'

'Home? Home? Didn't you hear what Fazio said? We've just come from Palermo, we came straight back! When we got to the Anti-Mafia Commission and turned over Tano the Greek, they took us one by one and put us in separate rooms. Since my nose was still hurting, I wanted to put a wet handkerchief over it. I'd been sitting there for half an hour, and still nobody'd shown up, so I opened the door and found an officer standing in front of me. Where you going? he says. I'm going to get a little water for my nose. You can't leave, he says, go back inside. Get that, Inspector? I was under guard! Like *I* was Tano the Greek!'

'Don't mention that name and lower your voice!' Montalbano scolded him. 'Nobody is supposed to know that we caught him! The first one who talks gets his arse kicked all the way to Asinara.'

'We were all under guard,' Fazio cut in, indignant.

Galluzzo continued his story: 'An hour later some guy I know entered the room, a colleague of yours who was kicked upstairs to the Anti-Mafia Commission. I think his name is Sciacchitano.'

A perfect arsehole, the inspector thought, but said nothing.

'He looked at me as if I smelt bad or something, like some beggar. Then he kept on staring at me, and finally he said: "You know, you can't very well present yourself to the Prefect looking like that."'

Still feeling hurt by the absurd treatment, he had trouble keeping his voice down.

'The amazing thing was that he had this pissed-off look in his eye, like it was all my fault! Then he left, muttering to himself. Later a cop came in with a clean shirt and jacket.'

'Now let me talk,' Fazio butted in, pulling rank. 'To make a long story short, from three o'clock in the afternoon to midnight yesterday, every one of us was interrogated eight times by eight different people.'

'What did they want to know?'

'How the arrest came about.'

'Actually, I was interrogated ten times,' said Germanà with a certain pride. 'I guess I tell a good story, and for them it was like being at the movies.'

'Around one o'clock in the morning they gathered us together,' Fazio continued, 'and put us in a great big room, a kind of large office, with two sofas, eight chairs and four tables. They unplugged the telephones and took them away. Then they sent in four stale sandwiches and four warm beers that tasted like piss. We got as comfortable as we could, and at eight the next morning some guy came in and said we could go back to Vigàta. No good morning, no goodbye, not even "get outta here" like you say to get rid of the dog. Nothing.'

'All right,' said Montalbano. 'What can you do? Go on home now, rest up, and come back here in the late afternoon. I promise you I'll take this whole business up with the commissioner.'

✳

'Hello? This is Inspector Salvo Montalbano from Vigàta. I'd like to speak with Inspector Arturo Sciacchitano.'

'Please hold.'

Montalbano grabbed a sheet of paper and a pen. He

started doodling without paying attention and only later noticed he had drawn a pair of buttocks on a toilet seat.

'I'm sorry, the inspector's in a meeting.'

'Listen, please tell him I'm also in a meeting, that way we're even. He can interrupt his for five minutes, I'll do the same with mine, and we'll both be happy as babies.'

He appended a few turds to the shitting buttocks.

'Montalbano? What is it? Sorry, but I haven't got much time.'

'Me neither. Listen, Sciacchitanov—'

'Eh? Sciacchitanov? What the hell are you saying?'

'Isn't that your real name? You mean you don't belong to the KGB?'

'I'm not in the mood for jokes, Montalbano.'

'Who's joking? I'm calling you from the commissioner's office, and he's very upset over the KGB-style treatment you gave my men. He promised me he'd write to the interior minister this very day.'

The phenomenon cannot be explained, and yet it happened: Montalbano actually saw Sciacchitano, universally known as a pusillanimous arse-lick, turn pale over the telephone line. His lie had the same effect on the man as a baton to the head.

'What are you saying? You have to understand that I, as defender of public safety—'

Montalbano interrupted him.

'Safety doesn't preclude politeness,' he said pithily, sounding like one of those road signs that say: BE POLITE, FOR SAFETY'S SAKE.

'But I was extremely polite! I even gave them beer and sandwiches!'

'I'm sorry to say, despite the beer and sandwiches, there will be consequences higher up. But cheer up, Sciacchitano, it's not your fault. You can't fit a square peg into a round hole.'

'What do you mean?'

'I mean that you, being a born arsehole, will never be a decent, intelligent person. Now, I demand that you write a letter, addressed to me, praising my men to the skies. And I want it by tomorrow. Goodbye.'

'Do you think if I write the letter, the commissioner will let it drop?'

'To be perfectly honest, I don't know. But if I were you, I'd write that letter. And I might even date it yesterday. Got that?'

*

He felt better now, having let off some steam. He called Catarella.

'Is Inspector Augello in his office?'

'No sir, but he just now phoned. He said that, figuring he was about ten minutes away, he'd be here in about ten minutes.'

Montalbano took advantage of the time to start writing the fake report. The real one he'd written at home the night before. At a certain point Augello knocked and entered.

'You were looking for me?'

'Is it really so hard for you to come to work a little earlier?'

'Sorry, but in fact I was busy till five o'clock in the morning. Then I went home and drifted off to sleep, and that was that.'

'Busy with one of those whores you like so much? The kind that pack two hundred and fifty pounds of flesh into a tight little dress?'

'Didn't Catarella tell you?'

'He told me you'd be coming in late.'

'Last night, around two, there was a fatal car accident. I went to the scene myself, thinking I'd let you sleep, since the thing was of no importance to us.'

'To the people who died, it was certainly important.'

'There was only one victim. He took the downhill stretch of the Catena at high speed – apparently his brakes weren't working – and ended up wedged under a truck that had started coming up the slope in the opposite direction. The poor guy died instantly.'

'Did you know him?'

'I sure did. So did you. Cavaliere Misuraca.'

*

'Montalbano? I just got a call from Palermo. They want us to hold a press conference. And that's not all: they want it to make some noise. That's very important. It's part of their strategy. Journalists from other cities will be there, and it will be reported on the national news. It's going to be a big deal.

'They want to show that the new government is not letting up in the fight against the Mafia, and that, on the contrary, they will be more resolute, more relentless than ever—

'Is something wrong, Montalbano?'

'No. I was just imagining the next day's headlines.'

'The press conference is scheduled for noon tomorrow. I just wanted to give you advance warning.'

'Thank you, sir, but what have I got to do with any of it?'

'Montalbano, I am a nice man, a kind man, but only up to a point. You have everything to do with it! Stop being so childish!'

'What am I supposed to say?'

'Good God, Montalbano! Say what you wrote in the report.'

'Which one?'

'I'm sorry, what did you say?'

'Nothing.'

'Just try to speak clearly, don't mumble, and keep your head up. And – Oh, yes, your hands. Decide once and for all where you're going to put them and keep them there. Don't do like last time, where the correspondent of the *Corriere* offered aloud to cut them off for you, to make you feel more comfortable.'

'And what if they question me?'

'Of course they'll "question" you, to use your odd phrasing. They're journalists, aren't they? Good-day.'

*

Too agitated by everything that was happening and was going to happen the following day, Montalbano had to leave the office. He went out, stopped at the usual shop, bought a small bag of *càlia e simenza*, and headed towards the jetty. When he was at the foot of the lighthouse and about to turn back, he found himself face to face with Ernesto Bonfiglio, the owner of a travel agency and a very good friend of the recently deceased Cavaliere Misuraca.

'Isn't there anything we can do?' Bonfiglio blurted out at him aggressively.

Montalbano, who was trying to dislodge a small fragment of peanut stuck between two teeth, merely looked at him, befuddled.

'I'm asking if there's anything we can do,' Bonfiglio repeated resentfully, giving him a hostile look in return.

'Do about what?'

'About my poor dead friend.'

'Would you like some?' asked the inspector, holding out the bag.

'Thanks,' said the other, taking a handful of *càlia e simenza*.

The pause allowed Montalbano to put the man he was speaking to in better perspective: Bonfiglio, aside from being

like a brother to the late cavaliere, was a man who held
extreme right-wing ideas and was not all there in the head.

'You mean Misuraca?'

'No, I mean my grandfather.'

'And what am I supposed to do?'

'Arrest the murderers. It's your duty.'

'And who would these murderers be?'

'Who they *are*, not "would be". I'm referring to the
local party leaders, who were unworthy to have him in their
ranks. *They* killed him.'

'I beg your pardon. Wasn't it an accident?'

'Oh, I suppose you think accidents just happen acci-
dentally?'

'I would say so.'

'You would be wrong. If someone's looking for an
accident, there's always somebody else ready to send one
his way. Let me cite an example to illustrate my point. This
last February Mimì Crapanzano drowned when he went for
a swim. An accidental death, they said. But here I ask you:
how old was Mimì when he died? Fifty-five years old. Why,
at that age, did he get this brilliant idea to go for a swim
in the cold, like he used to do when he was a kid? The
answer is because less than three months before, he had got
married to a Milanese girl twenty-four years younger than
him, and one day, when they were out strolling on the
beach, she asked him: "Is it true, darling, that you used to
swim in this sea in February?" "It sure is," replied Crapanzano. The girl, who apparently was already tired of the old
man, sighed. "What's wrong?" Crapanzano asked, like an

idiot. "I'm sorry I won't ever have a chance to see you do it again," said the slut. Without saying a word, Crapanzano took off his clothes and jumped into the water. Does that clarify my point?'

'Perfectly.'

'Now, to get back to the party leaders of Montelusa province. After a first meeting ended with harsh words, they held another last night. The cavaliere, along with a few other people, wanted the chapter to issue a press release protesting against the government's ordinance granting amnesty to crooks. Others saw things differently. At a certain point, some guy called Misuraca a geezer, another said he looked like something out of the puppet theatre, a third man called him a senile wreck. I learned all these things from a friend who was there. Finally, the secretary, some jerk who's not even Sicilian and goes by the name of Biraghìn, asked him please to vacate the premises, since he had no authorization whatsoever to attend the meeting. Which was true, but no one had ever dared say this before. So Gerlando got in his little Fiat and headed back home to Vigàta. His blood was boiling, no doubt about it, but the others had made him lose his head on purpose. And you're going to tell me it was an accident?'

The only way to reason with Bonfiglio was to put oneself squarely on his level. The inspector knew this from experience.

'Is there one television personality you find particularly obnoxious?' he asked him.

'There are a hundred thousand, but Mike Bongiorno is

the worst. Whenever I see him, my stomach gets all queasy and I feel like smashing the screen.'

'Good. And if, after watching this particular MC, you get in your car, drive into a wall, and kill yourself, what am I supposed to do, in your opinion?'

'Arrest Mike Bongiorno,' the other said firmly.

*

He went back to the office feeling calmer. His encounter with the logic of Ernesto Bonfiglio had distracted and amused him.

'Any news?' he asked as he walked in.

'There's a personal letter for you that came just now in the mail,' said Catarella, repeating, for emphasis, 'Person-al.'

On his desk he found a postcard from his father and some office memos.

'Hey, Cat! Where'd you put the letter?'

'I said it was personal!' Catarella said defensively.

'What's that supposed to mean?'

'It means that you have to receive it in person, it being personal and all.'

'Okay. The person is here in front of you. Where's the letter?'

'It's gone where it was supposed to go. Where the person personally lives. I told the postman to deliver it to your house, Chief, your personal residence, in Marinella.'

*

Standing in front of the Trattoria San Calogero, catching a breath of air, was the cook and owner.

'Where you going, Inspector? Not coming in?'

'I'm eating at home today.'

'Whatever you say. But I've got some rock lobster ready for the grill that'll seem like you're not eating them, but dreaming them.'

Montalbano went inside, won over by the image more than the desire. Then, after finishing his meal, he pushed the dishes away, crossed his arms on the table, and fell asleep. He always ate in a small room with three tables, and so it was easy for Serafino, the waiter, to steer customers towards the big dining room and leave the inspector in peace. Around four o'clock, with the restaurant already closed, the proprietor, noticing that Montalbano was showing no signs of life, made him a cup of coffee, then gently woke him up.

SIX

As for the personally personal letter earlier announced by
Catarella, he'd completely forgotten about it. It came back
to him only when he stepped right on it upon entering his
home: the postman had slipped it under the door. The
address made it look like an anonymous letter: MONTALBANO
— POLICE HEADQUARTERS — CITY. Then, on the upper left,
the inscription: PERSONAL. Which had then set Catarella's
earthquake-damaged wits in motion.

Anonymous it was not, however. On the contrary. The
signature that Montalbano immediately looked for at the
end went off in his brain like a gunshot.

Esteemed Inspector,

*It occurred to me that in all probability I won't be able to come
to see you tomorrow morning as planned. If the meeting of the Party
leadership of Montelusa, which I shall attend upon completing this letter,
were by chance — as appears quite likely — to spell failure for my
positions, I believe it would be my duty to go to Palermo to try and
awaken the souls and consciences of those comrades who make the
decisions within the Party. I am even ready to fly to Rome to request*

an audience with the National Secretary. These intentions, if realized, would necessitate the postponement of our meeting, and thus I beg you please to excuse me for putting in writing what I ought properly to have told you in person.

As you will surely recall, the day after the strange robbery/ non-robbery at the supermarket, I came of my own accord to police headquarters to report what I had happened to see — that is, a group of men quietly at work, however odd the hour, with lights on and under the supervision of a uniformed man who looked to me like the night watchman. No passer-by would have seen anything unusual in this scene; had I noticed anything out of the ordinary, I would have made sure to alert the police myself.

The night following my testimony, I was too upset from the arguments I'd had with my Party colleagues to fall asleep, and thus I had occasion to review the scene of the robbery in my mind. Only then did I remember a detail that could prove to be very important. On my way back from Montelusa, agitated as I was, I took the wrong approach route for Vigàta, one that has been recently made very complicated by a series of incomprehensible one-way streets. Instead of taking the Via Granet, I turned onto the old Via Lincoln and found myself going against the flow of traffic. After realizing my mistake about fifty yards down the street, I decided to retrace my path in reverse, completing my manoeuvre at the corner of Vicolo Trupìa, thinking I would back into this street, so that I could then point my car in the right direction. I was unable to do this, however, because the vicolo was entirely blocked by a large car, a model heavily advertised these days but available only in very limited quantities, the 'Ulysses', licence plate Montelusa 328280. At this point I had no choice but to proceed in my directional violation. A few yards down the street, I came out into the Piazza Chiesa Vecchia, where the supermarket is.

To spare you further investigation: that car, the only one of its kind in town, belongs to Mr Carmelo Ingrassia. Now, since Ingrassia lives in Monte Ducale, what was his car doing a short distance away

from the supermarket, also belonging to Mr Ingrassia, at the very
moment when it was being burgled? I leave the answer to you.
    Yours very sincerely,
                Cav. Gerlando Misuraca

'You've fucked me royally this time, Cavaliere!' was
Montalbano's only comment as he glared at the letter he
had set down on the dining table. And dining, of course,
was now out of the question. He opened the refrigerator
only to pay glum homage to the culinary mastery of his
housekeeper, a deserved homage, for an enveloping fragrance
of poached baby octopus immediately assailed his senses.
But he closed the fridge. He wasn't up to it; his stomach
was tight as a fist. He undressed and, fully naked, went for
a walk along the beach; at that hour there was nobody
around anyway. Couldn't eat, couldn't sleep. Around four
o'clock in the morning he dived into the icy water, swam
a long time, then returned home. He noticed, laughing,
that he had an erection. He started talking to it, trying to
reason with it.

'It's no use deluding yourself.'

The erection told him a phone call to Livia might be
just the thing. To Livia lying naked and warm with sleep
in her bed.

'You're just a dickhead telling me dickheaded things.
Teenage jerk-off stuff.'

Offended, the erection withdrew. Montalbano put on a
pair of briefs, threw a dry towel over his shoulder, grabbed
a chair and sat down on the veranda, which gave onto the
beach.

He remained there watching the sea as it began to lighten slowly, then take on colour, streaked with yellow sunbeams. It promised to be a beautiful day, and the inspector felt reassured and ready to act. He'd had a few ideas, after reading the cavaliere's letter; the swim had helped him to organize them.

*

'You can't show up at the press conference looking like that,' pronounced Fazio, looking him over severely.

'What, are you taking lessons from the Anti-Mafia Commission now?' Montalbano opened the padded nylon bag he was holding. 'In here I've got trousers, jacket, shirt and tie. I'll change before I go to Montelusa. Actually, do me a favour. Take them out and put them on a chair; otherwise they'll get wrinkled.'

'They're already wrinkled, Chief. But I wasn't talking about your clothes; I meant your face. Like it or not, you've got to go to the barber.'

Fazio had said 'like it or not' because he knew him well and realized how much effort it cost the inspector to go to the barber. Running a hand behind his head, Montalbano agreed that his hair could use a little trim, too. His face darkened.

'Not one fucking thing's going to go right today!' he predicted.

Before exiting, he left orders that, while he was out beautifying himself, someone should go and pick up Carmelo Ingrassia and bring him to headquarters.

'If he asks why, what should I tell him?' asked Fazio.

'Don't tell him anything.'

'What if he insists?'

'If he insists, tell him I want to know how long it's been since he last had an enema. Good enough?'

'There's no need to get upset.'

*

The barber, his young helper and a client who was sitting in one of the two rotating chairs that barely fitted into the shop — which was actually only a recess under a staircase — were in the midst of an animated discussion, but fell silent as soon as the inspector appeared. Montalbano had entered with what he himself called his 'barber-shop face', that is, mouth shrunken to a slit, eyes half-closed in suspicion, eyebrows furrowed, expression at once scornful and severe.

'Good morning. Is there a wait?'

Even his voice came out deep and gravelly.

'No sir. Have a seat, Inspector.'

As Montalbano took his place in the vacant chair, the barber, in accelerated, Chaplinesque movements, held a mirror behind the client's head to let him admire the finished product, freed him of the towel round his neck, tossed it into a bin, took out a clean one and put it over the inspector's shoulders. The client, denied even the customary brush-down by the assistant, literally fled from the shop after muttering 'Good-day.'

The ritual of the haircut and shave, performed in

absolute silence, was swift and funereal. A new client appeared, parting the beaded curtain, but he quickly sniffed the atmosphere and, recognizing the inspector, said, 'I'll pass by later.' Then he disappeared.

On the street, as he headed back to his office, Montal-bano noticed an indefinable yet disgusting odour wafting around him, something between turpentine and a certain kind of face powder prostitutes used to wear some thirty years back. The stink was coming from his own hair.

※

'Ingrassia's in your office,' Tortorella said in a low voice, sounding conspiratorial.

'Where'd Fazio go?'

'Home to change. The commissioner's office called. They said Fazio, Gallo, Galluzzo and Germanà should also take part in the press conference.'

I guess my phone call to that arsehole Sciacchitano had an effect, thought Montalbano.

Ingrassia, who this time was dressed entirely in pastel green, started to rise.

'Don't get up,' said the inspector, sitting down behind his desk. He distractedly ran a hand through his hair, and immediately the smell of turpentine and face powder grew stronger. Alarmed, he brought his fingers to his nose and sniffed them, confirming his suspicion. But there was nothing to be done; there was no shampoo in the office bathroom. Without warning, he resumed his 'barber-shop face'. Seeing him suddenly transformed, Ingrassia became worried and started squirming in his chair.

'Is something wrong?' he asked.

'In what sense do you mean?'

'Well . . . in every sense, I suppose,' said Ingrassia, flustered.

Montalbano shrugged evasively and went back to sniffing his fingers. The conversation stalled.

'Have you heard about poor Cavaliere Misuraca?' the inspector asked, as if chatting among friends in his living room.

'Ah! Such is life!' The other sighed sorrowfully.

'Imagine that, Mr Ingrassia. I'd asked him if he could give me some more details about what he'd seen the night of the robbery, we'd agreed to meet again, and now this . . .'

Ingrassia threw his hands up in the air, inviting Montalbano, with this gesture, to resign himself to fate. He allowed a respectful pause to elapse, then, 'I'm sorry,' he said, 'but what other details could the poor cavaliere have given you? He'd already told you everything he saw.'

Montalbano wagged his forefinger, signalling 'no'.

'You don't think he told you everything he saw?' asked Ingrassia, intrigued.

Montalbano wagged his finger again.

Stew in your own juices, scumbag, he was thinking.

The green Ingrassia started to tremble like a leafy branch in the breeze.

'Well, then, what did you want him to tell you?'

ANDREA CAMILLERI

'What he thought he didn't see.'

The breeze turned into a gale, the branch began to lurch.

'I don't understand.'

'Let me explain. You're familiar, are you not, with a painting by Pieter Brueghel called *Children's Games*?'

'Who? Me? No,' said Ingrassia, worried.

'Doesn't matter. But you must be familiar with the works of Hieronymus Bosch?'

'No sir,' said Ingrassia, starting to sweat. Now he was really getting scared, his face starting to match the colour of his outfit — green.

'Never mind, then, don't worry about it,' Montalbano said magnanimously. 'What I meant was that when someone sees a scene, he usually remembers the first general impression he has of it. Right?'

'Right,' said Ingrassia, prepared for the worst.

'Then, little by little, a few other details may start coming back to him, things that registered in his memory but were discarded as unimportant. An open or closed window, for example, or a noise, a whistle, a song — what else? — a chair out of place, a car where it's not supposed to be, a light . . . That sort of thing. You know, little details that can later turn out to be extremely important.'

Ingrassia took a white handkerchief with a green border out of his pocket and wiped the sweat from his face.

'You had me brought here just to tell me that?'

'No. That would be inconveniencing you for no reason. I would never do a thing like that. I was wondering if you'd

72

heard from the people who, in your opinion, played that joke on you, you know, the phony robbery.'

'Not a word from anyone.'

'That's odd.'

'Why?'

'Because the best part of any practical joke is enjoying it afterward with the person it was played on. Well, if you do hear from anybody, please let me know. Good-day.'

'Good-day,' muttered Ingrassia, standing up. He was dripping wet, his trousers sticking to his bottom.

✳

Fazio showed up all decked out in a shiny new uniform.

'I'm here,' he said.

'And the pope is in Rome.'

'I know, Inspector, I know: today is not your day.'

He started to leave but stopped in the doorway.

'Inspector Augello called, said he had a terrible tooth-ache. He says he's not coming unless he has to.'

'Listen, do you have any idea where the wreck of Cavaliere Misuraca's Fiat ended up?'

'It's still here, in our garage. If you ask me, it's just envy.'

'What are you talking about?'

'Inspector Augello's toothache. It's just a bout of envy.'

'Who's he envious of?'

'You. Because it's your press conference and not his. And he's probably also pissed off because you wouldn't tell him who you'd arrested.'

'Would you do me a favour?'

'All right, all right, I'm going.'

When Fazio had closed the door, Montalbano dialed a number. The voice of the woman who answered sounded like a parody of an African in a dubbed film.

'Hallo? Who dare? Who you callin' dare?'

Where did the Cardamones find these housekeepers?

'Is Signora Ingrid there?'

'Ya, but who callin'?'

'This is Salvo Montalbano.'

'You wait dare.'

Ingrid's voice, on the other hand, was the very same as the voice the Italian dubber had given to Greta Garbo, who was herself Swedish.

'Ciao, Salvo. How are you? Long time no see.'

'I need your help, Ingrid. Are you free tonight?'

'Actually, no. But if it's really important I can drop everything.'

'It's important.'

'Tell me where and when.'

'Nine o'clock tonight, at the Marinella Bar.'

*

For Montalbano, the press conference proved, as of course he knew it would, to be a long, painful embarrassment. Anti-Mafia Vice-Commissioner De Dominicis came from Palermo and sat on the Montelusa police commissioner's right. Imperious gestures and angry glances prevailed upon

Montalbano, who had wanted to remain in the audience, to sit on his superior's left. Behind him, standing, were Fazio, Germanà, Gallo and Galluzzo. The commissioner spoke first and began by naming the man they had arrested, the number one of the number twos: Gaetano Bennici, known as 'Tano the Greek', wanted for multiple murders and long a fugitive from justice. It was literally a bombshell. The journalists, who were there in great numbers – there were even four TV cameras – jumped out of their chairs and started talking to one another, making such a racket that the commissioner had difficulty re-establishing silence. He stated that credit for the arrest went to Inspector Montalbano who, with the assistance of his men – and here he named and introduced them one by one – had been able to exploit a golden opportunity with skill and courage. Then De Dominicis spoke, explaining Tano the Greek's role within his criminal organization, certainly a prominent one, though not of the utmost prominence. As the Anti-Mafia Vice-Commissioner sat back down, Montalbano realized he was being thrown to the dogs.

The questions came in rapid-fire bursts, worse than a Kalashnikov. Had there been a gunfight? Was Tano alone? Were any law enforcement personnel injured? What did Tano say when they handcuffed him? Had he been sleeping or awake? Was there a woman with him? A dog? Was it true he took drugs? How many murders had he committed? How was he dressed? Was he naked? Was it true he rooted for the Milan soccer team? Did he have a photo of

Ornella Muti on his person? Could the inspector explain a little better the golden opportunity the commissioner had alluded to?

Montalbano struggled to answer the questions as best he could, seeming to understand less and less what he was saying.

It's a good thing the TV's here, he thought. *That way, at least, I can watch and make some sense of the bullshit I've been telling them.*

And just to make things even harder, there were the adoring eyes of Corporal Anna Ferrara, staring at him from the crowd.

Nicolò Zito, newsman from the Free Channel and a true friend, tried to rescue him from the quicksand in which he was drowning.

'Inspector, with your permission,' said Zito. 'You said you met Tano on your way back from Fiacca, where you'd been invited to eat a *tabisca* with friends. Is that correct?'

'Yes.'

'What is a *tabisca*?'

They'd eaten *tabisca* many times together. Zito was simply tossing him a life preserver. Montalbano seized it. Suddenly confident and precise, the inspector went into a detailed description of that extraordinary, multi-flavoured pizza.

SEVEN

In the alternately desperate, stammering, hesitant, bewildered, flabbergasted, lost but always wild-eyed man framed pitilessly in the foreground by the Free Channel's videocamera, Montalbano scarcely recognized himself under the storm of questions from vile snake-in-the-grass journalists. And the part where he'd explained how *tabisca* was made — the part in which he came off best — had been cut out. Maybe it wasn't strictly in keeping with the principal subject, the capture of Tano the Greek.

The aubergine Parmesan his housekeeper had left for him in the oven suddenly tasted flavourless. But that was impossible, it couldn't be right. It must have been some sort of psychological effect from seeing himself look like such a stupid shit on television.

All at once he felt like crying, like throwing himself down on his bed and wrapping himself up in the sheet like a mummy.

*

'Inspector Montalbano? This is Luciano Acquasanta from the newspaper *Il Mezzogiorno*. Would you be so kind as to grant me an interview?'

'No.'

'I won't waste your time, I promise.'

'No.'

*

'Is this Inspector Montalbano? Spingardi here, Attilio Spingardi, from the RAI office in Palermo. We're putting together a round table to discuss—'

'No.'

'At least let me finish!'

'No.'

*

'Darling? It's Livia. How are you feeling?'

'Fine. Why?'

'I just saw you on TV.'

'Oh, Christ! You mean they showed that all over Italy?'

'I think so. But it was very brief, you know.'

'Could you hear what I was saying?'

'No, one could only hear the commentator speaking. But I could clearly see your face, and that's what got me worried. You were yellow as a lemon.'

'It was even in colour?'

'Of course it was in colour. You kept putting your hand over your eyes and rubbing your forehead.'

'I had a headache and the lights were bothering me.'

'Are you better now?'
'Yes.'

*

'Inspector Montalbano? My name is Stefania Quattrini, from the magazine *Essere Donna*. We'd like to do a telephone interview with you. Could you remain on the line?'
'No.'
'It'll only take a few seconds.'
'No.'

*

'Do I have the honour of actually speaking with the famous Inspector Montalbano who holds press conferences?'
'Don't break my balls.'
'No, don't worry about your balls, we won't break them. It's your arse we're after.'
'Who is this?'
'It's your death, that's who. You're not gonna wiggle out of this one so easy, you lousy fucking actor. Who'd you think you were fooling with that little song and dance you put on with your pal Tano? You're gonna pay for trying to fuck with us.'
'Hello? Hello?'

*

The line had gone dead. But Montalbano didn't have a chance to take in those threatening words and mull them over, because he realized that the insistent noise he'd been hearing for some time amid the flurry of phone calls was the doorbell ringing. For some reason he was convinced it must be a journalist more clever than the rest who'd decided to show up at his house. Exasperated, he ran to the entrance and without opening, yelled, 'Who the hell is it?'

'It's the commissioner.'

What could *he* want from him, at home, at that hour, without even having called to alert him? He released the bolt with a swat of the hand and yanked the door wide open.

'Hello, come on in, make yourself comfortable,' he said, standing aside to let him in.

'We haven't got any time. Get yourself in order, I'll wait for you in the car.'

He turned around and walked away. Passing in front of the large mirror on the armoire, Montalbano realized what the commissioner had meant by 'Get yourself in order'. He was completely naked.

*

The car had none of the usual police markings; it looked, rather, like a rental car. At the wheel, in civilian clothing, was an officer from the Montelusa station whom he knew. As soon as he sat down, the commissioner began to speak.

'I apologize for not calling beforehand, but your phone was always busy.'

'I know.'

The commissioner could have cut into the line, of course, but that wasn't in keeping with his polite, gentlemanly way of doing things. Montalbano didn't explain why the telephone had given him no peace. It didn't matter. His boss was gloomier than he'd ever seen him before, face drawn, mouth half twisted in a kind of grimace.

*

After they'd been driving on the highway to Palermo for some forty-five minutes with the driver going full tilt, Montalbano started looking out on that part of his island's landscape which charmed him most.

'You like it? Really?' an astonished Livia had asked him once, a few years earlier, when he brought her to this area.

Arid hills like giant tumuli, covered only by a yellow stubble of dry grass and abandoned by the hand of man after sudden failures owing to drought, extreme heat, or more simply to the weariness of a battle lost from the outset, were interrupted here and there by a group of rocky peaks rising absurdly out of nothing or perhaps fallen from above, stalactites or stalagmites of the deep, open-air cave that is Sicily. The few houses one saw, all single-storey, domed structures, cubes of dry stone, stood askew, as if by chance alone they'd survived the violent bucking of an earth that didn't want them on its back. Still there was the rare spot of green, not of trees or cultivation, but of agaves, sword grass, buckthorn and sorghum, beleaguered and dusty, they too on the verge of surrender.

ANDREA CAMILLERI

As if he had been waiting for the appropriate scenery, the commissioner finally began to speak, though Montalbano realized the words were addressed not to him but to the commissioner himself, in a kind of painful, furious monologue.

'Why did they do it? Who decided to decide? If an investigation were held – an impossible conjecture – it would turn out that either nobody took the first step, or they were acting on orders from above. So let's see who these superiors who gave the orders are. The head of the Anti-Mafia Commission would deny all knowledge, as would the minister of the interior and the prime minister, the head of state. Which leaves the pope, Jesus Christ, the Virgin Mary, and God the Father, in that order. All would cry in outrage: how could anyone think it was *they* who gave the order? That leaves only the Devil, notorious for being the cause of all evil. He's the guilty one! Satan! . . . Anyway, to make a long story short, they decided to transfer him to another prison.'

'Tano?' Montalbano ventured to ask. The commissioner didn't even answer.

'Why? We'll never know, that much is certain. And while we were holding our press conference, they were putting him in an ordinary car with two plainclothes men as escort – ah! how clever! – so as not to attract attention, of course! And so, when the requisite high-powered motorcycle appeared from an alley with two men aboard, rendered utterly unrecognizable by their helmets . . . Final tally: two

82

policemen dead, Tano in the hospital, on death's doorstep. And there you have it.'

Montalbano absorbed it all, thinking cynically that if only they'd killed Tano a few hours earlier, he would have been spared the torture of the press conference. He started asking questions only because he sensed that the commissioner had calmed down a little after his outburst.

'But how did they know—'

The commissioner slammed the seat in front of him, making the driver start and the car veer slightly.

'What do you think, Montalbano? A mole, no? That's what's driving me so crazy!'

The inspector let a minute or two pass before asking another question.

'Where do we come in?'

'He wants to talk to you. He knows he's dying, and he wants to tell you something.'

'I see. So why did you go to all this trouble? I could have gone by myself.'

'I came along to prevent any snags or delays. In their sublime intelligence, these guys are capable of denying you access to him.'

*

In front of the hospital gate there was an armoured car, as well as some ten guards scattered about the yard, submachine guns in hand.

'Idiots,' said the commissioner.

They passed through at least five checkpoints, growing more irritated each time, then finally reached the ward where Tano's room was. All the other patients had been cleared out, transferred elsewhere amid curses and obscenities. At each end of the corridor were four armed policemen, plus two outside the door of the room Tano was obviously in. The commissioner showed them his pass.

'Congratulations,' he said to the corporal.

'For what, Mr Commissioner?'

'For maintaining order.'

'Thank you,' said the corporal, brightening, the commissioner's irony sailing far over his head.

'You go in alone,' the commissioner said to Montalbano, 'I'll wait outside.'

Only then did he notice how ashen the inspector was, his forehead bathed in sweat.

'My God, Montalbano, what's wrong? Do you feel ill?'

'I'm perfectly fine,' the inspector replied through clenched teeth.

He was lying. In fact, he felt terrible. The dead left him utterly indifferent. He could sleep with them, pretend to break bread with them, play hearts or spades with them. They didn't bother him in the least. The dying, on the other hand, made him break into a sweat: his hands would start to tremble, he would go cold all over, a hole would open up in his stomach.

*

Under the sheet that covered him, Tano's body looked shrunken, smaller than the inspector remembered it. His arms lay stretched along his sides, the right arm wrapped in thick bandages. Oxygen tubes sprouted from his nose, which had turned almost transparent, and his face looked unreal, as if it belonged to a wax doll. Overcoming the desire to run away, Montalbano pulled up a metal chair and sat down beside the dying man, who kept his eyes shut, as if asleep.

'Tano? Tano? It's Inspector Montalbano.'

The other reacted immediately, opening his eyes and making as if to sit up in bed, a violent start surely triggered by the animal instinct of one who has long been hunted. Then his eyes brought the inspector into focus, and the tension in his body visibly relaxed.

'You wanted to talk to me?'

Tano nodded yes, and gave a hint of a smile. He spoke very slowly, with great effort.

'They ran me off the road anyway.'

He was referring to the discussion they'd had in the cottage. Montalbano didn't know what to say.

'Come closer,' the old man said.

Montalbano rose from his chair and leaned over.

'Closer.'

The inspector bent down so far forward, his ear actually touched Tano's lip. The man's burning breath made him feel disgusted. Tano then told him what he had to tell, lucidly and precisely. But the talking had worn him out, and he closed his eyes again. Montalbano didn't know what to do, whether to leave or stay a little while longer. He decided to sit down, and Tano said something again, in a gurgly voice. The inspector stood back up and leaned over the dying man.

'What did you say?'

'I'm spooked.'

Tano was afraid, and in his present state he didn't hesitate to admit it. Was it pity, this sudden wave of heat, this flutter of the heart, this agonizing surge of emotion? He put a hand on Tano's forehead, and the intimate words came out spontaneously.

'You needn't be ashamed to say so. It's one more thing that makes you a man. We'll all be scared when our time comes. Goodbye, Tano.'

He walked out quickly, closing the door behind him. In the hallway, together with the commissioner and policemen, were De Dominicis and Sciacchitano. He ran up to them.

'What did he say?' De Dominicis asked anxiously.

'Nothing. He didn't manage to say anything. He wanted to, but couldn't. He's dying.'

'Hah!' said Sciacchitano, doubtful.

Very calmly, Montalbano placed his open hand on Sciacchitano's chest and gave him a violent push. The man reeled three steps backward, stunned.

'Stay right where you are and don't come any closer,' the inspector said through clenched teeth.

'That's enough, Montalbano,' the commissioner intervened.

De Dominicis seemed to pay no mind to the two men's differences.

'Who knows what he wanted to tell you,' he persisted, eyeing Montalbano inquisitively, as if to say: you're not talking straight.

'If you'd like, I can try and guess,' Montalbano retorted insolently.

✳

Before leaving the hospital, Montalbano knocked back a double J&B, neat, at the bar. Then they headed back to Montelusa. He figured he'd be back in Vigàta by 7.30, and therefore could keep his appointment with Ingrid.

'He talked, didn't he?'

'Yes.'

'Anything important?'

'Yes, in my opinion.'

'Why did he choose you?'

'He said he wanted to give me a present, for playing fair with him throughout this whole business.'

'I'm listening.'

Montalbano told him everything, and when he had finished, the commissioner looked pensive. Then he sighed.

'You work it all out yourself, with your men. It's better if this remains a secret. Nobody else should know about it, not even in my office. As you've just seen, there are moles everywhere.'

He visibly sank back into the bad mood he'd been in during the drive to the hospital.

'So it's come to this!' he said angrily.

Halfway home, the cellphone rang.

'Yes?' answered the commissioner.

Somebody spoke briefly at the other end.

'Thank you,' said the commissioner. He turned to Montalbano. 'That was De Dominicis. He kindly informed me that Tano died virtually as we were leaving the hospital.'

'They'd better be careful,' said Montalbano.

'Careful?'

'Not to let anyone steal the body,' the inspector said with bitter irony.

They rode another while in silence.

'Why did De Dominicis bother to inform you that Tano was dead?'

'That call, for all practical purposes, was meant for you, my friend. Obviously De Dominicis, who's no fool, correctly believes that Tano managed to tell you something. And he would like a share of the pie, if not the whole thing.'

✣

Back at headquarters, he found only Catarella and Fazio. It was better this way; he preferred talking to Fazio with nobody around. Out of a sense of duty more than curiosity, he asked: 'Where are the others?'

'They went chasing after four kids who were racing each other on two motorbikes.'

'Jesus! The whole squad is gone chasing after a pair of racing motorbikes?'

'It's a special kind of race,' Fazio explained. 'One motorbike is green, the other yellow. The yellow one starts out first and races the whole length of a street, snatching whatever's there to be snatched. An hour or two later, after the people have calmed down, the green one takes off and swipes whatever's still there to be swiped. Then they change street and neighbourhood, but this time the green one goes first. It's a race to see who can steal the most.'

'I see. Listen, Fazio, this evening I want you to drop by the Vinti warehouse and ask the manager, in my name, to lend us some shovels, pickaxes, mattocks and spades, ten or so. We'll all meet here tomorrow morning at six. Inspector Augello and Catarella will stay behind at headquarters. I want two cars – no, make that one car, 'cause you're going to ask Vinti's to give you a Jeep, too. By the way, who has the key to our garage?'

'Whoever's on duty always has it. At the moment, that would be Catarella.'

'Get it from him and give it to me.'

'Right away. But if you don't mind my asking, what do we need shovels and pickaxes for?'

'We're changing profession. As of tomorrow, we're going into farming, the healthy life, working in the fields. What do you say?'

'You know, Inspector, for the last few days there's just no reasoning with you. Maybe you could tell us what's got into you? You're always obnoxious and rude.'

EIGHT

He first met Ingrid in the course of an investigation in which, through a series of false leads, she'd been offered up to him, though completely innocent, as the scapegoat. Since then a strange sort of friendship had developed between the inspector and that splendid woman. From time to time Ingrid would call him up and they would spend the evening chatting. The young woman would talk about her problems, confiding in Montalbano, and he would dispense wise, brotherly advice. He was a kind of spiritual father – a role he'd had to impose on himself by force, since Ingrid didn't exactly arouse spiritual feelings – and his recommendations were always studiously ignored. At none of their meetings – there'd been six or seven – had Montalbano ever shown up before she did. Ingrid had a mania for punctuality.

This time too, after parking in the Marinella Bar's car park, he noticed her car was already there, beside a Porsche convertible that looked like a rocket and was painted a tasteless shade of yellow that offended the eyes.

When he entered the bar, Ingrid was standing at the

counter drinking a whisky. Beside her was a man aged fortyish dressed in a fancy canary-yellow suit, sporting a Rolex and ponytail, and talking to her confidentially.

When he has to change clothes, thought the inspector, does he also change cars?

As soon as she saw him, Ingrid came running and embraced him, kissing him lightly on the lips. She was obviously happy to see him. Montalbano, too, was pleased: Ingrid looked like a gift from God, with her jeans painted on her very long legs, her sandals, her light-blue see-through blouse affording a glimpse of her round breasts, her blonde hair hanging loose around her shoulders.

'Sorry,' he said to the canary who was with her. 'See you around.'

They went and sat down at a table. Montalbano didn't feel like drinking anything. The man with the Rolex and ponytail took his whisky out to the seaside terrace. Ingrid and the inspector smiled at each other.

'You're looking well,' she said. 'A lot better than you did on TV today.'

'Yeah,' said Montalbano, then changed the subject. 'You look like you're doing all right yourself.'

'Did you want to see me to exchange compliments?'

'I wanted to ask a favour of you.'

'Here I am.'

The man with the ponytail was eyeing them from the terrace.

'Who's that?'

'Somebody I know. I passed him on my way here. He followed and offered me a drink.'

'In what sense do you know him?'

Ingrid turned serious, a line creasing her forehead.

'Are you jealous?'

'No, you know better than that. Anyway, there'd be no reason, with him. It's just that he got on my nerves from the minute I saw him. What's his name?'

'Come on, Salvo. What do you care?'

'Tell me his name.'

'Beppe . . . Beppe De Vito.'

'And what does he do to earn his Rolex, Porsche and everything else?'

'Trades in leather goods.'

'Ever slept with him?'

'Yes, about a year ago, only once. And he was just suggesting we do it again. But I don't have a very pleasant memory of it.'

'Some kind of degenerate?'

Ingrid eyed him for a moment, then let out a laugh that made the bartender jump.

'What's so funny?'

'The face you just made: the good cop full of indignation. No, Salvo, he's just the opposite. Totally lacking in imagination. All I can remember is that it seemed suffocating and pointless.'

Montalbano gestured for the man with the ponytail to come over to their table, and as he approached, smiling, Ingrid gave the inspector a worried look.

'Hello. Don't I know you? You're Inspector Montal-bano, aren't you?'

'Unfortunately for you, you're going to get to know me even better.'

The other became flustered, his whisky trembling in his glass, ice cubes tinkling.

'Why "unfortunately"?'

'Your name is Giuseppe De Vito and you deal in leather goods, am I correct?'

'Yes, but . . . I don't understand.'

'You'll understand in due time. One of these days you're going to be called in to Montelusa police headquarters. I'll be there, too. I think we'll have a lot to talk about.'

The man with the ponytail, face suddenly pale, set his glass down on the table, unable to hold it any longer.

'Couldn't you . . . at least give me a hint . . . some explanation . . .?'

Montalbano assumed the expression of someone just overcome by an irresistible wave of generosity.

'All right, but only because you're a friend of the lady. Do you know a German man by the name of Kurt Suckert?'

'Never heard of him, I swear,' the man said, digging a canary-coloured handkerchief out of his pocket and mopping his brow with it.

'Well, if that's your answer, I have nothing more to say to you,' the inspector said icily. He looked him up and down, then gestured for him to come closer. 'I'll give you my advice: don't try to be too clever. Goodbye.'

'Goodbye,' De Vito replied mechanically. And without even looking back at Ingrid, he raced out of the bar.

'You're a shit,' Ingrid said calmly, 'and an arsehole.'

'Yes, you're right. Every now and then something comes over me, and I get that way.'

'Does this Suckert really exist?'

'He used to. But he called himself Curzio Malaparte. He was a writer.'

They heard the roar of the Porsche, burning rubber as it pulled out.

'So did you get it out of your system?' Ingrid asked.

'I think so.'

'I could tell right away, you know, that you were in a bad mood. What is it? Can you tell me?'

'I could, but it's not worth going into. Problems at work.'

*

Montalbano suggested that Ingrid leave her car in the bar's car park; they would come back later to get it. Ingrid didn't ask him where they were going, nor what they were going to do. All of a sudden Montalbano asked her, 'How's it going with your father-in-law?'

'Fine!' Ingrid said cheerfully. 'I'm sorry, I should have mentioned it sooner. Things are fine with my father-in-law. He's left me in peace for two months now. He's no longer after me.'

'What happened?'

'I don't know. He hasn't told me anything. The last time was on our way back from Fela, where we'd been to a wedding. My husband couldn't make it and my mother-in-law wasn't feeling well, so the two of us were left alone again. At some point he turned off onto a side road, continued for a mile or two, then stopped in a wooded area. He made me get out of the car, tore off my clothes, threw me to the ground, and fucked me with his usual brutality. The next day I left for Palermo with my husband, and when I got back a week later, my father-in-law seemed like he'd aged. He was trembling. Since then, he's sort of been avoiding me. Now when I find myself face to face with him in some corridor of the house, I'm no longer afraid he's going to push me up against the wall with one hand on my tits and the other on my cunt.'

'It's better this way, isn't it?'

*

The story Ingrid had just told him Montalbano knew better than she did. The inspector had learned of Ingrid's relations with her father-in-law the very first time he met her. Then one night, as they were talking, without warning, Ingrid had burst into convulsive sobs; she could no longer bear the situation with her husband's father. An absolutely liberated woman, she felt soiled, demeaned by this quasi-incestuous relationship that was being forced on her. She thought of leaving her husband and returning to Sweden.

Being an excellent mechanic, she would manage to earn a living.

That was when Montalbano had made up his mind to help get her out of that mess. The following day, he'd invited Corporal Anna Ferrara to his house for dinner. Young Anna was in love with him and convinced that he and Ingrid were lovers.

'I'm desperate,' he had told her, opening the evening with a face worthy of a great tragic actor.

'Oh my God, what's wrong?' asked Anna, squeezing one of his hands in hers.

'Ingrid is cheating on me.'

He let his head fall to her breast and by some miracle managed to make his eyes grow moist.

Anna suppressed an exclamation of triumph. She'd been right all along! Meanwhile the inspector was hiding his face in his hands, and the girl felt overwhelmed by this exhibition of despair.

'You know, I never told you anything because I didn't want to upset you, but I did a little investigation about Ingrid. You're not the only man.'

'But I knew that!' said the inspector, his hands still over his face.

'What is it, then?'

'It's different this time! It's not some little fling like all the rest, which I could even forgive. She's in love, and he feels the same way!'

'Do you know who she's in love with?'

'Yes, her father-in-law.'

'Oh, Christ!' said Anna, giving a start. 'She told you herself?'

'No, I found out on my own. Actually, she denies it. She denies everything. I need some kind of irrefutable proof, something to throw in her face. Do you know what I mean?'

Anna had offered to provide him with this irrefutable proof. And she'd gone to such lengths that she even managed to take some pictures of that rustic episode in the woods. She'd had them enlarged by a trusted girlfriend of hers in the crime lab and then turned them over to the inspector. Ingrid's father-in-law, aside from being chief physician at Montelusa Hospital, was also a prominent local politician. And so Montalbano sent the man some eloquent initial documentation at his provincial party office, the hospital, and to his home. On the back of each photo were only the words: *We've got you now.* The barrage of images had apparently scared him to death: in a flash he'd seen his career and family jeopardized. In case of need, the inspector had another twenty or so photographs. He'd said nothing about this to Ingrid. The woman might throw a fit if she knew her Swedish sense of privacy had been violated.

Montalbano accelerated, now satisfied that the complex machinations he'd set in motion had achieved their desired goal.

*

'You bring the car inside,' said Montalbano, getting out and starting to raise the metal grille of the police garage.

Once she'd pulled in, he turned on the lights and lowered the grille.

'What do you want me to do?' Ingrid asked.

'See that wrecked Fiat 500 over there? I want to know if its brakes have been tampered with.'

'I don't know if I'll be able to tell.'

'Try.'

'There goes my blouse.'

'No, wait. I brought something.'

He reached into the back seat of his car and pulled out a shirt and pair of jeans that belonged to him.

'Here. Put these on.'

While Ingrid was changing, he went to look for a portable mechanic's lamp, found one on the counter, and plugged it in. Without saying a word, Ingrid took the lamp, a monkey wrench and a screwdriver and slid under the little Fiat's twisted chassis. It took her only about ten minutes. She came out from under the car covered with dust and grease.

'I was lucky. The brake cable was partly cut, I'm sure of it.'

'What do you mean "partly"?'

'I mean, it wasn't cut all the way through. They left just enough so the car wouldn't crash right away. But with the first hard pull, the cable would certainly have snapped.'

'Are you positive it didn't break all by itself? It was a very old car.'

'The cut is too clean. There's no shredding. Or very little.'

'Now listen closely,' said Montalbano. 'The man who was at the wheel drove from Vigàta to Montelusa, stopped there a little while, then headed back to Vigàta. The accident occurred on the steep descent right before you come into town, the Catena hillside. He slammed straight into a truck, and that was that. Clear so far?'

'Yes.'

'What I want to know is this: in your opinion, was this slick little job done in Vigàta or in Montelusa?'

'In Montelusa,' said Ingrid. 'If they'd done it in Vigàta, he would definitely have crashed much sooner. Anything else?'

'No. Thanks.'

Ingrid didn't change her clothes, and didn't even wash her hands.

'I'll do it at your house.'

*

Ingrid got out in the bar's car park, took her car, and followed the inspector. It was a warm evening, not yet midnight.

'You want to take a shower?' he asked her when they got to his place.

'No, I'd rather go for a swim. I'll shower later, if I feel like it.'

She took off the grease-stained clothes of Montalbano's that she was wearing and slipped out of her panties. The inspector meanwhile had to make some effort to reassume his much-suffered guise as spiritual adviser.

'Come on. Take your clothes off and join me,' she said.

'No. I like watching you from the veranda.'

The full moon was actually too bright. Montalbano remained in his deck chair, enjoying the sight of Ingrid's silhouette as she reached the water's edge and began a dance of little hops in the water, arms extended. He saw her dive in, following awhile the small black dot that was her head, and then, suddenly, he fell asleep.

*

When he awoke, day was already dawning. He got up, slightly chilled, made coffee and drank three cups in a row. Before leaving, Ingrid had cleaned the house: there was no trace of her having been there. Ingrid was worth her weight in gold: she'd done everything he'd asked of her and hadn't even wanted an explanation. As far as curiosity was concerned, she was certainly not female. But only as far as curiosity was concerned.

Feeling a pang of hunger, he opened the refrigerator. The aubergine Parmesan he hadn't eaten at lunchtime was gone, dispatched by Ingrid. He had to content himself with a piece of bread and some processed cheese. Better than nothing. He took a shower and put on the clothes he had lent to Ingrid. They still bore a trace of her scent.

As was his habit, he arrived at headquarters about ten minutes late. His men were all ready with one squad car and the Jeep on loan from Vinti's, which was loaded up with shovels, mattocks, pickaxes and spades. They looked like labourers on their way to earn a day's pay working the land.

*

The Crasto mountain, which for its part would never have dreamed of calling itself a mountain, was a rather bald little hill that rose up west of Vigàta barely five hundred yards from the sea. It had been carefully pierced by a tunnel, now boarded up, that was supposed to have been an integral part of a road that started nowhere and led nowhere, a very useful bypass route for diverting funds into bottomless pockets. It was, in fact, called 'the bypass'. Legend had it that deep in the mountain's bowels was a *crasto*, a ram, made of solid gold. The tunnel-diggers never found it, but those who won the bid for the government contract certainly did. Attached to the mountain, on the landward side, was a kind of stronghold of rock called the Crasticeddru, the 'little Crasto'. The earthmovers and trucks had never reached this area, and it preserved an untamed beauty.

Having come down some virtually impassable roads to avoid attracting attention, the two cars headed straight for the Crasticeddru. In the absence of any further path or trail, it was very hard to go on, but the inspector insisted that the cars pull right up to the foot of the rocky spur.

Montalbano ordered everyone out of the cars. The air was cool, the morning bright.

'What do you want us to do?' asked Fazio.

'Search the Crasticeddru, all of you, very carefully. Look everywhere, and look hard. There's supposed to be

an entrance to a cave somewhere. It's been covered up, cam-
ouflaged by rocks or vegetation. Keep your eyes peeled. We
have to find it. I assure you it's there.'

They fanned out.

＊

Two hours later, discouraged, they met back up beside the
cars. The sun was beating down, they were sweating, but
far-sighted Fazio had brought along thermoses of coffee
and tea.

'Let's try again,' said Montalbano. 'But don't look only
around the rock; search also along the ground, you might
see something that looks fishy.'

They resumed their hunt, and half an hour later
Montalbano heard Galluzzo call from afar.

'Inspector! Inspector! Come here!'

The inspector went over to the policeman, who had
assigned himself the side of the spur closest to the highway
that went to Fela.

'Look.'

Someone had tried to make them disappear, but at a
certain point along the ground, there were clearly visible
tracks left behind by a large truck.

'They lead over there,' said Galluzzo, pointing to the
rock face. As he was saying this, he suddenly stopped,
mouth agape.

'Jesus God!' said Montalbano.

How had they managed not to see it before? There was
a huge boulder placed in an odd position, with shoots of

withered grass sticking out from behind. As Galluzzo was calling to his mates, the inspector ran towards the boulder, grabbed a tuft of sword grass and tugged hard. He almost fell backward: the clump had no roots. It had merely been stuck there with bunches of sorghum to camouflage the entrance to the cave.

NINE

The boulder was a great stone slab, roughly rectangular in shape, that appeared to be of a piece with the rock around it and rested on a sort of giant step, also rock. At a glance Montalbano determined that it was about six feet tall and four and a half feet wide; moving it by hand was out of the question. And yet there had to be a way. Halfway up its right side, about four inches from the edge, was a perfectly natural-looking hole.

'If this was an actual wooden door,' the inspector reasoned, 'that opening would be at the right height for inserting a doorknob.'

He took a pen out of his pocket and stuck it in the hole. The pen fitted all the way inside, but when Montalbano was about to put it back in his pocket, he noticed that the pen had soiled his hand. He looked at his fingers, then smelled them.

'That's grease,' he said to Fazio, the only person remaining beside him.

The other policemen had taken shelter in the shade.

Gallo had found a clump of sheep's sorrel and offered some to the others.

'Suck the stalk,' he said, 'it's delicious and quenches your thirst.'

Montalbano thought of the only possible solution.

'Do we have a steel cable?'

'Sure do, inside the Jeep.'

'All right, then pull the car up here as close as you can.'

As Fazio was walking away, the inspector, now convinced he'd found the proper expedient for moving the big slab, looked at the surrounding landscape with different eyes. If this was indeed the place that Tano the Greek had revealed to him on his deathbed, there must be some spot nearby from which one could keep it under surveillance. The area seemed deserted and remote; one would never have imagined that right behind the bluff, a few hundred yards away, was the highway with all its traffic. Not far from there, on a rise of dry, rocky terrain, was a minuscule cottage, a cube consisting of a single room. He called for some binoculars. The little structure's wooden door, which was closed, looked solid. Next to the door, at the height of a man's head, was a small window without shutters, protected by two crisscrossing iron bars. The cottage appeared uninhabited, and it was the only possible observation point in the vicinity. All the other houses were too far away. Still doubtful, he called to Galluzzo.

'Go have a look at that little house. Do what you can to open the door, but don't break it in. Be careful, we may need to use it. See if there are any recent signs of life inside, if anyone's been living there in the last few days. But leave everything exactly as it was, as if you'd never been there.'

The Jeep had meanwhile backed almost all the way up to the base of the boulder. The inspector took the end of the steel cable, inserted it easily into the hole and started pushing it inside. This required little effort, for the cable slid into the boulder as if following a well-greased, unobstructed groove. In fact, a few seconds later, the cable end popped out on the other side of the slab, looking like the head of a snake.

'Take this end,' Montalbano told Fazio, 'fix it to the Jeep, put the engine in gear and pull away, but very, very gently.'

As the Jeep began to move, so did the boulder, its right side starting to come detached from the rock face as if turning on invisible hinges.

'Open sesame . . .' Germanà murmured in amazement, recalling the children's formula that magically served to open all doors.

*

'I assure you, Commissioner, that stone slab was turned into a door by a superb master craftsman. Just imagine, the iron hinges were totally invisible from the outside. Closing the door was as easy as opening it. We went in with flashlights. Inside, the cave was very carefully and intelligently fitted out. They'd made a floor, for example, out of a dozen or so puncheons nailed together and set down on the bare earth.'

'What's a puncheon?'

'I can't think of the proper word. Let's just say they're very thick planks. They built a floor to keep the crates of weapons from coming into direct contact with the damp ground. The walls are covered with lighter boards. The whole inside of the cave is a sort of giant wooden box without a top. They obviously worked a long time on it.'

'What about the weapons?'

'A veritable arsenal. About thirty machine guns and sub-machine guns, a hundred or so pistols and revolvers, two bazookas, thousands of ammunition rounds, cases of every kind of explosive, from TNT to Semtex. And a large quantity of police and carabinieri uniforms, bullet-proof vests, and various other things. All in perfect order, with each item wrapped in cellophane.'

'We've really dealt them a serious blow, eh?'

'Absolutely. Tano avenged himself well, just enough to avoid looking like a traitor or repenter. I want you to know that I didn't sequester the weapons; I left them in the cave. I've arranged for my men to stand guard, in two shifts, round the clock. They're in an uninhabited cottage a few hundred yards away from the arms depot.'

'You're hoping someone will come for supplies?'

'That's the idea.'

'Good, I agree with that. We'll wait a week, keep everything under close watch, and if nothing happens, we'll go ahead with the seizure. Ah, Montalbano, do you remember my dinner invitation for the day after tomorrow?'

'How could I forget?'

'I'm afraid we'll have to postpone it a few days. My wife has the flu . . .'

*

There was no need to wait a week. The third day after they had discovered the weapons, Catarella, having completed his midnight-to-midday shift on guard, went to report to Montalbano, asleep on his feet. The inspector had asked them all to do the same as soon as they went off duty.

'Any news?'

'Nothing, Chief. All peacefulness and quietude.'

'Good. Actually, bad. Go get some sleep.'

'Uh, wait. Now that I put my head to it, there was something, nothing, really, I just thought I'd tell you more out of consciousness than duty, but it's nothing.'

'What kind of nothing?'

'A tourist came by.'

'Explain a little better, Cat.'

'It looked to be around twenty-one hundred hours in the morning.'

'If it was morning, it was nine, Cat.'

'Whatever you say. Then right then and there I heard the roar of a motorcycle. So I grabbed the binoculars around my neck and precautiously looked out the window for confirmation. The motorcycle was red.'

'The colour is of no importance. Then what?'

'Then a tourist of the male sex descended from off said motorcycle.'

'What made you think he was a tourist?'

'He was wearing a camera around his neck, a really big camera, so big it looked like a cannon.'

'Must have been a telephoto lens.'

'Yessir, that it was. Then he started taking telephotos.'

'Of what?'

'Everything, Chief, everything. The countryside, the Crasticeddru, even the location I was located in.'

'Did he get close to the Crasticeddru?'

'Never, sir. But when he climbed back on his motorcycle to leave, he waved at me with his hands.'

'He saw you?'

'No. I stayed inside the whole time. But as I was saying, once he started up, he waved goodbye to the little house.'

*

'Commissioner? I've got some news, and it's not good. Looks like they somehow got wind of our discovery and sent somebody on reconnaissance to confirm.'

'And how do you know this?'

'This morning the man on duty in the cottage saw some guy arrive on a motorcycle and take photographs of the whole area with a powerful telephoto. They must have set up a very specific marker around the boulder blocking the entrance, like, say, a stick pointing in a certain direction, a rock placed a certain distance away . . . It simply would not have been possible for us to put everything back exactly the way it was.'

'Excuse me, but had you given precise instructions to the officer on duty?'

'Of course. The man on duty should have stopped the motorcyclist, identified him, confiscated the camera, and brought him to the station . . .'

'So why didn't he?'

'For one very simple reason: the officer was Catarella, whom we both know well.'

'Ah,' was the commissioner's laconic reply.

'What do we do now?'

'We'll go ahead and sequester the arms immediately, today. Palermo has ordered me to give it maximum coverage.'

Montalbano felt his armpits getting soaked in sweat.

'Another press conference?'

'I'm afraid so. Sorry.'

*

As he was about to leave for the Crasticeddru with two cars and a van, Montalbano noticed Galluzzo imploring him with his eyes, like a battered dog. He called him aside.

'What's the problem?'

'Think I could invite my brother-in-law, the newsman?'

'No,' Montalbano said at once, but he immediately reconsidered. Another idea had come into his mind, and he felt very pleased with himself for having thought of it. 'Listen,' he said, 'okay, as a favour to you. Give him a call and tell him to come.'

The idea was that if Galluzzo's brother-in-law was there on the spot and gave the discovery sufficient publicity, the need for the press conference might just go up in smoke.

＊

Montalbano not only allowed Galluzzo's brother-in-law and his TeleVigàta cameraman a free hand, he actually helped them stage their scoop by acting as director. He had his men assemble a bazooka, which Fazio then mounted on his shoulder as if to fire, then had the cave brightly illuminated so that every cartridge clip, every magazine, could be filmed or photographed.

After two hours of serious work, the cave was completely emptied of its cargo. The news reporter and his cameraman raced off to Montelusa to edit their feature, and Montalbano called the commissioner on a cellphone.

'It's all loaded up.'

'Good. Send it here to me, in Montelusa. And one more thing: leave a man on duty. Jacomuzzi will soon be there with the crime lab team. Congratulations.'

＊

It was Jacomuzzi, in the end, who took care of setting the idea of the press conference definitively to rest. Wholly involuntarily, of course, since Jacomuzzi was blissfully in his element at press conferences and interviews. In fact, before coming to the cave to gather evidence, the crime lab chief had taken the trouble to alert some twenty journalists from the press and television. Thus, while the report put together by Galluzzo's brother-in-law quickly reverberated in the local news, the commotion unleashed by the stories on Jacomuzzi and his men had national resonance. The commissioner – as Montalbano had correctly foreseen – decided to call off the press conference, since everyone already knew everything, and settled for issuing a detailed press release instead.

At home in his underpants, and with a large bottle of beer in his hand, Montalbano relished the sight of Jacomuzzi's face on TV, the whole time in close-up, as the head of the crime lab explained how his men were dismantling the wooden construction inside the cave, piece by piece, searching for the slightest clue, any hint of a fingerprint, any trace of a footprint. When the cave was stripped bare, restored to its primordial state, the Free Channel cameraman did a long, slow pan of the whole interior. And in the course of this shot, the inspector saw something that didn't look right to him. It was just an impression, nothing more. But he might as well check it out. He phoned the Free Channel and asked for Nicolò Zito, the Communist journalist and his friend.

'No problem, I'll have it sent over to you.'

'But I haven't got one of those thingamajigs, whatever the hell they're called.'

'Then come and watch it here.'

'Would tomorrow morning around eleven be all right?'
'That's fine. I won't be here, but I'll leave word.'

*

At nine o'clock the next morning, Montalbano went to Montelusa, to the headquarters of the party that Cavaliere Misuraca had served. The plaque next to the main door indicated that the offices were on the fifth floor. But the treacherous sign did not specify that the only way to get there was on foot, since the building was not equipped with a lift. After climbing at least ten flights of stairs, and a little out of breath, Montalbano knocked and knocked on a door that remained stubbornly closed. He went back down the stairs and out into the street. Right next door was a greengrocer; inside, an elderly man was serving a customer. The inspector waited until the greengrocer was alone.

'Did you know Cavaliere Misuraca?'

'And who, may I ask, gives a fuck who I know and who I don't?'

'I give a fuck. I'm with the police.'

'All right. And I'm Lenin.'

'Are you trying to be funny?'

'Not at all. That's really my name. My father named me Lenin and I'm proud of it. But maybe you're of the same stripe as the people next door?'

'No, I'm not. Anyway, I'm only here on a case. So I'll repeat my question: did you know Cavaliere Misuraca?'

'I certainly did. He spent his whole life going in and out of that door and busting my balls with his rattletrap Fiat 500.'

'Did the car bother you?'

'Did it bother me? He always parked it in front of my store! Even on the day he smashed into that truck!'

'He parked it right here?'

'Do I speak Turkish or something? Right here, he parked it. And I asked him to move it, but he went nuts and started yelling and said he didn't have any time to waste on me. So I got really mad and gave him hell. Anyway, to make a long story short, we were about to go at it when luckily some kid passed by and told the late cavaliere he'd be happy to move the car for him. So Misuraca gave him the keys.'

'Do you know where he parked it?'

'No sir.'

'You think you could recognize this kid? Had you ever seen him before?'

'I seen him sometimes going in next door. Must be a member of their fancy club.'

'The party chief's name is Biraghìn, isn't it?'

'Something like that. He's from around Venice some- where. Works at the Public Housing Office; he's probably there now. This place here won't re-open till after six; right now it's too early.'

*

'Mr Biraghìn?' he shouted into the public phone. 'This is Inspector Montalbano of Vigàta Police. Sorry to disturb you at work.'

'Not at all. What can I do for you?'

'I need you to remember something for me. The last party meeting attended by Cavaliere Misuraca, what kind of meeting was it?'

'I don't understand the question.'

'No need to get touchy, sir, this is just a routine investigation to clarify the circumstances of the cavaliere's death.'

'Why, was there something unclear about it?'

A real pain in the arse, this Ferdinando Biraghìn.

'It's all clear as day, I assure you.'

'So what's the problem?'

'I have to close the file, understand? I can't leave a dossier incomplete.'

Upon hearing the words 'file' and 'dossier', Biraghìn, a bureaucrat from the Public Housing Office, changed his tune at once.

'Yes, of course, I know how it is. Well, it was a meeting of the local party leadership, which the cavaliere was not entitled to attend. But we stretched the rules a little.'

'So it was a rather small meeting.'

'About ten people.'

'Did anyone come looking for the cavaliere?'

'No. We'd locked the door. I would remember something like that. Actually, he did get a phone call.'

'Pardon my asking, but I assume you're unfamiliar with the tenor of that conversation?'

'I'm not only familiar with the tenor, I also know the bass, the baritone and the soprano!' He laughed.

Such a wit, this Ferdinando Biraghìn.

'You know how the cavaliere spoke, of course,' Biraghìn continued. 'As if everyone else were deaf. It was hard not to overhear when he was talking. Just imagine, on one occasion—'

'I'm sorry, sir, I haven't got much time. So you were able to grasp the—' he stopped, discarding the word 'tenor' to spare himself another dose of Biraghìn's tragic sense of humour – 'the gist of that phone call?'

'Of course. Somebody had done the cavaliere the favour of moving his car. And by way of thanks, the cavaliere only scolded him for parking it too far away.'

'Were you able to tell who it was that called?'

'No. Why do you ask?'

'Because,' said Montalbano. And he hung up.

So the kid, having completed his deadly little service in the shelter of some complicitous garage, had also decided, just for fun, to make the cavaliere get a little exercise.

*

At the Free Channel studios, Montalbano explained to a polite young woman that he was utterly hopeless when it came to anything electronic. Turning on a television, yes, flipping the channels, turning it off, no problem. As for the rest, utter darkness. With patience and grace, the girl put in the cassette, then started to rewind it, stopping the image every time Montalbano asked. By the time he left the Free Channel offices, the inspector was convinced he'd seen exactly what had aroused his interest. But what had aroused his interest seemed not to make any sense.

TEN

He stood outside the Trattoria San Calogero, undecided. It was indeed time to eat, and his stomach certainly felt empty; and yet an idea that had come to him while watching the videotape and which demanded to be verified was pushing him to continue on to the Crasticeddru. The scent of fried mullet coming from the restaurant won the duel. He ate a special appetizer of shellfish, then had them bring him two sea perches so fresh they seemed to be still swimming in the sea.

'You're eating without conviction, Inspector.'

'It's true. The fact is, I've got something on my mind.'

'The mind should be forgotten when the Lord in His grace puts such perches in front of you,' Calogero said solemnly, walking away.

*

He passed by the office to see if there was any news.

'Jacomuzzi called several times for you,' Germanà informed him.

'If he calls again, tell him I'll get back to him later. Do we have a very powerful flashlight?'

After turning off the main road and stopping near the Crasticeddru, he abandoned the car and decided to proceed on foot. It was a beautiful day, with a light breath of wind that cooled the air and lifted Montalbano's spirits. The ground around the rocky spur was marked by tyre tracks apparently left by people who had come up there out of curiosity. The boulder that served as the door had been pulled open several yards, the cave entrance now entirely exposed. As he was about to enter, he stopped, pricking up his ears. From inside came a low murmur occasionally interrupted by some stifled moans. He became alarmed: want to bet they're torturing someone in there? There wasn't time to run back to the car to get his pistol. He bounded inside, simultaneously turning on the powerful flashlight.

'Everybody freeze! Police!'

The two people inside the cave froze, but the greatest chill was felt by Montalbano himself. They were a very young couple, completely nude, making love: she with her hands braced against the wall, arms extended, he glued to her from behind. In the glare of the flashlight they looked like statues, beautiful. The inspector felt his face burning with shame. Turning off the flashlight, he started to withdraw, awkwardly muttering:

'I'm sorry . . . It was a mistake . . . Don't let me bother you.'

They came out less than a minute later. (It doesn't take long to put one's jeans and T-shirt back on.) Montalbano was truly sorry for having interrupted them. In their way, the two youngsters had been reconsecrating the cave, now that it was no longer a depository of death. The boy passed in front of him, head bowed and hands in his pockets; the girl instead glanced at him a moment, smiling faintly, an amused glint in her eye.

A simple, superficial reconnaissance of the site was all the inspector needed to confirm that what he had noticed in the videotape corresponded to what he was seeing in reality: that while the sides of the cave were relatively smooth and solid, the lower part of the rear wall, that is, the surface opposite the entrance, was quite uneven in texture, with protuberances and recesses, and might at first glance appear sloppily chiselled. But there was nothing chiselled about it. In fact, it consisted of stones stacked one atop and beside the other. Time had since taken care of binding and cementing them, camouflaging them with dust, earth, seeping water and saltpetre, finally transforming the rough surface into an almost natural wall.

He continued looking very closely, exploring inch by inch, and in the end he no longer had any doubt: at the back of the cave, there must be an opening at least three feet square that had been covered over quite a few years ago.

*

'Jacomuzzi? Montalbano here. I absolutely need you to—'

'Do you mind telling me where you've been hiding your arse? I spent the whole morning looking for you!'

'Well, I'm here now.'

'I found a piece of cardboard, from a parcel or, rather, from a large box, the kind used for shipping.'

'You tell a secret, I tell a secret: I once found a red button.'

'What an arsehole you are! I'm not going to say any more.'

'Oh, come on, honeybuns, don't be offended.'

'On this piece of cardboard are some printed letters. I found it under the wooden underframe of the cave; it must have slipped through one of the interstices between the planks.'

'What was that word you said?'

'Underframe?'

'No, after that.'

'Interstices?'

'Yes. My, my, aren't we educated? And so well spoken! Did you find anything else under this whatever-it-was you called it?'

'Yes. Rusted nails, a button, in fact – but this one was black – a pencil stub and some scraps of paper, but the dampness had turned them all to mush. That piece of cardboard is still in good condition because it had apparently been there only a few days.'

'Send it down to me. Listen, have you got an echo sounder and anyone who might know how to use it?'

'Yes. We used it at Misilmesi just last week to look for three dead bodies, which we eventually found.'

'Could you have it here to me in Vigàta by five o'clock?'

'Are you insane? It's four-thirty! Let's say in two hours. I'll bring it myself, along with the cardboard. But what do you need it for?'

'To sound your little behind.'

＊

'Headmaster Burgio is here for you. Says if you'll see him, he has something to tell you. It won't take more than five minutes.'

'Show him in.'

Headmaster Burgio had already been retired for ten years or so, but everyone still called him by that title because he'd been headmaster of the Vigàta Business School. He and Montalbano were well acquainted. The headmaster was a very cultured, energetic man, with a keen interest in life despite his age, and he sometimes accompanied the inspector on his restful walks along the jetty. The inspector stood up to greet him.

'How nice to see you! Please sit down.'

'Since I was in the neighbourhood, I thought I'd ask if I could talk to you. If I hadn't found you in the office, I would have phoned.'

'What can I do for you?'

'I wanted to let you know a few things about the cave where you found those weapons. I'm not sure it'll be of any interest, but—'

'Are you kidding? Tell me everything you know.'

'Well, let me state first that what I'm about to say is

based on what I've heard on the local TV and read in the newspapers. It's possible they got a few things wrong. In any case, somebody said that the boulder covering the cave entrance had been made into a door by mafiosi or by whoever was trafficking in weapons. It's not true. This work of . . . let's call it adjustment, was done by the grandfather of a very dear friend of mine, Lillo Rizzitano.'

'How long ago? Do you know?'

'Of course I know. It was in about 1941, when oil, flour and wheat were growing scarce because of the war. At that time, all the land around the Crasto and the Crasticeddru belonged to Giacomo Rizzitano, Lillo's grandfather, who had made a lot of money in America by less than legitimate means, or at least that's what people in town said. Anyway, it was Giacomo Rizzitano's idea to seal off the cave by turning that boulder into a door. Inside it they kept all sorts of good things, selling them on the black market with the help of his son Pietro, Lillo's father. They were unscrupulous men, who'd been implicated in other affairs which decent people at the time never talked about, including, apparently, some acts of violence. Lillo, on the other hand, had turned out differently. He was sort of literary, he wrote nice poems and read a lot. It was he who first introduced me to Pavese's *Paesi tuoi*, Vittorini's *Conversazione in Sicilia*, and so on. I used to go to visit him, usually when his parents weren't there, in a small house right at the foot of the Crasto, on the seaward side.'

'Was it demolished to build the tunnel?'

'Yes. Or, more precisely, the earthmovers working on the tunnel merely got rid of the ruins and foundations, since the house was literally pulverized during the bombings that preceded the Allied landing in 1943.'

'Think you could track down this Lillo friend of yours?'

'I don't even know whether he's dead or alive, or where he's lived since then. I say this because you should bear in mind that Lillo was, or is, four years older than me.'

'Tell me, Mr Burgio, have you ever been inside that cave?'

'No. I once asked Lillo, but he said no. He had strict orders from his father and grandfather. He was very afraid of them; the fact that he'd even told me the secret of the cave was already a lot.'

*

Officer Balassone, despite his Piedmontese name, spoke Milanese dialect and always wore a haggard face worthy of the Day of the Dead.

'*L'è el dì di mort, alegher!*' Montalbano thought upon seeing him, reminded of the title of a poem by Delio Tessa.

After half an hour of fussing about with his instrument at the back of the cave, Balassone removed his headset and gave the inspector an even more disconsolate look than usual, if that was possible.

I was wrong, thought Montalbano, *and now I'm going to look like a stupid shit in Jacomuzzi's eyes.*

Jacomuzzi, for his part, after ten minutes inside the

cave, had made it known he suffered from claustrophobia and gone outside.

Maybe because now there aren't any TV cameras pointed at you? Montalbano thought maliciously.

'So?' the inspector finally asked Balassone, to confirm his failure.

'It's there, behind the wall,' Balassone said mysteriously. He was not only a melancholic, but also a man of few words.

'Would you please tell me – if it's not asking too much – exactly *what* is there behind the wall?' asked Montalbano, who was becoming dangerously polite.

'*On sit voeuij.*'

'Would you please have the courtesy to speak Italian?'

The appearance and tone seemed those of an eighteenth-century gentleman of the court. Baldassone had no idea that, if he went on at this rate, he was in line to have his nose rearranged. Luckily for him, he obeyed.

'There's a hollow,' he said, 'and it's as big as this cave here.'

The inspector took comfort. He'd seen right. At that moment Jacomuzzi came in.

'Find anything?'

With his immediate superior, Baldassone's tongue suddenly loosened. Montalbano gave him a dirty look.

'Yessir,' said the Piedmontese. 'There apparently is another cave behind this one. It's like something I saw once on television. There was this Eskimo's house – what do you call them? – oh, yes, this igloo, and right next to it was another igloo. And the two igloos were connected by a kind of passageway, a short, low corridor. It's the same here.'

'At a rough glance,' said Jacomuzzi, 'I'd say the passage between the two caves must date from a good number of years ago.'

'Yessir,' said Baldassone, looking more and more weary. 'If any weapons were hidden in the other cave, they'd have to go back as least as far as the Second World War.'

＊

The first thing Montalbano noticed about the piece of cardboard, which the crime lab had dutifully inserted in a little transparent plastic bag, was that it had the same shape as Sicily. In the middle of it were some letters printed in black: ATO-CAT.

'Fazio!'

'At your service!'

'Get Vinti's to lend you the Jeep and shovels and pick axes again. We're going back to the Crasticeddru tomorrow, you, me, Germanà and Galluzzo.'

'This is becoming a bad habit!' Fazio cried out.

＊

Montalbano felt tired. In the fridge he found some boiled squid and a slice of nicely aged caciocavallo cheese. He set himself up on the veranda. When he had finished eating, he went to look in the freezer, and there he found a tub of lemon ice, which the housekeeper made regularly for him by following a one-two-four formula: one glass of lemon juice, two of sugar, and four of water. A finger-licking delight. Then he decided to stretch out on the bed and finish the novel by Montalbán. He was unable to read even a chapter. Despite his interest, sleep got the better of him. He woke up with a start less than two hours later. He looked at his watch: barely eleven o'clock. As he was putting the watch back on the bedside table, his eye fell on the piece of cardboard, which he'd brought with him. He picked it up and went into the bathroom. Sitting on the toilet in the cold fluorescent light, he studied it closely. Suddenly an idea flashed in his brain. For a moment it seemed as if the bathroom light were growing steadily in intensity, until it exploded in a luminescent burst. He started laughing.

Is it possible ideas only come to me when I'm on the loo?

He studied the piece of cardboard again and again.

I'll try again tomorrow morning, with a cooler head.

But it was not to be. After fifteen minutes of tossing and turning in bed, he got up, grabbed the phonebook, and looked up the number of Captain Aliotta of the Customs Police in Montelusa, who was a friend of his.

'Sorry to call so late, but I urgently need some information. Have you ever done any inspections at the supermarket of a certain Carmelo Ingrassia in Vigàta?'

'The name doesn't ring a bell. And if I can't remember, it probably means that there was an inspection, but it turned up nothing irregular.'

'Thanks.'

'Wait. The person responsible for these kinds of procedures is Sergeant Laganà. If you want, I'll have him phone you at home. You're at home, right?'

'Yes.'

'Give me ten minutes.'

He had enough time to go into the kitchen and drink a glass of cold water before the telephone rang.

'Laganà speaking. The captain filled me in. The last inspection check at that supermarket was two months ago. Everything was in order.'

'Was it done at your own instigation?'

'Just a routine check. Nothing out of order. In fact, it's not that often we come across a store owner with his papers in such good order. If somebody wanted to screw him, they'd have nothing to grab on to.'

'And you checked everything? Accounts, invoices, receipts?'

'Excuse me, Inspector, but how do you think we do our checks?' asked the sergeant, starting to sound a little testy.

'For heaven's sake, Sergeant, I didn't mean to cast any doubt . . . That wasn't the reason for my question. You see, I'm unfamiliar with certain procedures, and that's why I'm asking for your help. How do these supermarkets get their stocks?'

'From wholesalers. They might use five or ten different ones, depending on what they need.'

'I see. Would you be able to tell me who the suppliers of the Ingrassia supermarket are?'

'I think so. I should have some notes around here somewhere.'

'I really appreciate this. I'll call you tomorrow at the barracks.'

'But I'm at the barracks right now! Stay on the line.'

Montalbano heard some whistling.

'Hello, Inspector? Here we are. The wholesalers that stock Ingrassia . . . there's three from Milan, one from Bergamo, one in Taranto, one in Catania. Take this down. In Milan—'

'Wait. Excuse me for interrupting. Start with Catania.'

'The corporate name of the Catanian company is "Pan", you know, like "frying pan". Owned by Salvatore Nicosia, who resides at—'

It didn't add up.

'Thanks, that's enough.'

'Wait, here's something else I'd forgotten about. The supermarket is also supplied by another wholesaler, also in Catania, for its household goods. That one's called Brancato.'

ATO-CAT, the piece of cardboard said. Brancato-Catania: it added up, and how! Montalbano's cry of joy thundered in the sergeant's earpiece, frightening him.

'Inspector? Inspector! Oh, my God, what happened? Are you all right, Inspector?'

ELEVEN

Fresh and smiling, in jacket and tie and enveloped in a haze of cologne, Montalbano showed up at the home of Francesco Lacommare, manager of the Ingrassia supermarket, at seven o'clock in the morning. The manager greeted him not only with legitimate astonishment, but also in his underwear, with a glass of milk in his hand.

'What is it?' he asked, turning pale upon recognizing the inspector.

'Two simple little questions and I'll get out of your hair. But, first, one very serious stipulation: this meeting must remain between you and me. If you speak to anyone at all about it, even your boss, I'll find an excuse to throw your arse in jail, and you can bank on that.'

As Lacommare was struggling to recover his breath, a shrill, annoying female voice exploded inside the apartment:

'Ciccino! Who's that at this hour?'

'It's nothing, Carmelina, go back to sleep,' Lacommare reassured her, pulling the door shut behind him.

'Do you mind, Inspector, if we talk over here on the

landing? The top floor, the one right above us, is vacant, so there's no danger anyone will bother us.'

'Who do you buy from in Catania?'

'From Pan and Brancato.'

'Do they have fixed delivery schedules?'

'Once a week for Pan, once a month for Brancato. We've coordinated it with the other supermarkets that use the same wholesalers.'

'Very good. So, as I understand it, Brancato will load up a truck with merchandise and send it out to make the rounds of the supermarkets. Now, where on these rounds is your store situated? Let me explain better—'

'I understand, Inspector. The truck leaves Catania, services the Caltanissetta area first, then Trapani, then Montelusa. The Vigàta markets are the last ones the truck visits before heading back to Catania.'

'One last question. The merchandise those thieves took and then left behind—'

'You're very intelligent, Inspector.'

'You are, too, if you can answer me before I've asked you a question.'

'The fact is, this whole story's been keeping me up at night. Here's the problem: the Brancato merchandise was delivered early. We were expecting it first thing the next morning, but it arrived the evening before, just as we were closing. The driver told us one of his supermarkets in Trapani had been suddenly closed for mourning, so he was ahead of schedule. Mr Ingrassia, to free up the truck, had it unloaded, checked the list, and counted the crates. But he didn't have anyone open them up. Said it was too late. He didn't want to pay anybody overtime and said we could do everything the next day. A few hours later, the store was robbed. So, my question is: who told the robbers the merchandise had arrived early?'

Lacommare was putting some passion into his reasoning. Montalbano decided to play devil's advocate. After all, the manager must not be allowed to get too close to the truth; that might cause trouble. Most of all, it was obvious he was unaware of Ingrassia's trafficking.

'The two things aren't necessarily connected,' the inspector said. 'The thieves could have come to rob what you already had in storage and ended up finding the freshly delivered merchandise instead.'

'Yes, but then why leave it all behind?'

That was indeed the question. Montalbano was hesitant to give an answer that might satisfy Lacommare's curiosity.

'But who the fuck is that anyway?' asked the now enraged female voice from within.

She must have been a woman of delicate sentiment, this Signora Lacommare. Montalbano took advantage of the interruption to leave. He'd found out what he wanted to know.

'My respects to your lovely wife,' he said, starting back down the stairs.

When he reached the front door, however, he sprang back upstairs like a tethered ball and rang the doorbell.

'You again?' Lacommare had drunk his milk but was still in his underwear.

'I'm sorry, I forgot something. Are you sure the truck was completely empty after you unloaded it?'

'No, I didn't say that. There were still about fifteen large crates. The driver said they belonged to that supermarket in Trapani that he'd found closed.'

'But what is all this fucking commotion so early in the morning?' Signora Carmelina shrieked from within, and Montalbano fled without even saying goodbye.

*

'I think I've determined, with reasonable accuracy, the route the weapons travelled before reaching the cave. Bear with me, Mr Commissioner. Here goes: in some way that we have yet to discover, the weapons come to the Brancato firm in Catania from some other part of the world. Brancato warehouses them and puts them in big boxes with the company name on them, so they look like they contain normal electrical appliances to be sold in supermarkets. When they receive the order to deliver, the Brancato people load the boxes with the weapons onto the truck, along with the rest. As a precaution, along some stretch of road between Catania and Caltanissetta, they replace the company truck with a stolen one. That way, if anybody finds the weapons, Brancato's can claim they had nothing to do with it, they know nothing about it, the truck isn't theirs, and, in fact, they themselves were robbed. The stolen truck begins its circuit, dropping off the . . . uh . . . "clean" crates at the various supermarkets it supplies, then heads off to Vigàta. Before arriving, however, it stops in the middle of the night at the Crasticeddru and unloads the weapons in the cave. Early that morning – according to Lacommare, the store manager – they deliver their final packages to the Ingrassia supermarket and then leave. On the way back to Catania, the stolen truck is then replaced by the company's actual truck, which returns home as if it has made its full journey. Maybe they take care to tinker with the odometer each time. And they've been playing this little game for at least three years, since Jacomuzzi said that the outfitting of the cave in fact goes back three years.'

'Your explanation makes excellent logical sense,' said the commissioner. 'But I still don't understand the whole charade of the phony robbery.'

'They acted out of necessity. Do you remember that gunfight between a patrol of carabinieri and three thugs in the Santa Lucia countryside, where one carabiniere was wounded?'

'Yes, I do remember it, but what's that got to do with this?'

'The local radio stations broadcast the news around nine p.m., right when the truck was on its way to the Crasticeddru. Santa Lucia is only about a mile and a half away from the cave. The traffickers must have heard the news on the radio. It would have been stupid to let themselves be spotted in a deserted place by some patrol – of which there were many that night, racing to the site of the shoot-out. So they decided to push on to Vigàta. They were certain to run into a roadblock, but that was the lesser evil at this point, since they stood a good chance of slipping through. And that's what happened. So, they arrive well ahead of schedule and make up the story about the supermarket closed for mourning in Trapani. Ingrassia, who's been alerted of the hitch, has his employees unload the truck, which then pretends to head back to Catania. It's still carrying the weapons, those same crates which they told Lacommare, the manager, were supposed to have gone to the supermarket in Trapani. The truck is then hidden somewhere around Vigàta, on Ingrassia's or some accomplice's property.'

'I ask you again: why fake the heist? From where they'd hidden it, the truck could have easily gone back to the Crasticeddru without having to pass through Vigàta.'

'But it did have to pass through Vigàta. If they'd been stopped by the carabinieri, the Customs Police, or whomever, with those fifteen crates aboard, unaccompanied by any delivery note, they would have aroused suspicion. They'd have been forced to open one, and that would have been the end of that. They absolutely did have to take back the packages that Ingrassia had unloaded, and which he had every reason not to open.'

'I'm beginning to understand.'

'So, at a certain hour of the night, the truck returns to the supermarket. The night watchman is in no position to recognize either the delivery men or the truck because he wasn't yet on duty when they came the previous evening. They load the still-sealed packages, head off to the Crasti-ceddru, unload the weapons crates, turn back round, ditch the truck in the car park behind the filling station, and their work is done.'

'But can you tell me why they didn't simply get rid of the stolen merchandise and head back to Catania?'

'That's the stroke of genius. By leaving the truck behind with all the stolen merchandise inside, they throw us off their trail. We're automatically forced to assume some kind of flap – a threat, a warning for not paying one's protection dues. In short, they force us to investigate at a lower level, the kind of stuff that is unfortunately an everyday matter in this part of Italy. And Ingrassia plays his part very well, absurdly calling it all a practical joke.'

'A real stroke of genius,' said the commissioner.

'Yes, but if you look closely enough, you can always uncover a mistake. In our case, they didn't realize that a piece of cardboard had slipped under the planks that served as the cave's floor.'

'Right, right,' the commissioner said pensively. Then, as if to himself 'Who knows where the empty boxes ended up?' he queried.

Now and then the commissioner would pause in idiotic wonder over meaningless details.

'They probably loaded them into some car and burned them out in the country. Because some accomplices brought at least two cars to the Crasticeddru, perhaps to take the driver away after he'd ditched the truck behind the petrol station.'

'So without that piece of cardboard we would never have discovered anything,' the commissioner concluded.

'Well, not exactly,' said Montalbano. 'I was following another path that would eventually have led me to the same conclusions. They were forced, you see, to kill a poor old man.'

The commissioner gave a start, darkening.

'A murder? Why was I not informed of this?'

'Because it was made to look like an accident. I only ascertained a couple of nights ago that the brakes on his car had been tampered with.'

'Was it Jacomuzzi who told you?'

'For the love of God! Jacomuzzi, bless his soul, is certainly competent, but mixing him up in this would have been like issuing a press release.'

'One of these days I'm going to give that Jacomuzzi a good dressing down . . . I'm going to skin him alive,' said the commissioner, sighing. 'Now tell me the whole story, but slowly, and in chronological order.'

Montalbano told him about Misuraca and the letter the cavaliere had sent him.

'He was murdered needlessly,' he concluded. 'His killers didn't know he'd already written to me and told me everything.'

'Listen, explain to me what reason Ingrassia had for being near his supermarket while the phony robbery was taking place, if we're to believe Misuraca.'

'If there were any other snags — an untimely visit, for example — he could jump out and readily explain that everything was all right and they were sending the merchandise back because the people at Brancato's had got the order wrong.'

'And what about the night watchman in the freezer?'

'He was no longer a problem. They would have bumped him off.'

'How should we proceed?' the commissioner asked after a pause.

'Tano the Greek has given us a tremendous gift, even without naming any names,' Montalbano began, 'and we shouldn't waste it. If we go about this carefully, we could get our hands on a network the size of which we can't even imagine. But we've got to be cautious. If we immediately arrest Ingrassia or someone from the Brancato firm, we'll come up empty for all our effort. We need to aim for the bigger fish.'

'I agree,' said the commissioner. 'I'll call Catania and tell them to put a tail on—'

He broke off with a grimace, painfully remembering the mole who'd talked in Palermo and brought about Tano's death. There might well be another in Catania.

'Let's start at the bottom,' he decided. 'We'll put only Ingrassia under surveillance.'

'All right. I'll get the court order from the judge,' said the inspector.

As he was heading out the door, the commissioner called him back inside.

'By the way, my wife is feeling much better. How would Saturday evening do for you? We have a lot to discuss.'

✻

He found Judge Lo Bianco in an unusually good mood, his eyes sparkling.

'You look well,' the inspector couldn't help saying.

'Yes, yes, I'm quite well, in fact.' He then looked around, assumed a conspiratorial air, leaned towards Montalbano, and said in a low voice: 'Did you know that Rinaldo had six fingers on his right hand?'

Montalbano faltered a moment, befuddled. Then he remembered that the judge had been working devotedly for years on a ponderous book entitled *The Life and Deeds of Rinaldo and Antonio Lo Bianco, Masters of Law at the University of Girgenti at the time of King Martin the Younger (1402–1409)*. Lo Bianco had got it into his head that the two ancient barristers were his ancestors.

'Oh, really?' Montalbano asked with jovial surprise. It was best to humour him.

'Yes, indeed. Six fingers, on his right hand.'

Jerking off must have been heaven, Montalbano was about to say sacrilegiously, but managed to restrain himself.

He told the judge everything about the weapons traffic and Misuraca's murder. He even detailed the strategy he wanted to follow and asked him for a court order to tap Ingrassia's phone lines.

Normally, Lo Bianco would have raised objections,

created obstacles, imagined problems. This time, delighted with his discovery of Rinaldo's six-fingered hand, he would have granted Montalbano an order to torture, impale, or burn someone at the stake.

*

He went home, put on his bathing suit, went for a long, long swim, came back inside, dried himself off, but did not get dressed again. There was nothing in the refrigerator, but in the oven sat, as on a throne, a casserole with four huge servings of *pasta 'ncasciata*, a dish worthy of Olympus. He ate two portions, put the casserole back in the oven, set his alarm clock, slept like a rock for one hour, got back up, took a shower, put his already dirty jeans and shirt back on, and went to the station.

Fazio, Germanà and Galluzzo were waiting for him in their work clothes. As soon as they saw him, they grabbed their shovels, pickaxes and mattocks and struck up the old day labourers' chorus, shaking their tools in the air, 'Give land to those who work! Give land to those who work!'

'Fucking idiots,' was Montalbano's only comment.

*

Prestìa, Galluzzo's newsman brother-in-law, was already there, at the entrance of the Crasticeddru cave, along with a camera man who had brought along two large battery-powered floodlights.

Montalbano gave Galluzzo a dirty look.

'Well,' the latter said, blushing, 'I just thought that since you allowed him last time—'

'All right, all right,' the inspector cut him off.

They entered the weapons cave, and when Montalbano gave the order, Fazio, Germanà and Galluzzo started working on removing the stones that had fused together over the years. They laboured for a good three hours, and even Prestìa, the cameraman, and the inspector joined in, periodically relieving the three men. In the end the wall came down. They could clearly see the little passageway, just as Balassone had said. The rest was lost in darkness.

'You go in first,' Montalbano said to Fazio.

The sergeant took a flashlight, started crawling on his belly, and disappeared. A few seconds later, they heard an astonished voice from the other side.

'Oh, my God! Inspector! You have to see this.'

'The rest of you come in when I call you,' said Montalbano to the others, looking especially at the newsman, who upon hearing Fazio had started forward and was about to throw himself to the ground and start crawling.

The little tunnel was roughly the same length as the inspector's body. An instant later he was on the other side, and he turned on his flashlight. The second cave was smaller than the first and immediately gave the impression of being perfectly dry. In the very middle was a rug still in good condition. In the far left corner of the rug, a bowl. To the right, in the symmetrically corresponding position, a jug. Forming the vertex of this upside-down triangle, at the near end of the rug, was a life-size shepherd dog, made of terracotta. And on the rug were two dead bodies, all shrivelled up as in a horror film, embracing.

Montalbano felt short of breath; he couldn't open his mouth. He remembered the two youngsters he had surprised in the act of making love in the other cave. The men took advantage of his silence and, unable to resist, came in one after the other. The cameraman turned on his floods and began frantically filming. Nobody spoke. The first to recover was Montalbano.

'Call the crime lab, the judge and Dr Pasquano,' he said.

He didn't even turn around towards Fazio to give the order. He just stood there, in a trance, staring at that scene, afraid that his slightest gesture might wake him from the dream he was living.

TWELVE

Rousing himself from the spell that had paralysed him, Montalbano started shouting to everyone to stand with their backs to the wall and not to move, not to tread on the floor of the cave, which was covered with a very fine, reddish sand. Where it had filtered in from was anyone's guess. Maybe it was on the walls. There was no trace of this sand whatsoever in the other cave; perhaps it had somehow halted the decomposition of the corpses. These were a man and a woman, their ages impossible to determine by sight. That they were of different sex the inspector could tell by the shapes of their bodies and not, of course, by any sexual attributes, which had been obliterated by natural process. The man was lying on his side, arm extended across the breast of the woman, who was supine. They were therefore embracing, and would remain in that embrace forever. In fact, what had once been the flesh of the man's arm had sort of stuck to and fused with the flesh of the woman's breast. No, they would be separated soon enough, by the hand of Dr Pasquano. Standing out under the wizened, shrivelled flesh was the white of their bones. The lovers had been dried out, reduced to pure form. They looked as if they were laughing, the lips pulled back, stretched about the mouth and showing the teeth. Next to the dead man's head was the bowl, with some round objects inside; next to the woman was the earthenware jug, the kind in which peasants used to carry cool water around with them as they worked. At the couple's feet, the terracotta dog. It was about three feet long, its colours, grey and white, still intact. The craftsman who made it had portrayed it with front legs extended, hind legs folded, mouth half-open with the pink tongue hanging out, eyes watchful. Lying down, in short, but on guard. The rug had a few holes through which one could see the sand of the cave floor, but these may well have been already there when the rug was put in the cave.

'Everybody out!' Montalbano ordered. Then, turning to Prestìa and the cameraman 'And turn off those lamps. Now.'

He had suddenly realized how much damage the heat of the floodlights and their own mere presence must be causing. He was left alone in the cave. By the beam of the flashlight, he carefully examined the contents of the bowl: those round objects were metal coins, oxydized and covered with verdigris. Gently, with two fingers, he picked one up, seemingly the best preserved: it was a twenty-centesimo piece, minted in 1941, with a portrait of King Victor Emmanuel on one side and a female profile with the Roman fasces on the other. When he aimed the light at the dead man's head, he noticed a hole in his temple. He was too well versed in such matters not to realize that it had been made by a firearm. The man had either committed suicide or been killed. But if it had been a suicide, where was the weapon? The woman's body, on the other hand, bore no trace of violent, induced death. Montalbano remained pensive. The two were naked, yet there was no clothing in the cave. What did it mean? Without growing first yellow and dim, the flashlight suddenly went out. The battery had died. He was momentarily blinded and couldn't get his bearings. To avoid damaging anything, he crouched down on the sand, waiting for his eyes to adjust to the dark; in a minute he would surely start to glimpse the faint glow of the passageway. Yet those few seconds of total darkness and silence were enough for him to notice an unusual odour that he was certain he had smelt before. He tried to remember where, even if it was of no importance. Ever since childhood he had always associated a colour with every smell that caught his attention; this smell, he decided, was dark green. From this association he was able to remember where he had first noticed it. It was in Cairo, inside the pyramid of Cheops, in a corridor off-limits to tourists which he had been able to visit courtesy of an Egyptian friend. And all at once he felt like a *quaquaraquà*, a worthless man, with no respect for anything. That morning, by surprising the two kids making love, he had desecrated life; and now, by exposing the two bodies that should have remained forever unknown to the world in their embrace, he had desecrated death.

*

Perhaps because of this feeling of guilt, Montalbano did not wish to take part in the evidence-gathering, which Jacomuzzi and his crime lab team, along with Dr Pasquano, began at once. He had already smoked five cigarettes, seated on the boulder that served as a door to the weapons cave, when he heard Pasquano call to him in an agitated, irritated voice.

'Where the hell is the judge?'

'You're asking me?'

'If he doesn't get here soon, things are going to turn nasty. I've got to get these corpses to Montelusa and put them in the fridge. They're practically decomposing before our eyes. What am I supposed to do?'

'Have a cigarette with me,' Montalbano said, trying to pacify him.

Judge Lo Bianco arrived fifteen minutes later, after the inspector had smoked another two cigarettes.

Lo Bianco glanced distractedly at the scene and, since the dead were not from the time of King Martin the Younger, said hastily to the coroner, 'Do whatever you want with them. It's ancient history, in any case.'

*

TeleVigàta had immediately discovered the proper angle from which to present the story. The first thing one saw on the evening news at 8.30 was Prestìa's excited face announcing an extraordinary scoop for which, he said, they were indebted to 'one of those ingenious intuitions that make Inspector Salvo Montalbano of Vigàta a figure perhaps unique among crime investigators across the island of Sicily and – why not? – in all of Italy.' He went on to recount the inspector's dramatic arrest of the fugitive Tano the Greek, the bloodthirsty Mafia boss, and his discovery of the weapons cache inside the Crasticeddru cave. Then they played some footage of the press conference held after Tano's arrest, in which an insane-looking, stammering man who answered to the name and title of Inspector Montalbano was having trouble putting together four consecutive words. Prestìa resumed his account of how this exceptional detective had become convinced that behind the cave of weapons there must be another cave connected to it.

'Trusting in the inspector's intuition,' said Prestìa, 'I followed him, assisted by my cameraman, Gerlando Schirirò.'

At this point Prestìa, adopting a tone of mystery, raised a few questions: what sort of secret, paranormal powers did the inspector possess? What was it made him think that an ancient tragedy lay hidden behind a few rocks blackened by time? Did the inspector have X-ray vision, like Superman?

Upon hearing this last question, Montalbano – who was watching the broadcast from his home and for the last half-hour had been unsuccessfully searching for a clean pair of underpants, which he knew must be around somewhere – told the newsman to go fuck himself.

As the chilling images of the bodies in the cave started rolling, Prestìa expounded his thesis with conviction. Since he didn't know about the hole in the man's head, he spoke of two people who had died for love. In his opinion, the lovers, their passion opposed by their families, had shut themselves up in the cave, sealing off the passageway and letting themselves starve to death. They had furnished their final refuge with an old rug and a jug full of water, and had waited for death in each other's arms. Of the bowl full of coins he said nothing: it would have clashed with the scene he was painting. The two – Prestìa went on – had not been identified; their story had taken place at least fifty years ago. Then another newscaster started talking about the day's events: a six-year-old girl raped and bludgeoned to death with a stone by a paternal uncle; a corpse discovered in a well; a shoot-out at Merfi resulting in three dead and four injured; a labourer killed in an industrial accident; the disappearance of a dentist; the suicide of a businessman who had been squeezed by loan sharks; the arrest of a town councillor in Montevergine for graft and corruption; the suicide of the provincial president, who had been indicted for receiving stolen goods; a dead body washed ashore . . .

Montalbano fell into a deep sleep in front of the television.

*

'Hello, Salvo? Gegè here. Let me talk, and don't interrupt with your usual bullshit. I need to see you. I need to tell you something.'

'Okay, Gegè. Even tonight's okay, if you want.'

'I'm not in Vigàta, I'm in Trapani.'

'So when?'

'What day is today?'

'Thursday.'

'How about Saturday midnight at the usual place?'

'Listen, Gegè, Saturday night I'm having dinner with someone, but I can come anyway. If I'm a little late, wait for me.'

*

The phone call from Gegè, who from his tone of voice sounded worried – enough not to tolerate any joking – had woken him up just in time. It was ten o'clock, and he tuned in to the Free Channel. Nicolò Zito, with his intelligent face, red hair, and red ideas, opened the news broadcast with the story of a labourer who died at his workplace in Fela, roasted alive in a gas explosion. He listed a series of examples to demonstrate how, in at least 90 per cent of the cases, management was blithely indifferent to safety standards. He then moved on to the arrest of some public officials charged with various forms of embezzlement and used this instance to remind viewers of how several different elected governments had tried in vain to pass laws that might prevent the clean-up operation currently under way.

His third item was the suicide of the businessman strangled by debts to a loan shark, and here he criticized the government's provisions against usury as utterly inadequate. Why, he asked, were those investigating this scourge so careful to keep loan-sharking and the Mafia separate? How many different ways were there to launder dirty money?

Finally, he came to the news of the two bodies found in the cave, but he approached it from a peculiar perspective, indirectly challenging the angle that Prestìa and TeleVigàta had taken on the story. Somebody, he said, once asserted that religion is the opium of the people; today, instead, one would have to say that the real opium is television. For example: why had certain people presented this case as a story of two lovers thwarted in their love? What facts authorized anyone to advance such a hypothesis? The two were found nude: what had happened to their clothes? No trace of any weapon was found in the cave. How would they have killed themselves? By starving to death? Come on! Why did the man have a bowl beside him containing coins no longer current today but still valid at the time of their deaths? To pay Charon's toll? The truth, claimed the newsman, is that they want to turn a probable crime into a certain suicide, a romantic suicide. And in our dark days, with so many threatening clouds on the horizon, he concluded, we puff up a story like this to drug people, to distract their attention from the serious problems and divert them with a Romeo and Juliet story, one scripted, however, by a soap-opera writer.

*

'Darling, it's Livia. I wanted to tell you I've booked our tickets. The flight leaves from Rome, so you'll have to buy a ticket from Palermo to Fiumicino; I'll do the same from Genoa. We'll meet at the airport and board together.'

'Mm-hmm.'

'I've also reserved our hotel. A friend of mine has stayed there and said it's really nice without being too fancy. I think you'll like it.'

'Mm-hmm.'

'We leave in two weeks and a day. I'm so happy. I'm counting the days and the hours.'

'Mm-hmm.'

'Salvo, what's wrong?'

'Nothing. Why should there be anything wrong?'

'You don't sound very enthusiastic.'

'Of course I am, what do you mean?'

'Look, Salvo, if you wiggle out of this at the last minute, I'll go anyway, by myself.'

'Come on.'

'But what's wrong with you?'

'Nothing. I was sleeping.'

*

'Inspector Montalbano? Good evening. This is Headmaster Burgio.'

'Good evening. What can I do for you?'

'I'm very sorry to disturb you at home. I just heard on television about the two bodies that were found.'

'Could you identify them?'

'No. I'm calling about something that was said in passing on TV, but which might be of interest to you. I'm talking about the terracotta dog. If you have no objection, I thought I'd come to your office tomorrow morning with Burruano, the accountant. Do you know him?'

'I know who he is. Ten o'clock all right?'

*

'Here,' said Livia. 'I want to do it here, right away.'

They were in a kind of park, dense with trees. Crawling about at their feet were hundreds of snails of every variety, garden snails, tree snails, escargots, slugs, periwinkles.

'Why right here? Let's get back in the car and in five minutes we'll be home. Around here, somebody might see us.'

'Don't argue, jerk!' Livia shot back, grabbing his belt and trying awkwardly to unbuckle it.

'I'll do it,' he said.

In an instant Livia was naked, while he was still struggling with his trousers, then his underpants.

She's accustomed to stripping in a hurry, he thought, in a surge of Sicilian jealousy.

As Livia threw herself down on the wet grass, legs spread, caressing her breasts with her hands, he heard, to his disgust, the sound of dozens of snails being crushed under the weight of her body.

'Come on, hurry up,' she said.

Montalbano finally managed to strip down naked, shuddering in the chill air. Meanwhile, a few snails had started slithering over Livia's body.

'And what do you expect to do with that?' she asked critically, eyeing his cock. With a look of compassion, she got up on her knees, took it in her hands, caressed it, and put her lips around it. When she felt he was ready, she resumed her prior position.

'Fuck me to kingdom come,' she said.

When did she become so vulgar? he wondered, bewildered.

As he was about to enter her, he saw the dog a few steps away, a white dog with its pink tongue sticking out, growling menacingly, teeth bared, a string of slobber dribbling from its mouth. When did it get there?

'What are you doing? Has it gone soft again?'

'There's a dog.'

'What the hell do you care? Give it to me.'

At that exact moment the dog sprang into the air and he froze, terrified. The dog landed a few inches from his head, turned stiff, its colour lightly fading, then lay down, its front legs extended, hind legs folded. It became fake, turned into terracotta. It was the dog in the cave, the one guarding the dead couple.

Then all at once the sky, trees, and grass disappeared, walls of rock formed around them and overhead, and in horror he realized that the dead couple in the cave were not two strangers, but Livia and himself.

He awoke from the nightmare breathless and sweating,

and immediately in his mind he begged Livia's forgiveness for having imagined her as so obscene in the dream. But what was the meaning of that dog? And those disgusting snails slithering all over the place?

That dog had to have a meaning, he was sure of it.

*

Before going to the office, he stopped at a kiosk and bought Sicily's two newspapers. Both of them prominently featured the story of the bodies found in the cave; as for the discovery of the weapons, they had prominently forgotten about that. The paper published in Palermo was certain that it had been a love suicide, whereas the one published in Catania was also open to the possibility of murder, while not, of course, discounting suicide, and indeed its headline read: DOUBLE SUICIDE OR DUAL HOMICIDE? – implying some vague, mysterious distinction between 'double' and 'dual'. On the other hand, no matter what the issue, this newspaper customarily never took a position. Whether the subject was a war or an earthquake, it always liked to play both sides of the fence, and for this had gained a reputation as an independent, freethinking daily. Neither of the two dwelt on the jug, the bowl, or the terracotta dog.

The instant Montalbano appeared in the doorway, Catarella asked him what he should say to the hundreds of journalists who were certain to phone, wanting to speak with the inspector.

'Tell them I've gone on a mission.'

'What, you've become a missionary?' quipped the policeman, lightning-quick, chuckling noisily to himself.

Montalbano concluded that he'd been right, the previous evening, to unplug the telephone before going to bed.

THIRTEEN

'Dr Pasquano? Montalbano here. Just wondering if there's any news.'

'Yes, there certainly is. My wife has a cold and my granddaughter lost a baby tooth.'

'Are you angry, Doctor?'

'I certainly am!'

'With whom?'

'You ask me if there's any news! Well, let me ask you how you can have the gall to ask me anything at nine o'clock in the morning! What do you think, that I've just spent the night opening up those two corpses' bellies like some kind of vulture? I happen to sleep at night! And, at the moment, I'm working on that guy who drowned around Torre Spaccata. Who didn't drown at all, since before being tossed into the sea he'd been stabbed three times in the chest.'

'Shall we make a bet, Doctor?'

'On what?'

'On whether or not you spent the night with those two corpses.'

'All right, all right. You win.'

'What did you find out?'

'Right now I can't tell you much; I still have to look at a few other things. One sure thing is that they were killed by gunshot wounds. He to the head, she to the heart. You couldn't see the woman's wound because his hand was covering it. A textbook execution, while they were sleeping.'

'Inside the cave?'

'I don't think so. They were probably already dead when they were brought there, then were rearranged, still naked and all.'

'Have you managed to establish their ages?'

'I wouldn't want to be wrong, but I'd say they were young, very young.'

'And when did the crime take place, in your opinion?'

'I could venture a guess, which you can take with a pinch of salt. About fifty years ago, more or less.'

*

'I'm not here for anyone. No phone calls for the next fifteen minutes,' Montalbano told Catarella. Then he locked the door to his office, returned to his desk, and sat down. Mimì Augello was also sitting there, but stiff as a poker, bolt upright.

'Who goes first?' asked Montalbano.

'I do,' said Augello, 'since it was I who asked to talk to you. Because I think it's time I said something.'

'Well, I'm here to listen.'

'Could you please tell me what I've done to you?'

'You? To me? Nothing at all. Why do you ask?'

'Because I feel like I've become a stranger in this place. You don't tell me what you're doing, you keep me at a distance, and I feel insulted. For example, was it right, in your opinion, to keep me in the dark about Tano the Greek? I'm not Jacomuzzi, who shouts these things from the rooftops. I can keep a secret. I didn't find out what happened at my own police station until I heard it at the press conference. Does that seem like the right way to treat someone who's your second-in-command until proved otherwise?'

'But do you realize how sensitive this matter was?'

'It's precisely because I realize it that I'm so pissed off. Because it must mean that for you, I'm not the right person for sensitive matters.'

'I've never thought that.'

'You've never thought it, but you've always done just that. Like with the weapons, which I found out about by accident.'

'Come on, Mimì, I was overwhelmed by the pressure and anxiety. It didn't occur to me to inform you.'

'That's bullshit, Salvo. That's not the real story.'

'Oh, yeah? What's the real story?'

'I'll tell you. You've created a police station in your own image and likeness. Fazio, Germanà, Galluzzo, take anyone you want, they're all just limbs that obey one single head: yours. They never contradict you, never ask questions: they just follow orders. There are two foreign bodies here: Catarella and me. Catarella, because he's too stupid, and me—'

'Because you're too intelligent.'

'See? That's not what I was going to say. You make me out to be arrogant, which I'm not, and you do it maliciously.'

Montalbano looked at him, stood up, put his hands in his pockets, circled round the chair in which Augello was sitting, then stopped.

'It wasn't malicious, Mimì. You really are intelligent.'

'If you seriously believe that, then why do you cut me out? I could be at least as useful to you as the others.'

'That's just it, Mimì. Not *as* useful, but more so. I'm speaking to you quite frankly, since you're making me think seriously about my attitude towards you. And maybe this is what bothers me most.'

'So, just to please you, I ought to dumb myself down a little?'

'Listen, if you want to have it out with me, let's go. That's not what I meant. The fact is that over the course of time, I've realized I'm sort of a solitary hunter – I'm sorry if that sounds idiotic, maybe it's not the right term. Because I do like to go hunting with others, but I want to be the only one to organize the hunt. That's the one necessary precondition for making my brain function properly. An intelligent observation made by someone else merely upsets me – it throws me off, sometimes for a whole day, and can even prevent me from following my own train of thought.'

'I get it,' said Augello. 'Actually, I got it some time ago, but I wanted to hear you say it yourself. So I'm telling you now, without any hostility or hard feelings: I'm going to write to the commissioner today and request a transfer.'

Montalbano looked him over, drew near, and leaned forward, putting his hands on Augello's shoulders.

'Will you believe me if I tell you that would hurt me very deeply?'

'So fucking what!' Mimì exploded. 'Do you expect everyone to give you everything? What kind of man are you? First you treat me like shit, then you try the affectionate approach? Do you realize how monstrously egotistical you are?'

'Yes, I do,' said Montalbano.

*

'Allow me to introduce Mr Burruano, the accountant who so kindly consented to come here with me today,' said Headmaster Burgio with stuffed-shirt ceremoniousness.

'Please sit down,' said Montalbano, gesturing towards two small, old armchairs in a corner of the room, which were reserved for distinguished guests. For himself he pulled up one of the two straight-back chairs in front of his desk, normally reserved for people who were decidedly undistinguished.

'These last few days I feel it's been up to me to correct

or at least clarify what gets said on television,' Burgio began.

'Then correct and clarify,' Montalbano said, smiling.

'Mr Burruano and I are almost the same age. He's four years older, but we remember the same things.'

Montalbano heard a note of pride in the headmaster's voice. There was good reason for it: the twitchy Burruano, who was a bit milky-eyed to boot, looked at least ten years older than his friend.

'You see, right after the TeleVigàta news, which showed the inside of the cave in which they found th—'

'Excuse me for interrupting, but the last time we spoke you mentioned the weapons cave, but said nothing about this other cave. Why?'

'Because I simply didn't know it existed. Lillo never said anything about it to me. Anyway, right after the news, I called Mr Burruano because I'd seen that statue of the dog before, and I wanted confirmation.'

The dog! That was why it appeared in his nightmare, because the headmaster had alluded to it on the phone. Montalbano felt overcome by a childish feeling of gratitude.

'Would you gentlemen like some coffee? Eh? A cup of coffee? They make it so well at the corner cafe.'

The two men shook their heads in unison.

'An orangeade? Coca-Cola? Beer?'

If they didn't stop him, he would soon be offering them ten thousand lire each.

'No, no, thank you, we can't drink anything. Old age, you know,' said Burgio.

'All right, then, tell me your story.'

'It's better if Mr Burruano tells it.'

'From February 1941 to July 1943,' the accountant began, 'though still very young, I was *podestà* of Vigàta. Either because Fascism claimed to like the young – in fact it liked them so much it ate them all, roasted or frozen, made no difference – or because the only people left in town were women, children and the elderly. Everybody else was at the front. I couldn't go because I was consumptive. I really was.'

'I was too young to be sent to the front,' Burgio interjected, to avoid any misunderstanding.

'Those were terrible times. The British and Americans were bombing us every day. In one thirty-six-hour period I counted ten bombing raids. Very few people were left in town, most had been evacuated, and we were living in the shelters that had been dug into the hill of marl above the city. Actually, they were tunnels with two exits, very safe. We even took our beds in there. Vigàta's grown a lot over the years. It's no longer the way it was back then, a handful of houses around the port and a strip of buildings between the foot of the mountain and the sea. Up on the hill, the Piano Lanterna, which today looks like New York with its highrises, had just four structures along a single road, which led to the cemetery and then disappeared into the countryside. The enemy aircraft had three targets: the power station, the port with its warships and merchant ships, and the anti-aircraft and naval batteries along the ridge of the hill. When it was the British overhead, things went better than with the Americans.'

Montalbano was impatient. He wanted the man to get to the point – the dog, that is – but didn't feel like interrupting his digressions.

'Went better in what sense, Mr Burruano? It was still bombs they were dropping.'

Lost within some memory, Burruano had fallen silent, and so Headmaster Burgio spoke for him.

'The British, how shall I say, played more fairly. When they dropped their bombs they tried to hit only military targets, whereas the Americans dropped them helter-skelter, come what may.'

'Towards the end of 1942,' Burruano resumed, 'the situation got even worse. We had nothing: no bread, no medicine, no water, no clothing. So for Christmas I decided to make a nativity scene that we could all pray to. We had nothing else left. I wanted it to be a very special nativity. That way, I thought, for a few days at least, I could take people's minds off their worries – there were so many – and distract them from the terror of the bombings. There wasn't a single family that didn't have at least one man fighting far from home, in the ice of Russia or the hell of Africa. We'd all become edgy, difficult, quarrelsome – the slightest thing would set people off; our nerves were frayed. Between the anti-aircraft machine guns, the exploding bombs, the roar of the low-flying planes, and the cannon-blasts from the ships at sea, we couldn't get a wink of sleep at night. And everyone would come to me or to the priest to ask one thing or another and I didn't know which way to turn. I didn't feel so young any more. I felt then the way I feel now.'

He stopped to catch his breath. Neither Montalbano nor Burgio felt like filling that pause.

'Anyway, to make a long story short, I mentioned my idea to Ballassaro Chiarenza, who was a real artist with terracotta. He did it for pleasure, since he was a carter by trade. It was his idea to make the statues all life-size. Baby Jesus, the Virgin Mary, Saint Joseph, the ox, the donkey, the shepherd with the lamb over his shoulders, a sheep, a dog and the other shepherd, the one who's always portrayed with his arms raised in a gesture of wonder. So he made the whole thing, and it came out really beautiful. We even decided not to put it in the church, but to set it up under the arch of a bombed-out house, so it would look like Jesus had been born amid the suffering of our people.'

He put a hand in his pocket and pulled out a photograph, which he passed to the inspector. The nativity really was beautiful; Mr Burruano was right. It seemed so ephemeral, so perishable, and at the same time conveyed a comforting warmth, a superhuman serenity.

'It's astonishing,' Montalbano complimented him, his emotions welling up. But only for an instant, as the cop in him got the upper hand and began carefully examining the dog. There was no doubt about it: that was the same dog he had found in the cave. Burruano put the photo back in his pocket.

'The nativity performed a miracle, you know. For a few days we were considerate towards one another.'

'What became of the statues?'

This was where Montalbano's real interest lay. The old man smiled.

'I sold them at auction, all of them. I made enough to pay Chiarenza, who wanted only to be reimbursed for his expenses, and to give alms to those who needed them most. And there were many.'

'Who bought the statues?'

'Well, that's the problem. I don't remember. I had the receipts and all, but they were lost when the town hall caught fire during the American invasion.'

'During the period you're talking about, had you heard any news about a young couple disappearing?'

Burruano smiled, but Headmaster Burgio actually laughed out loud.

'Was that a stupid question?'

'I'm sorry, Inspector, but it really was,' remarked the headmaster.

'You see, in 1939, the population of Vigàta was fourteen thousand,' Burruano explained. 'I know my numbers. By 1942, we were down to eight thousand. The people who could leave, did, finding temporary refuge in the inland towns, the tiny little villages of no importance to the Americans. Then, between May and July of 1943, our numbers dropped, give or take a few, to four thousand, without counting the Italian and German soldiers, and the sailors. Everyone else had scattered across the countryside, living in caves, in barns, in any hole they could find. How could we have known about one disappearance or another? Everybody disappeared!'

They laughed again. Montalbano thanked them for the information.

*

Good, at least he'd managed to find a few things out. The moment the headmaster and accountant left, the surge of gratitude the inspector had felt towards them turned into an uncontrollable attack of generosity which he knew he would sooner or later regret. He called Mimì Augello into his office, made a full apology for his misdeeds towards his friend and collaborator, put his arm around the young man's shoulders, walked around the room with him, expressed his 'unconditional faith' in him, spoke at great length of the investigation he was conducting in weapons trafficking, told him about the murder of Misuraca, and informed him he'd requested a court order to tap Ingrassia's telephone lines.

'So what do you want me to do?' asked Augello, overcome with enthusiasm.

'Nothing. You must only listen to me,' said Montalbano, suddenly himself again. 'Because if you do the slightest thing on your own initiative, I'll break your neck.'

*

The telephone rang. Picking up the receiver, Montalbano heard the voice of Catarella, who served as phone operator.

'Hullo, Chief? There's – what's he called? – Chief Jacomuzzi to talk to you.'

'Put him on the line.'

'Talk with the chief, Chief, over the phone,' he heard Catarella say.

'Montalbano? Since I was passing by here on the way back from the Crasticeddru—'

'But where are you?'

'What do you mean where am I? I'm in the room next to yours.'

Montalbano cursed the saints. Was it possible to be stupider than Catarella?

'Come on in.'

The door opened and Jacomuzzi entered, covered with red sand and dust, dishevelled and rumpled.

'Why would your officer only let me talk to you by phone?'

'Jacomù, what's more idiotic, Carnival or the people who celebrate it? Don't you know what Catarella's like? You should have just given him a kick in the pants and come in.'

'I've finished my examination of the cave. I had the sand sifted. Worse than the gold-seekers in American movies! We found absolutely nothing. And that can mean only one thing, since Pasquano told me they both had entrance and exit wounds.'

'That the two were shot somewhere else.'

'Right. If they'd been killed in the cave, we would have found the bullets. Oh, and another thing, rather odd. The sand inside the cave was mixed together with very tiny fragments of snail shells. There must have been thousands of the creatures in there.'

'Jesus!' Montalbano muttered. The dream, the nightmare, Livia's naked body with the slimy things crawling over her . . . What could it mean? He brought a hand to his forehead and found it drenched in sweat.

'Are you ill?' asked Jacomuzzi, concerned.

'It's nothing, a little dizziness. I'm tired, that's all.'

'Call Catarella and have him bring you a cordial from the cafe.'

'Catarella? Are you joking? Once, when I asked him to bring me an espresso, he brought me a postal envelope.'

Jacomuzzi put three coins on the desk.

'These were from the bowl. I sent the rest to the lab. They won't be of any use to you. You can keep 'em as souvenirs.'

FOURTEEN

With Adelina, it was possible for an entire season to go by without the two of them ever seeing each other. Every week Montalbano would leave shopping money for her on the kitchen table, and every thirty days her monthly wages. Between them, however, a tacit system of communication had developed: when Adelina needed more shopping money, she would leave the *caruso* – the little clay money box he had bought at a fair and kept because it looked nice – on the table for him to see; when new supplies of socks or underwear were needed, she would leave a pair on the bed. Naturally the system did not work in one direction only; Montalbano, too, would tell her things by the strangest means, which she, however, understood. For some time now, the inspector had noticed that, when he was tense, troubled, and nervous, Adelina would somehow know it from the way he left the house in the morning, and in these instances she would make special dishes for him to find on his return, to lift his spirits. That day, Adelina had been back in action: in the fridge Montalbano found a squid sauce, dense and black, just the way he liked it. Was there or wasn't there a hint of oregano? He inhaled the aroma deeply before putting it on the heat, but this investigation, too, came to nothing. Once he'd finished eating, he donned his bathing suit with the intention of taking a brief stroll on the beach. After walking only a little while, he felt tired, the balls of his feet sore.

> Sex standing up and walking on sand
> will bring any man to a bad end.

He'd once had sex standing up and afterward did not feel so destroyed as the proverb implied; whereas it was true that if you walked on sand, even the firm sand nearest the sea, you tired quickly. He glanced at his watch and was amazed: some little while! He'd been walking for two hours. He collapsed on the beach.

'Inspector! Inspector!'

The voice came from far away. He struggled to his feet and looked out at the sea, convinced that someone must be calling him from a boat or dinghy. But the sea was deserted all the way to the horizon.

'Inspector, over here! Inspector!'

He turned around. It was Tortorella, waving his arms from the highway that for a long stretch ran parallel to the beach.

*

As Montalbano quickly washed and dressed, Tortorella told him they'd received an anonymous telephone call at the station.

'Who took the call?' asked Montalbano.

If it was Catarella, who knows what harebrained idiocies he might have understood or reported?

'Don't worry,' said Tortorella smiling, having guessed what his chief was thinking. 'He'd gone out to the bathroom for a minute, and I was manning the switchboard for him. The voice had a Palermo accent, putting *i*'s in the place of *r*'s, but he might have been doing it on purpose. He said we would find some bastard's corpse at the Pasture, inside a green car.'

'Who went to check it out?'

'Fazio and Galluzzo did, and I raced over here to get you. I'm not sure that was the right thing; maybe the phone call was only a joke.'

'What a bunch of jokers we Sicilians are!'

*

Montalbano arrived at the Pasture at five o'clock, the hour of what Gegè called the 'changing of the guard', the time of day when the unpaid couples – that is, lovers, adulterers, boyfriends and girlfriends – got off (*in every sense*, thought Montalbano), giving way to Gegè's flock, bitchin' blondes from Eastern Europe, Bulgarian transvestites, ebony Nigerian nymphs, Brazilian *viados*, Moroccan queens, and so on in procession, a veritable UN of cock, arse and cunt. And there indeed was the green car, trunk open, surrounded by three carabinieri vehicles. Fazio's car was stopped a short distance away. Montalbano got out and Galluzzo came up to him.

'We got here late.'

They had an unwritten understanding with the National Police. Whoever arrived first at the scene of a crime would shout 'Bingo!' and take the case. This prevented meddling, polemics, elbowing and long faces. But Fazio was gloomy.

'They got here first.'

'So what? What do you care? We're not paid by the corpse, on a job-by-job basis.'

By a strange coincidence, the green car was right next to the same bush beside which an 'outstanding corpse' had been found a year earlier, a case in which Montalbano had become very involved. The lieutenant of the carabinieri, who was from Bergamo and went by the name of Donizetti, approached, and they shook hands.

'We were tipped off by a phone call,' said the lieutenant.

Someone had really wanted to make sure the body was found. The inspector studied the curled-up corpse in the trunk. The man appeared to have been shot only once, with the bullet entering his mouth, shattering his teeth and lips, and exiting through the back of the neck, opening a wound the size of a fist. Montalbano didn't recognize the face.

'I'm told you know the manager of this open-air whore-house,' the lieutenant enquired with some disdain.

'Yes, he's a friend of mine,' Montalbano replied in a tone of obvious defiance.

'Do you know where I could find him?'

'At home, I would imagine.'

'He's not there.'

'Excuse me, but why do you think I can tell you where he is?'

'You're his friend, you said so yourself.'

'Oh, and I suppose you can tell me, at this exact moment, where all your friends from Bergamo are and what they're doing?'

Cars were continually arriving from the main road, turning onto the Pasture's small byways, noticing the swarm of carabinieri squad cars, shifting into reverse, and quickly returning to the road they'd come from. The blondes from the East, Brazilian *viados*, Nigerian nymphs, and the rest of the gang were coming to work, smelling something fishy, and scattering in every direction. It promised to be a miserable night for Gegè's business.

The lieutenant walked back towards the green car. Montalbano turned his back to him and without saying a word returned to his own vehicle. He said to Fazio, 'You and Galluzzo stay here. See what they're doing and what they find out. I'm going to the station.'

*

Montalbano stopped in front of Sarcuto's Stationery and Book Shop, the only one in Vigàta that was true to its sign; the other two sold not books but satchels, notebooks and pens. He remembered he'd finished the Vasquez Montalbán novel and had nothing else to read.

'We've got the new book on Falcone and Borsellino!' Signora Sarcuto announced as soon as she saw him enter.

She still hadn't understood that Montalbano hated books that talked about the Mafia, murder and Mafia victims. He didn't know why she couldn't grasp this, since he never bought them and didn't even read their jacket copy. He bought a book by Luigi Consolo, who'd won an important literary prize some time before. After he'd taken a few steps outside, the book slid out from under his arm and fell onto the pavement. He bent down to pick it up, then got back in his car.

At headquarters Catarella told him there was no news. Montalbano obsessively wrote his name in every book he bought. As he reached for one of the pens on his desk, his eye fell on the coins that Jacomuzzi had left him. The first one, a copper coin dated 1934, had the king's profile and the words 'Victor Emmanuel III, King of Italy' on one side, and a spike of wheat and 'C. 5', five centesimi, on the other. The second coin, dated 1936 and also copper, was a little bigger and had the same king's head with the same words on one side, and a bee resting on a flower with the letter 'C' and the number '10', ten centesimi, on the other. The third was made of a light metal alloy, with the inevitable king's head and accompanying words on one side, on the other an eagle displayed, with a Roman fasces partially visible behind it. This side also had four inscriptions: 'L. I', which meant one lira; 'ITALIA', which meant Italy; '1942', which was the date of minting; and 'XX', which meant year twenty of the Fascist era. As he was staring at this last coin, Montalbano remembered what it was he had seen when bending down to pick up the book he'd dropped in front of the bookshop. He'd seen the front window of the shop next door, which featured a display of antique coins.

He got up from his desk, informed Catarella he was going out and would be back in half an hour at the most, and headed off to the shop on foot. It was called Things, and things were what it sold: desert roses, stamps, candlesticks, rings, brooches, coins, semi-precious stones. He went inside, and a neat, pretty girl welcomed him with a smile. Sorry to disappoint her, the inspector explained that he wasn't there to buy anything, but since he'd seen some ancient coins displayed in the window, he wanted to know if there was anyone, there in the shop or in Vigàta, with expertise in numismatics.

'Of course there is,' said the girl, still smiling delightfully. 'There's my grandfather.'

'Where might I disturb him?'

'You wouldn't be disturbing him at all. Actually, he'd be happy to help you. He's in the back room. Just wait a moment while I go tell him.'

He hadn't even had time to look at a hammerless late-nineteenth-century pistol when the girl reappeared.

'You can go inside.'

The back room was a glorious jumble of old phonographs with horns, prehistoric sewing machines, copying presses, paintings, prints, chamber pots and pipes. And it was entirely lined with bookshelves on which sat, higgledy-piggledy, an assortment of incunabula, parchment-bound tomes, lampshades, umbrellas and opera hats. In the middle of it all was a desk with an old man sitting behind it, an art nouveau lamp shedding light on his labours. He was holding a stamp with a pair of tweezers and examining it under a magnifying glass.

'What is it?' he asked gruffly, without looking up.

Montalbano laid the three coins down in front of him. The old man took his eyes momentarily off the stamp and glanced distractedly at them.

'Worthless,' he said.

Of the various old men he'd been encountering in his investigation of the Crasticeddru deaths, this one was the grumpiest.

I ought to gather them all together at an old people's home, the inspector thought. *That'd make it easier to question them.*

'I know they're worthless.'

'So what is it you want to know?'

'When they went out of circulation.'

'Use your brain a little.'

'When the Republic was proclaimed?' Montalbano hesitantly guessed.

He felt like a student who hadn't studied for the exam. The old man laughed, and his laugh sounded like the noise of two empty tin cans rubbing together.

'Am I wrong?'

'Very wrong. The Americans landed here the night of July 9–10, 1943. In October of that same year, these coins went out of use. They were replaced by Amlire, the paper

money printed up by Amgot, the Allied military adminis-
tration of the occupied territories. And since these bills
were for one, five and ten lire, the centesimo coins disappeared from circulation.'

＊

By the time Fazio and Galluzzo returned, it was already
dark. The inspector scolded them.

'Damn you both! You certainly took your time!'

'Who, us?' Fazio shot back. 'You know what the lieutenant's like! Before he could touch the body, he had to wait
for Pasquano and the judge to arrive. And *they* certainly did
take their time!'

'And so?'

'A new-laid corpse if I ever saw one, fresh as can be.
Pasquano said less than an hour had passed between the
killing and the phone calls. The guy had an ID card on
him. Pietro Gullo's his name, forty-two years old, blue
eyes, blond hair, fair complexion, born in Merfi, resident
of Fela, Via Matteotti 32, married, no distinguishing
features.'

'You ought to get a job at the Records Office.'

Fazio nobly ignored the provocation and continued.

'I went to Montelusa and checked the archives. This
Gullo had an uneventful youth, two robberies and a brawl.
Then he straightened himself out, at least apparently. He
dealt in grain.'

＊

'I really appreciate you seeing me right away,' Montalbano said to Headmaster Burgio, who had answered the door.

'What are you saying? The pleasure's all mine.'

He let the inspector in, led him into the living room, and asked him to sit down.

'Angelina!' the headmaster called.

A tiny old woman appeared, curious about the unexpected visit, looking smart and well groomed, her lively, attentive eyes sparkling behind thick glasses.

The old peoples home! thought Montalbano.

'Allow me to introduce my wife, Angelina.'

Montalbano gave her an admiring bow. He sincerely liked elderly ladies who kept up appearances, even at home.

'Please forgive me for bothering you at supper time.'

'No bother at all. On the contrary, Inspector, are you busy this evening?'

'Not at all.'

'Why don't you stay and have supper with us? We're just having some old-people fare, since we're supposed to eat lightly: soft vegetables and striped mullet with oil and lemon.'

'Sounds like a feast to me.'

Mrs Burgio exited, content.

'What can I do for you?' asked the headmaster.

'I've managed to discover the time frame in which the double homicide of the Crasticeddru took place.'

'Oh. So when did it happen?'

'Definitely between early 1943 and October of the same year.'

'How did you come to that conclusion?'

'Easy. The terracotta dog, as Mr Burruano told us, was sold after Christmas of 1942, which reasonably means after the Epiphany of 1943. The coins found inside the bowl went out of circulation in October that same year.' He paused. 'And this can mean only one thing,' he added.

But what that one thing was, he didn't say. He patiently waited while Burgio collected his thoughts, stood up, and took a few steps around the room.

'I get it,' said the old man. 'You're saying that during this period, the Crasticeddru cave belonged to the Rizzitanos.'

'Exactly. And as you told me, the cave was already sealed off by the boulder at the time, because the Rizzitanos kept merchandise to be sold on the black market in it. They must have known about the other cave, the one where the dead couple were brought.'

The headmaster gave him a confused look.

'Why do you say they were 'brought' there?'

'Because they were killed somewhere else. Of that I am absolutely certain.'

'But it doesn't make any sense. Why put them there and set them up as if they were asleep, with the jug, the bowl of money and the dog?'

'I've been asking myself the same question. And maybe the only person who could tell us something is your friend Lillo Rizzitano.'

Signora Angelina came in.

'It's ready.'

The soft vegetables, which consisted of the leaves and

flowers of Sicilian courgettes – the long, smooth kind, which are white, lightly speckled with green – had come out so tender, so delicate, that Montalbano actually felt deeply moved. With each bite he could feel his stomach purifying itself, turning clean and shiny the way he'd seen happen with certain fakirs on television.

'How do you find them?' asked Signora Angelina.

'Beautiful,' said Montalbano. Seeing the couple's surprise, he blushed and explained himself. 'I'm sorry. Sometimes I abuse my adjectives.'

The striped mullet, boiled and dressed in olive oil, lemon, and parsley, was every bit as light as the vegetables. Only when the fruit was brought to the table did the headmaster come back to the question Montalbano had asked him – but not before he'd had his say on the problem of the schools and the reform the new minister of education had decided to carry out, which would abolish mandatory secondary-school attendance.

'In Russia at the time of the tsars,' said Burgio, 'they had secondary schools, though they called them whatever they're called in Russian. In Italy it was Gentile who called them lyceums when he instituted his own reform, which placed humanistic studies above all others. Well, Lenin's Communists, being the kind of Communists they were, didn't have the courage to abolish secondary schools. Only an upstart, a semi-illiterate nonentity like our minister, could conceive of such a thing. What's he called, Guastella?'

'Vastella,' said Signora Angelina.

Actually, he was called something else as well, but the inspector refrained from pointing this out.

'Lillo and I were friends in everything, but not in school, since he was a few years ahead of me. When I entered my third year of lyceum, he had just graduated. On the night of the American landing, Lillo's house, which was at the foot of the Crasto, was destroyed. From what I was able to find out once the storm had passed, Lillo had been at home alone and was seriously injured. A peasant saw some Italian soldiers putting him on a truck; he was bleeding profusely. That was the last I heard of Lillo. I haven't had any news since, though God knows I've searched far and wide!'

'Is it possible nobody from his family survived?'

'I don't know.'

The headmaster noticed that his wife looked lost in thought, absent, her eyes half-closed.

'Angelina!' Burgio called.

The old woman roused herself, then smiled at Montalbano.

'Forgive me. My husband says I've always been a "woman of fantasy", but he doesn't mean it as a compliment. He means I sometimes let my fantasies run away with me.'

FIFTEEN

When he returned home after supper with the Burgios, it wasn't even ten o'clock. Too early to go to bed. On TV there was a debate on the Mafia, another on Italian foreign policy, still another on the economic situation, a round table on conditions in the Montelusa insane asylum, a discussion about freedom of information, a documentary on juvenile delinquency in Moscow, another documentary on seals, still another on tobacco farming, a gangster film set in thirties Chicago, a nightly programme in which a former art critic, now a parliamentary deputy and political opinion-maker, was raving against magistrates, leftist politicians and various adversaries, making himself into a little Saint-Just when his rightful place was among the ranks of carpet salesman, wart-healers, magicians and strippers who were appearing with increasing frequency on the small screen. Turning off the television, Montalbano switched on the outdoor light, went out on the veranda, and sat down on the little bench with a magazine to which he subscribed. It was nicely printed, with interesting articles, and edited by a group of young environmentalists in the province. Scanning the table of contents, he found nothing of interest and thus started looking at the photographs, which occasionally realized their ambition of illustrating news events in emblematic fashion.

The ring of the doorbell caught him by surprise. He wasn't expecting anyone, he said to himself, but a second later he remembered that Anna had called in the afternoon. When she had suggested coming by to see him, he couldn't say no. He felt indebted to the girl for having used her — contemptibly, he had to admit — in that whole story he'd concocted to save Ingrid from persecution by her father-in-law.

Anna kissed him on each cheek and handed him a package.

'I brought you a *petrafèrnula*.'

This was a cake now very hard to find, which Montalbano loved, but it was anyone's guess why the pastry shops had stopped making it.

'I had to go to Mittica for work and saw it in a window, so I bought it for you. Careful with your teeth.'

The harder the cake was, the tastier.

'What were you doing?'

'Nothing, just reading a magazine. Why don't you come outside?'

They sat down on the bench. Montalbano went back to looking at the photographs, while Anna rested her head on her hands and gazed out at the sea.

'It's so beautiful here!'

'Yes.'

'All you hear are the waves.'

'Yes.'

'Does it bother you if I talk?'

'No.'

Anna fell silent. After a brief pause, she spoke again.

'I'm going inside to watch TV. I feel a little chilly.'

'Mm-hmm.'

The inspector didn't want to encourage her. Anna clearly wanted to abandon herself to a solitary pleasure, that of pretending she was his partner, imagining they were spending a quiet evening together like so many others. On the very last page of the magazine, he saw a photo that showed the inside of a cave, the 'grotto of Fragapane', which was actually a necropolis, a network of Christian tombs dug out of ancient cisterns. The picture served in its way to illustrate the review of a recent book by one Alcide Maraventano entitled *Funerary Rites in the Montelusa Region*. The publication of this richly documented essay by Maraventano, the reviewer claimed, filled a void, giving us a work of great scholarly value that investigated, with keen intelligence, a subject spanning the period from prehistory to the Byzantine–Christian era.

He sat there a long time meditating on what he had just read. The idea that the jug, the bowl with coins and the dog might be part of some burial rite had never even crossed his mind. And perhaps he'd been wrong not to think of this; in fact, the investigation should probably have started from this very premise. He suddenly felt uncontrollably pressed. He went inside, unplugged the phone, then picked up the whole apparatus.

'What are you doing?' asked Anna, who was watching the gangster movie.

'I'm going into the bedroom to make some phone calls. I don't want to disturb you out here.'

He dialled the Free Channel's number and asked for his friend Nicolò Zito.

'Quick, Montalbà, I go on the air in a few seconds.'

'Do you know someone by the name of Maraventano who wrote—'

'Alcide? Sure, I know him. What do want from him?'

'I'd like to talk to him. Do you have his phone number?'

'He hasn't got a phone. Are you at home? I'll track him down myself and let you know.'

'I need to talk to him by tomorrow.'

'I'll call you back in an hour at the latest and tell you what to do.'

He turned off the bedside lamp. In the dark it was easier to think about the idea that had just come to him. He tried to imagine the Crasticeddru's cave the way it had looked when he first entered. If you removed the two bodies from the picture, that left the rug, a bowl, a jug and a terracotta dog. If you drew lines between the three objects, they formed a perfect triangle, though upside down with respect to the cave's entrance. At the centre of the triangle lay the two corpses. Did it mean anything? Maybe he needed to study the triangle's orientation?

Between thinking, musing and fantasizing, he ended up dozing off. After a spell of indeterminate length, he was awakened by the ring of the telephone. He answered in a thick voice.

'Did you fall asleep?'

'Yeah, nodded off.'

'And here I am putting myself out for you. So, Alcide is expecting you tomorrow afternoon at five-thirty. He lives in Gallotta.'

Gallotta was a village a few miles outside Montelusa, a handful of peasant houses once famous for being inaccessible in winter, when the rains were heavy.

'Give me the address.'

'What address? If you're coming from Montelusa, it's the first house on the left, a big tumbledown villa that would delight any horror-film director. You can't miss it.'

*

He fell back asleep as soon as he put down the receiver. Then he woke with a start, feeling something moving on his chest. It was Anna, whom he'd completely forgotten about, lying down beside him on the bed and unbuttoning his shirt. On every piece of skin she uncovered, she planted her lips and held them there a long time. When she reached his navel, the girl raised her head, slipped one hand under his shirt to caress his nipple, then plastered her mouth against Montalbano's. Since he made no sign of reacting to her passionate kiss, Anna let her hand slide farther down his body. She caressed him there as well.

Montalbano decided to speak.

'See, Anna? It's hopeless. Nothing happens.'

In a single bound Anna sprang out of bed and locked herself in the bathroom. Montalbano didn't move, not even when he heard her sobbing — a childish wail, like that of a little girl denied a toy or some sweets. Against the light of the bathroom, whose door she left open on her way out, Montalbano saw her fully dressed.

'A wild animal has more feelings than you,' she said, leaving.

Sleep then abandoned Montalbano. At four in the morning, he was still up, trying to finish even one game of solitaire, though it was clear he would never succeed.

*

He arrived at work grumpy and troubled, the encounter with Anna weighing on his mind. He felt remorseful for treating her the way he did. On top of this, that morning he'd started wondering: had it been Ingrid instead of Anna, would he have behaved the same way?

'I need to speak to you urgently,' said Mimì Augello, standing in his doorway looking agitated.

'What do you want?'

'To bring you up to date on the investigation.'

'What investigation?'

'Okay, I get the message. I'll come by later.'

'No, you stay right here and tell me what fucking investigation you're talking about.'

'What do you mean? The one into the weapons traffic!'

'And I, in your opinion, put you in charge?'

'In my opinion? We talked about it! Remember? It seemed implicit to me.'

'Mimì, the only implicit thing around here is that you're a goddamned son of a bitch, no offense to your mother, of course.'

'Let's do this: I'll tell you what I've done, and you can decide if I should continue.'

'All right, let's hear what you've done.'

'First of all, I thought Ingrassia should be kept on a leash, so I assigned two of our men to tail him day and night. He can't even take a piss without me knowing about it.'

'Two of our men? You put two of ours on his tail? Don't you know that that guy knows everything about our men down to the hairs on their arse?'

'I'm not stupid. They're not actually ours, not from the Vigàta force, I mean. They're two officers from Ragòna that the commissioner transferred to my service after I spoke to him.'

Montalbano looked at him in admiration.

'Ah, so you spoke to the commissioner. Well done, Mimì, you really do know how to get around!'

Augello did not respond in kind, preferring to continue his explanation.

'We also listened in on a phone conversation that might mean something. I've got the transcript in my room, I'll go and get it.'

'Do you know it by heart?'

'Yes, but if you hear it, you might be able to discover—'

'Mimì, at this point I think you've discovered everything there was to discover. Don't make me waste time. Now tell me what they said.'

'Well, from his supermarket, Ingrassia phones the Brancato company in Catania. He asks for Brancato himself, who comes to the phone. Ingrassia complains about the snags that occurred during the last delivery, he says you can't send the truck so far ahead of schedule, that this caused him a lot of problems. He wants them to meet so they can study different, safer means of delivery. Here Brancato's answer is shocking, to say the least. He raises his voice in anger and asks Ingrassia, "How dare you call me here?" Ingrassia, now stammering, asks for an explanation. Which Brancato provides, saying that Ingrassia is insolvent, and that the banks have advised him to cease doing business with him.'

'And how did Ingrassia react?'

'He didn't. He didn't even make a peep. He just hung up.'

'Do you realize what that phone call means?'

'Of course. Ingrassia was asking for help, and they cut him loose.'

'Stay on top of Ingrassia.'

'I already am, as I told you.'

There was a pause.

'What should I do?' continued Mimì. 'Continue the investigation?'

Montalbano wouldn't answer.

'You're such a fucking jerk!' commented Augello.

*

'Salvo? Are you alone in your office? Can I speak openly?'

'Yes. Where are you calling from?'

'From home. I'm in bed with a bit of fever.'

'I'm sorry.'

'Well, you shouldn't be. It's one of those growing fevers.'

'I don't understand. What do you mean?'

'It's one of those fevers little children get. They last two or three days, around one hundred and one or one hundred and two degrees, no cause for alarm. It's natural, it's a growing fever. When it passes, the child has grown an inch or so. And I'm sure that when my fever is over, I too will have grown. In my head, not my body. What I mean is, never, as a woman, have I been so offended as with you.'

'Anna—'

'Let me finish. You really did offend me. You're mean, Salvo, wicked. I didn't deserve that kind of treatment.'

'Be reasonable, Anna. What happened last night was for your own good—'

Anna hung up. Even though he had made her understand a hundred different ways that what she wanted was out of the question, Montalbano, realizing that the girl at that moment was suffering terribly, felt like considerably less than a pig, since pork, at least, can be eaten.

*

Montalbano easily found the villa upon entering Gallotta, but it did not seem possible to him that anyone could live in that ruin. Half the roof was visibly caved in, which must surely have let in the rain on the third floor. The faint wind in the air was enough to rattle a shutter that remained attached by means not immediately apparent. The outer wall on the upper part of the facade had cracks the width of a fist. The second, first and ground floors looked in better shape. The surface plaster had long disappeared; the shutters were all broken and flaking, but at least they closed, however askew. There was a wrought-iron gate, half open and leaning outward, apparently in this position since time immemorial, amid weeds and peaty soil. The yard was an amorphous mass of contorted trees and dense shrubbery, a thick, closely knit tangle. He proceeded up the path of disconnected stones and stopped when he reached the peeling front door. Darkness was already falling. The switch from daylight time to standard time really did shorten the days. There was a doorbell, and he rang it. Or, rather, he pushed it, since he heard no sound whatsoever, not even far away. He tried again before realizing that the doorbell hadn't worked since the discovery of electricity. He rapped on the door with the horse-head knocker, and finally, after the third rap, he heard some shuffling footsteps. The door opened, without any noise from a lock or bolt, only a long wail as of a soul in purgatory.

'It was open. You needed only to push, come inside and call me.'

It was a skeleton speaking to him. Never in his life had Montalbano seen anyone so thin. Or, rather, he had seen a few such people, on their deathbeds, dried up, shrivelled by illness. This man, however, was standing, though bent over in two, and appeared to be alive. He was wearing a priest's cassock whose original black now tended towards green, the once-stiff white collar now a dense grey. On his feet, two hobnailed peasant boots of the kind you couldn't buy any more. He was completely bald, and his face looked like a death's head on which somebody, as a joke, had placed a pair of gold eyeglasses with extremely thick lenses, behind which the eyes foundered. Montalbano thought the couple in the cave, who'd been dead for fifty years, had more flesh on their bones than this priest. Needless to say, he was very old.

In ceremonious fashion, the man invited him inside and led him into an enormous room literally crammed with books, not only on the shelves but stacked on the floor in piles that stretched nearly to the lofty ceiling and remained standing by means of some impossible equilibrium. No light entered through the windows; the books amassed on their ledges covered them completely. The furniture consisted of a desk, a chair and an armchair. The lamp on the desk looked to Montalbano like an authentic oil lantern. The old priest cleared the armchair of books and told the inspector to sit down.

'I cannot imagine how I could be of any use to you, but go ahead and talk.'

'As you were probably told, I'm a police inspector and I—'

'No, nobody told me anything, and I didn't ask. Late last night somebody from the village came and said a man from Vigàta wanted to see me, and I said to have him come at five-thirty. If you're an inspector, you've come to the wrong place. You're wasting your time.'

'Why am I wasting my time?'

'Because I haven't set foot outside this house for at least thirty years. What would I go out for? The old faces have all disappeared and I don't care much for the new ones. Somebody does my shopping every day, and in any case I only drink milk, and chicken broth once a week.'

'You probably heard on television—'

He had barely started the sentence when he interrupted himself; the word 'television' had sounded incongruous to him.

'There's no electricity in this house.'

'Well, you've probably read in the papers—'

'I don't read newspapers.'

Why did he keep setting off on the wrong foot? Taking a deep breath, he got a kind of running start and told him everything, from the arms traffic to the discovery of the dead couple in the Crasticeddru.

'Let me light the lamp,' said the old man, 'we'll talk better that way.'

He rummaged through some papers on the desktop, found a box of kitchen matches, and lit one with a trembling hand. Montalbano felt a chill come over him.

If he drops it, he thought, *we'll be roasted alive in three seconds.*

The operation, however, was a success, except that it made matters worse, in that the lamp shed a feeble light over half of the desktop and plunged the side on which the old man sat into total darkness. In amazement Montalbano saw the old man reach out with one hand and seize a small bottle with an odd sort of cork. There were three other such bottles on the desk, two empty and the other full with a white liquid. They weren't regular bottles, actually, but baby bottles, each furnished with a nipple. The inspector felt himself growing stupidly irritated as the old man started sucking.

'You'll have to forgive me. I haven't any teeth.'

'But why don't you drink the milk from a mug or a cup or, I don't know, a glass?'

'Because it gives me more pleasure this way. It's as if I were smoking a pipe.'

Montalbano decided to leave as quickly as possible. Standing up, he took from his jacket pocket two of the photos taken by Jacomuzzi and handed them to the priest.

'Might this have been some sort of burial rite?'

The old man looked at the photos, growing animated and groaning.

'What was inside the bowl?'

'Coins from the 1940s.'

'And in the jug?'

'Nothing . . . There was no trace of anything . . . It must have contained only water.'

The old man sat there sucking a good while, engrossed in thought. Montalbano sat back down.

'It makes no sense,' said the priest, setting the photos down on the desk.

SIXTEEN

Montalbano was at the end of his rope. Bombarded with questions by the priest, he felt his thoughts growing confused and, what was worse, every time he was unable to answer, Alcide Maraventano made a kind of whining sound and in protest began sucking louder than usual. He was already working on his second baby bottle.

In what directions were the heads of the dead pointed?

Was the jug made of absolutely normal clay or some other material?

How many coins were there inside the bowl?

Exactly how far from the two bodies were the jug, bowl and terracotta dog?

At last the third degree ended.

'It makes no sense.'

The interrogation's conclusion confirmed precisely what the priest had immediately surmised at the start. The inspector, with a certain, not very well-concealed relief, thought he could now get up, take his leave and go.

'Wait. What's the hurry?'

Montalbano sat back down, resigned.

'It's not a funerary rite, but maybe it's something else.'

All at once, the inspector roused himself from his lethargy and regained full possession of his mental faculties. This Maraventano was a thinking mind.

'Tell me, I'd much appreciate your opinion.'

'Have you read Umberto Eco?'

Montalbano began to sweat.

Jesus, now he's giving me a literature exam, he thought, but he managed to say: 'I've read his first novel and the two small diaries, which seemed to me—'

'Well, I haven't. I don't know the novels. I was referring to the *Treatise of General Semiotics*, a few of whose passages might be of use to us.'

'I'm embarrassed to say, I haven't read it.'

'And I suppose you haven't read Kristeva's *Semeiotiké* either?'

'No, and I have no desire to,' said Montalbano, starting to feel angry. He was beginning to suspect that the old man was pulling his leg.

'All right, then,' said Alcide Maraventano, sighing, 'I'll give you a down-to-earth example.'

'Something on my level,' Montalbano muttered to himself.

'If you, then, are a police inspector, and you find a man who's been shot and killed, and in whose mouth the killers have placed a stone, what conclusion might you draw?'

'That's old stuff, you know,' said Montalbano, bent on

regaining the upper hand. 'Nowadays they murder without giving any explanations.'

'I see. So for you that stone in the mouth is a kind of explanation.'

'Of course.'

'And what does it mean?'

'It means the dead man talked too much, said things he wasn't supposed to say, or was an informer.'

'Exactly. You, therefore, understood the explanation because you possessed the code of that language, which in this case was a metaphorical language. But if you'd been ignorant of the code, what would you have understood? Nothing. To you, that man would have been a murder victim in whose mouth the killers had in-ex-pli-ca-bly placed a stone.'

'I'm beginning to understand.'

'Now, to return to our discussion: somebody kills two young people for reasons we don't know. He could make the bodies disappear in many different ways, in the sea, underground, under the sand. But, no, he puts them in a cave instead. Not only that, but he arranges a bowl, a jug and a terracotta dog around them. What, therefore, has he done?'

'He's made a statement, sent a message,' said Montal-bano in a soft voice.

'That's right, a message, which you, however, can't read because you don't possess the code,' concluded the priest.

'Let me think,' said Montalbano. 'But the message must

have been directed at someone, just not at us, fifty years after the fact.'

'And why not?'

Montalbano thought about this a moment, then stood up.

'I'm going to go, I don't want to take up any more of your time. What you've told me has been very valuable to me.'

'I'd like to be even more useful to you.'

'How so?'

'You just said that nowadays they kill without providing any explanations. There is always an explanation and it is always provided, otherwise you wouldn't be in the line of work you're in. It's just that the codes have multiplied and diversified.'

'Thank you,' said Montalbano.

*

For dinner they'd eaten fresh anchovies *all'agretto*, which Signora Elisa, the commissioner's wife, had cooked with art and skill, the secret of success lying in correctly determining the infinitesimal length of time to keep the pan in the oven. Then, after the meal, the signora had retired to the living room to watch television, but not before having arranged, on the desk in her husband's study, a bottle of Chivas, another of bitters, and two glasses.

While they were eating, Montalbano had spoken enthusiastically of Alcide Maraventano and his peculiar way of life, his erudition, his intelligence. The commissioner, however, had shown only lukewarm curiosity, more out of politeness to his guest than out of real interest.

'Listen, Montalbano,' he broke in as soon as they were alone, 'I can easily understand the sense of urgency you might feel about the two murder victims you found in the cave. I daresay I've known you too long not to expect you to become fascinated by a case like this, because it defies explanation, but also – and I think this is the real reason – because even if you were to find the solution, it would prove utterly useless. Just the sort of uselessness that you would find amusing and – excuse me for saying so – almost congenial.'

'Useless in what way?'

'Useless, useless, don't play innocent. To be generous – since fifty or more years have since passed – the murderer, or murderers, are either dead or, in the best of cases, little old men at least seventy years old. Right?'

'Right,' Montalbano reluctantly agreed.

'Therefore – forgive me, because what I'm about to say is not normally part of my vocabulary – but what you're engaged in is not an investigation, but an act of mental masturbation.'

Montalbano, lacking the strength or arguments to rebut him, took it all in.

'Now, I could allow you this little exercise,' the commissioner continued, 'if I wasn't afraid you'd end up devoting the best of your brainpower to it, and neglecting other investigations of greater significance and reach.'

'No! That's not true!' the inspector bridled.

'But it is. Look, none of this is intended, in any way, as a reproach. We're here talking, at my home, between friends. Why, for example, did you assign the weapons trafficking case – an extremely delicate case – to your deputy, who is a very capable officer but certainly not on your level?'

'But I haven't assigned him anything! It's he who—'

'Don't be childish, Montalbano. You've been throwing the better part of the investigation on his shoulders. Because you're well aware that you can't devote all your energies to it, since three-fourths of your brain are tied up with the other case. Tell me, quite honestly, if you think I'm wrong.'

'You're right,' Montalbano honestly admitted, after a pause.

'So let's leave it at that, and move on to other matters. Why the hell don't you want me to recommend you for a promotion?'

'You really want to keep crucifying me.'

*

He left the commissioner's house pleased – with the anchovies *all'agretto*, but also because he'd managed to obtain a postponement of the recommendation of promotion. There was no rhyme or reason to the arguments he'd cited, but his superior politely pretended to accept them. Could Montalbano very well have told him that the mere idea of a transfer, of a change of habits, gave him a fever?

It was still early. His appointment with Gegè wasn't for another two hours. He dropped by the Free Channel studios, wanting to learn more about Alcide Maraventano.

'Extraordinary, isn't he?' said Nicolò Zito. 'Did he suck milk from a baby bottle in front of you?'

'And how.'

'It's all a put-on, you know. He's just play acting.'

'What do you mean? He has no teeth.'

'You have heard of an invention called dentures, I presume? He owns a set, and they work perfectly well. I'm told he sometimes wolfs down a quarter of veal or a roast suckling goat when nobody's looking.'

'So why does he do it?'

'Because he's a born tragedian. Or comedian, if you prefer.'

'Is he really a priest?'

'He quit the priesthood.'

'And the things he says, are they true or made up?'

'You don't have to worry about that. His knowledge is limitless, and when he says something, it's better than gospel. Did you know he shot somebody about ten years ago?'

'Come on.'

'Really. Some thief broke into his house, on the ground floor. He bumped into a pile of books and they came crashing down, making an infernal racket. Maraventano, who'd been asleep upstairs, woke up, came down, and shot him with a muzzle-loading rifle, a kind of household cannon. The blast made half the village jump out of bed.

When the smoke cleared, the robber was wounded in the leg, a dozen or so books were ruined, and the old man had a fractured shoulder from the gun's tremendous kick. The robber, however, maintained he'd entered the house not with any criminal intent, but because he'd been invited there by the priest, who at a certain point, for no apparent reason, picked up a rifle and shot him. And I believe him.'

'Whom?'

'The supposed thief.'

'But why would he shoot him?'

'I suppose you know what goes on inside the head of Alcide Maraventano? Maybe it was to see if the rifle still worked. Or just to make a scene, which is more likely.'

'Listen, before I forget, do you have Umberto Eco's *Treatise of General Semiotics*?'

'Me? Are you crazy?'

*

On his way to the car, which he'd left in the Free Channel's car park, Montalbano got soaked. It had started raining without warning, very fine drops but very dense. He got home with time to spare before the appointment. He changed clothes and sat down in the armchair in front of the TV, but then immediately got up again and went to his desk to fetch a postcard that had arrived that morning.

It was from Livia. As she'd informed him by telephone, she had gone to visit a cousin in Milan for ten days or so. On the glossy side, which showed the inevitable view of the cathedral, there was a luminescent trail of slime cutting the image in half. Montalbano touched it with the tip of his index finger: it was very fresh, and slightly sticky. He examined the desk more closely. A *scataddrizzo*, a large, dark brown snail, was slithering across the cover of the Consolo book. Montalbano did not hesitate. The horror he'd felt after the dream, which he was still carrying around with him, was too strong. Grabbing the Vasquez Montalbán novel, which he'd already read, he slammed it violently down on the one by Consolo. Caught in between, the *scataddrizzo* made such a noise as it was being crushed that Montalbano felt nauseated. He then tossed the two novels into the rubbish bin. He would buy new copies tomorrow.

*

Gegè wasn't there, but the inspector knew he wouldn't be long. His friend was never late by much. The rain had stopped, but there must have been quite a storm at sea: large puddles had formed along the beach, and the sand gave off a strong smell of wet wood. He lit a cigarette. All at once, by the faint light of the moon that had suddenly appeared, he saw the dark shape of a car approaching very slowly, lights extinguished, from the opposite direction to where he'd come in, which was the same direction Gegè should have come from. Alarmed, he opened the glove compartment, took out his pistol, cocked it and disengaged the car door, ready to jump out. When the other car came within range, he turned on his high beam all at once. The car was Gegè's, no doubt about that, but it might easily be somebody else at the wheel.

'Turn off your lights!' he heard someone shout from the car.

It was definitely Gegè's voice, and the inspector obeyed. They spoke one to the other, each in his own car, through their lowered windows.

'What the fuck are you doing? I nearly fired at you,' Montalbano said angrily.

'I wanted to see if they'd followed you.'

'If who'd followed me?'

'I'll tell you in a second. I got here half an hour ago and was hiding behind the jetty at Punta Rossa.'

'Come over here,' said the inspector.

Gegè got out of his car and into Montalbano's, almost huddling against him.

'What's wrong, you cold?'

'No, but I'm shivering anyway.'

He stank of fear. As Montalbano knew from experience, fear had a smell all its own, sour, yellow-green in colour.

'Do you know who that was who got killed?'

'Gegè, a lot of people get killed. Who are you talking about?'

'Pietro Gullo, that's who, the one they drove to the Pasture after they killed him.'

'Was he a client of yours?'

'A client? If anything, I was *his* client. He was Tano the Greek's man, his collector. The same guy who told me Tano wanted to meet you.'

'Why so surprised, Gegè? It's the usual story: winner take all. They use the same system in politics. Tano's businesses are changing hands, so they're liquidating everybody who worked with him. You were neither an associate nor a dependent of Tano's. So what are you worried about?'

'No,' Gegè said firmly, 'that's not how it is. That's not what they told me in Trapani.'

'So how is it, then?'

'They said there was an agreement.'

'An agreement?'

'Oh, yes. An agreement between you and Tano. They said the shoot-out was bogus, a sham, a masquerade. And they're convinced that the people who staged this masquerade were me, Pietro Gullo, and somebody else they're sure to kill one of these days.'

Montalbano remembered the telephone call he'd received after the press conference, when an anonymous voice had called him a 'lousy fucking actor'.

'They feel offended,' Gegè continued. 'They can't bear the thought that you and Tano spat in their faces, made them look like chumps. It means more to them than the weapons. Now you tell me: what am I supposed to do?'

'Are you sure they have it in for you too?'

'I swear to God. Why else did they bring Gullo all the way to the Pasture, which is my turf? You can't get any clearer than that!'

The inspector thought of Alcide Maraventano and what he'd said about codes.

It must have been a change in the density of the

darkness, or a split-second glimmer seen out of the corner of one eye, but the fact is that an instant before the explosion of gunfire, Montalbano's body obeyed a series of impulses frantically transmitted by his brain: he bent over, opening the car door with his left hand, and hurled himself out while all around him was a thunder of gunshots, shattering glass, plates of metal flying apart, quick red flashes brightening the dark. Montalbano remained motionless, wedged between Gegè's car and his own, and only then did he realize he had his pistol in his hand. When Gegè had come inside his car, he'd set it on the dashboard. He must have grabbed it by instinct. After the pandemonium, a leaden silence reigned. Nothing moved. There was only the sound of the agitated sea. Then, about twenty yards away, to the side where the beach ended and the hill of marl began, there was a voice, 'Everything okay?'

'Everything okay,' said another voice, this one very close.

'Make sure they're both finished, then we can go.'

Montalbano tried to picture the movements the man would have to make to verify that they were dead: *chuff, chuff* went his footsteps in the sodden sand. Now the man must be right beside the car; in a moment he would bend down to look inside.

Montalbano leapt to his feet and fired. A single shot. He clearly heard the thud of a body collapsing on the sand, then a gasping, a kind of gurgling, then nothing.

'Jujù, everything all right?' asked the distant voice.

Without getting back in his car, Montalbano, through the open door, put his hand on the high-beam switch and waited. He could hear nothing. He decided to try his luck and started counting in his head. When he got to fifty, he turned on the lights bright and stood straight up. Swathed in light, about ten yards away, appeared a man with a sub-machine gun in hand, frozen in surprise. Montalbano fired, the man immediately reacted, firing blindly into the dark. Feeling something like a tremendous punch in his left side, the inspector staggered, leaned his left hand against the car, then fired again, three shots in a row. The man sort of jumped in the air, turned around, and started running, as Montalbano saw the white beam of the headlights begin to turn yellow, his eyes clouding over, head spinning. He sat down on the sand, realizing that his legs could no longer support him, and leaned back against the side of the car.

He waited for the pain, and when it came it was so intense he started howling and crying like a child.

SEVENTEEN

As soon as he awoke, he realized he was in a hospital room, and he remembered everything in minute detail: the meeting with Gegè, the words they exchanged, the shooting. Memory failed him only from the moment he found himself between the two cars, lying on the wet sand with an unbearable pain in his side. But it did not fail him completely. He remembered, for example, Mimì Augello's contorted face, his cracking voice.

'How do you feel? How do you feel? The ambulance is coming now, it's nothing, just stay calm.'

How had Mimì managed to find him?

Then, already in the hospital, someone in a white smock, 'He's lost too much blood.'

After that, nothing. He tried to look around. The room was clean and white. There was a large window, the daylight pouring through. He couldn't move; his arms were stuck full of IVs. His side didn't hurt any more, however; it felt instead like a dead part of his body. He tried to move his legs but couldn't. He slipped slowly away into sleep.

He awoke again towards what must have been evening, since the lights were on. He closed his eyes at once when he saw that there were people in the room. He didn't feel like talking. Then, out of curiosity, he raised his eyelids just enough to see a little. Livia was there, sitting beside the bed in the only metal chair; behind her, standing, was Anna. On the other side of the bed, also standing, was Ingrid. Livia's eyes were wet with tears, Anna was crying without restraint, and Ingrid was pale, her face drawn.

Good God! Montalbano said to himself in terror.

He closed his eyes and escaped into sleep.

*

At 6.30 on what he thought was the next morning, two nurses washed him and changed his dressings. At seven the chief physician appeared, accompanied by five assistants, all of them in white smocks. The chief physician examined the chart at the foot of the bed, pulled the sheet aside, and began to touch him on his injured side.

'Seems to be coming along very nicely,' he declared. 'The operation was a complete success.'

Operation? What operation was he talking about? Ah, maybe to remove the bullet that had wounded him. But it's not often a machine-gun bullet stays inside the body instead of slicing right through it. He would have liked to ask questions, demand explanations, but the words wouldn't come out. The doctor, however, seeing his eyes, guessed what questions the inspector was formulating.

'We had to perform an emergency operation on you. The bullet passed through your colon.'

Colon? And what the hell was his colon doing in his side? The colon had nothing to do with one's sides, it was supposed to be in the belly. But if it had to do with the belly, did this mean – and here he gave such a start that the doctors noticed – that from this moment on, for the rest of his life, he could eat only mush?

'. . . mush?' Montalbano finally managed to mutter, the horror of that prospect reactivating his vocal cords.

'What did he say?' the chief physician asked, turning to his assistants.

'I think he said brush,' said one.

'No, no, he said ambush,' interjected another.

They left arguing over the question.

*

At 8.30 the door opened and Catarella appeared.

'Chief, how goes it? How you feeling?'

If there was one person in the entire world with whom Montalbano felt dialogue was useless, it was Catarella. He didn't answer, but merely moved his head as if to say that things were a little less bad.

'I'm on guard here, over you, I mean. This hospital's a revolving door, people come, people go, back and forth and back and forth. Somebody could maybe come in immotivated with bad intentions, trying to finish the job they didn't finish. You know what I mean?'

The inspector knew exactly what he meant.

'Know what, Chief? I gave blood for the transfusal.'

And he went back on guard against the badly immotivated. Montalbano thought bitterly of the dark years that lay ahead of him, surviving on Catarella's blood and eating semolina mush.

*

The first in the long series of kisses he would receive over the course of the day were from Fazio.

'Did you know, Chief, that you shoot like a god? You got one guy in the throat with a single shot, and you wounded the other.'

'I also wounded the other guy?'

'You certainly did. We don't know in what part of the body, but you wounded him all right. It was Jacomuzzi who noticed a red puddle about ten yards from the cars. Blood.'

'Have you identified the one who died?'

'Of course.'

Fazio pulled a piece of paper from his pocket.

'Munafò, first name Gerlando, born in Montelusa on the sixth of September, 1971, unmarried, resident of Montelusa, Via Crispi 43, no distinguishing features.'

He still hasn't given up his Records Office fetish, thought Montalbano.

'And how did he stand with the law?'

'Not a thing. Clean record.' Fazio put the sheet of

paper back in his pocket. 'For a job like that, they get half a million lire maximum.'

He paused. He obviously had something to say but didn't have the courage to say it. Montalbano decided to help him out.

'Did Gegè die on the spot?'

'Didn't suffer at all. The volley took half his head off.'

The others came in, and there was an orgy of kisses and embraces.

*

Jacomuzzi and Dr Pasquano came from Montelusa to see him.

'All the papers are talking about you,' said Jacomuzzi. He seemed moved but a little envious.

'I was truly sorry I didn't get to do your autopsy,' said Pasquano. 'I'd really like to know how you're put together inside.'

*

'I was the first on the scene,' said Mimì Augello, 'and when I saw you in that condition, in that situation, I got so scared I nearly shit my pants.'

'How did you find out?'

'There was an anonymous call to headquarters saying there'd been some shooting at the foot of the Scala dei Turchi. Galluzzo was on duty and phoned me right away. He also said something I didn't know. He said you were in the habit of meeting Gegè at the place where the shooting was heard.'

'He knew that?!'

'Apparently everybody knew! Half the town knew! So, anyway, I didn't even get dressed, I went right outside in my pyjamas—'

Montalbano raised a tired hand, interrupting him.

'You sleep in pyjamas?'

'Yes,' said Augello, confused. 'Why?'

'Never mind. Go on.'

'As I was racing there in my car, I called an ambulance with my cellphone. Which was a good thing, because you were losing a lot of blood.'

'Thanks,' Montalbano said gratefully.

'What do you mean, "thanks"? Wouldn't you have done the same for me?'

Montalbano did a little rapid soul-searching and decided not to answer.

'Oh, I also wanted to mention something strange,' Augello continued. 'The first thing you asked me, when you were still lying on the sand, groaning, was to remove the snails that were crawling on you. You were sort of delirious, so I said yes, I'd remove them, but there wasn't a single snail on you.'

*

Livia came and gave him a long hug, started crying, and lay down on the bed beside him as best she could.

'Stay like that,' said Montalbano.

He liked the scent of her hair as she rested her head on his chest.

'How did you find out?'

'From the radio. Actually, it was my cousin who heard the news. What a way to wake up!'

'What did you do?'

'First I called Alitalia and booked a flight to Palermo, then I called your office in Vigàta. They put Augello on, and he was very nice. He reassured me and even offered to come and get me at the airport. He told me the whole story in the car.'

'Livia, how am I?'

'You're doing well, considering what happened.'

'Am I ruined forever?'

'What are you talking about?!'

'Will I have to eat bland food for the rest of my life?'

*

'But you leave me no choice,' the commissioner said, smiling.

'Why?'

'Because you've been going about things like a sheriff, or, if you prefer, like some kind of nocturnal avenger, and it's going to end up all over the television and news-papers.'

'That's not *my* fault.'

'No, it's not, but neither will it be my fault if I'm forced to promote you. You're just going to have to behave for a little while. Fortunately you won't be able to leave this place for another twenty days.'

'Twenty days?!'

'By the way, Under Secretary Licalzi's in Montelusa at the moment. He says he's here to sensitize public opinion to the struggle against the Mafia. He's made it known he intends to pay you a visit this afternoon.'

'I don't want to see him!' Montalbano shouted, upset.

The under secretary was someone who had been up to his ears in sweetheart deals with the Mafia and was now recycling himself, as always with the Mafia's consent.

At that exact moment the head physician came in. Seeing there were six people in the room with Montalbano, he frowned.

'Don't take this the wrong way, but I beg you please to leave him alone. He needs to rest.'

They were starting to say their goodbyes when the doctor said to the nurse, in a loud voice, 'And no more visitors for the rest of the day.'

'The under secretary is supposed to leave this afternoon at five,' the commissioner whispered to Montalbano. 'Unfortunately, I suppose he won't be able to see you. Doctor's orders.'

They exchanged smiles.

*

A few days later they removed the IV from his arm and put a telephone on his bedside table. That same morning, he received a visit from Nicolò Zito, who came in like Santa Claus.

'I've brought you a TV, a VCR and a cassette. I've even brought the newspaper articles that talk about you.'

'What's on the cassette?'

'I taped and spliced together all the idiocies that I, TeleVigàta, and all the other TV stations said about the incident.'

*

'Hello, Salvo? It's Mimì. How are you feeling today?'

'Better, thanks.'

'I'm calling to let you know they killed our friend Ingrassia.'

'I expected as much. When did it happen?'

'This morning. They shot him as he was driving into town. Two guys on a high-powered motorcycle. The officer who was tailing him couldn't do anything but try to give him first aid, but it was too late. Listen, Salvo, I'm coming to see you tomorrow morning. You're going to have to tell me, for the record, every detail of your shoot-out.'

*

He told Livia to put in the cassette. Not that he was so curious; it was just to pass the time. On TeleVigàta, Galluzzo's brother-in-law indulged in a fantasy worthy of a scriptwriter for films like *Raiders of the Lost Ark*. In his opinion, the shooting was a direct consequence of the discovery of the two mummified bodies in the cave. What terrible, indecipherable secret lay behind that distant crime? The newsman did not blush to recall, however briefly, the sad end to which the discoverers of the pharaohs' tombs had come, and likened this to the ambush of the inspector.

Montalbano laughed so hard he felt a stab of pain in his side. Next appeared the face of Pippo Ragonese, the same station's political commentator, a former Communist, former Christian Democrat, and now a representative of the Renewal Party. Mincing no words, Ragonese asked himself: what was Montalbano doing in that place with a pimp and drug dealer who was rumoured to be his friend? Were such associations consistent with the rigorous moral standards that every public servant should abide by? Times have changed, the commentator noted sternly; thanks to the new government, an atmosphere of renewal was shaking up the country, and we must all march in step. The old attitudes, the old collusions, must end, once and for all.

Montalbano felt another stab of pain in his side, from rage this time, and he cried out. Livia got up at once and turned off the video.

'You're getting upset over what that arsehole says?'

*

After half an hour of insistence and entreaties, Livia gave in and turned the video back on. Nicolò Zito's commentary was affectionate, indignant and rational. Affectionate towards his friend, the inspector, to whom he sent his sincerest good wishes; indignant because, despite all the politicians' promises, the Mafia had a free hand across the island; and rational because it connected Tano the Greek's arrest with the discovery of the weapons. As the man responsible for these two powerful blows against organized crime, Salvo Montalbano had become a dangerous adversary, one who must be liquidated at all costs. Zito ridiculed the conjecture that the ambush might be an act of revenge for desecrating the dead. With what money would the assassins have been paid? With the obsolete coins that were found in the bowl?

The picture then switched back to the TeleVigàta newsman, who was now interviewing Alcide Maraventano, presented to the viewing public as a 'specialist in the occult'. The defrocked priest was wearing a cassock sewn with multicoloured patches and sucking from a baby's bottle. In response to a series of insistent questions intended to make him acknowledge a possible connection between the ambush of the inspector and the supposed desecration, Maraventano, like a masterly, consummate actor, both did and did not acknowledge the possibility, leaving everyone in nebulous suspense.

Zito's cassette concluded with the logo of Ragonese's editorial segment. But then an unknown newsman appeared, saying that his colleague was prevented from airing his commentary that evening because he'd been the victim of a brutal assault. A group of hoodlums, still unidentified, had roughed him up and robbed him the night before, as he was returning home from his job at TeleVigàta. The newsman then launched into a violent attack on the police, accusing them of no longer being able to guarantee the safety of the citizenry.

'Why did Zito want you to see that report, which has nothing to do with you?' naively asked Livia, who was from the North and didn't understand certain insinuations.

*

Augello interrogated him, and Tortorella took it all down. He explained that he'd been schoolmates and friends with Gegè, and that their friendship had endured over the years, even though they found themselves on opposite sides of the barricade. He had them write in the report that Gegè, that evening, had asked to see him, but they'd managed to exchange only a few words, barely more than a greeting.

'He started to mention the weapons traffic, said he'd heard talk of something that might interest me, but he didn't get a chance to tell me what it was.'

Augello pretended to believe this, and Montalbano went on to recount the various stages of the gunfight.

'Now it's your turn to tell me,' he said to Mimì.

'First sign the statement,' said Augello.

Montalbano signed, and Tortorella said goodbye and headed back to headquarters. There wasn't much to tell, said Augello. Ingrassia's car was overtaken by the motorcycle; the guy on the back turned round, opened fire, and that was that. Ingrassia's car ended up in a ditch.

'They were pruning a dead branch,' Montalbano commented. Then, with a touch of melancholy because he felt left out of the game. 'What do you think you'll do?'

'The people in Catania, whom I've informed, promised not to let Brancato get away.'

'We can always hope.'

Augello didn't realize it, but by informing his colleagues in Catania, he may have signed Brancato's death warrant.

'So who was it?' Montalbano asked bluntly after a pause.

'Who was what?'

'Take a look at this.'

He pressed the remote and showed him the segment reporting the news of the assault on Ragonese. Mimì played the part of someone in the dark to perfection.

'You're asking me? Anyway, it doesn't concern us; Ragonese lives in Montelusa.'

'You're such an innocent, Mimì! Here, bite my pinky.'

And he held out his little finger to him, as one does to teething babies.

EIGHTEEN

After a week, the visits, embraces, phone calls and congratulations gave way to loneliness and boredom. He had persuaded Livia to go back to her cousin in Milan; there was no point in wasting her holidays. The planned trip to Cairo, for the moment, was out of the question. They agreed that Livia would fly back down as soon as Montalbano got out of the hospital. Only then would she decide how and where to spend her two remaining weeks of vacation.

And little by little, the uproar surrounding the inspector and what had happened likewise died down to a mere echo, before disappearing entirely. Every day, however, Augello or Fazio would come to keep him company. But they didn't stay long, just enough to tell him the latest news and the state of certain investigations.

Every morning when he opened his eyes, Montalbano made a point of devoting his thoughts and speculations to the dead couple of the Crasticeddru. He wondered when he would again have the chance to be alone, in precious silence, with no disturbance of any kind, so he could develop a sustained line of reasoning from which he might receive a flash, a spark. He needed to take advantage of this situation, he would say to himself, and he'd begin to replay the whole affair in his mind with the speed of a galloping horse. Soon, however, he would find himself moving at a lazy trot, then at a walk, and finally a kind of torpor would ever-so-slowly overwhelm him, body and mind.

'Must be my convalescence,' he told himself.

He would sit down in the armchair, pick up a newspaper or magazine, and halfway through an article just a little longer than the rest, he would get fed up, his eyes would start to droop, and he would sink into a sweaty sleep.

✻

Sargint Fasio said you was comin home today. I am hapy and releved. The sargint also said for me to feed you lite foods. Adelina

The housekeeper's note was on the kitchen table. Montalbano rushed to the fridge to see exactly what she meant by 'lite'. There were two fresh hakes to be served with oil and lemon. He unplugged the phone; he wanted to reaccustom himself at an easy pace to living at home. There was a lot of mail, but he didn't open a single letter or read a single postcard. He ate and went to bed.

Before falling asleep, he asked himself a question: if the doctors reassured him that he would recover all his strength, why did he have that lump of sadness in his throat?

✻

For the first ten minutes he drove apprehensively, paying closer attention to the reactions of his side than to the road. Then, seeing that he was weathering the bumps without difficulty, he accelerated, passed through Vigàta, took the road to Montelusa, turned left at the Montaperto crossroads, drove another few miles, turned onto an unpaved trail, and pulled up at a small clearing in front of a farmhouse. He got out of the car. Mariannina, Gegè's sister, who had been his teacher at school, was sitting in a wicker chair beside the front door, mending a basket. The moment she saw the inspector, she ran up to meet him.

'Salvù! I knew you'd come.'

'You're the first person I'm visiting since leaving the hospital,' said Montalbano, embracing her.

Mariannina began weeping very softly, without a sound, only tears, and Montalbano's eyes welled up.

'Pull up a chair,' said Mariannina.

Montalbano sat down beside her. She took his hand and began to stroke it.

'Did he suffer?'

'No. I realized while they were still shooting that they'd snuffed out Gegè on the spot. This was later confirmed. I don't even think he ever realized what was happening.'

'Is it true you killed the one who killed Gegè?'

'Yeah.'

'Gegè will be happy, wherever he is.'

Mariannina sighed and squeezed the inspector's hand a little harder.

'Gegè loved you with all his soul.'

Meu amigo de alma, the title of a book, came to Montalbano's mind.

'I loved him, too,' he said.

'Do you remember how naughty he was?'

And a naughty boy he was, mischievous, bad. Clearly Mariannina was not referring to recent years, when Gegè had his run-ins with the law, but to a distant time when her younger brother was a restless little scamp. Montalbano smiled.

'Do you remember the time he threw a firecracker into a copper cauldron that someone was repairing, and the blast made the poor guy faint?'

'And the time he emptied his inkwell into Mrs Longo's purse?'

They talked about Gegè and his exploits for nearly two hours, recounting episodes that never went beyond his adolescence.

'It's getting late,' said Montalbano. 'I should go.'

'I'd like to tell you to stay for dinner, but what I made is probably too heavy for you.'

'What did you make?'

'*Attuppateddri* in tomato sauce.'

Attuppateddri were small light brown snails which, when they went into hibernation, would secrete a fluid that solidified into a white sheet, which served to close — *attuppari* in Sicilian — the entrance to the shell. Montalbano's first impulse was to decline in disgust. How long would this obsession continue to torment him? In the end, he coolly decided to accept, as a twofold challenge to his stomach and his psyche. With the plate in front of him giving off an exquisite, ochre-coloured scent, he had to steel himself, but after extracting the first *attuppateddru* with a pin and tasting it, he suddenly felt liberated: with the obsession gone and the melancholy banished, there was no doubt the belly, too, would adjust.

*

At headquarters he was smothered by embraces. Tortorella even wiped away a tear.

'I know what it means to come back after being shot!' said the officer.

'Where's Augello?'

'In his office, your office,' said Catarella.

He opened the door without knocking and Mimì leapt out of the chair behind the desk as if he'd been caught stealing. He blushed.

'I haven't touched anything. It's just that from here, the phone calls—'

'Mimì, you did absolutely the right thing,' Montalbano cut him short, repressing the urge to kick him in the arse for having dared to sit in his place.

'I was planning to come to your house today,' said Augello.

'To do what?'

'To arrange protection.'

'Protection? For whom?'

'For whom? For you, of course. There's no saying they won't try again, after coming up empty the first time.'

'You're wrong. Nothing more's going to happen to me. Because, you see, Mimì, it was you who had me shot.'

Augello turned so red, he looked as though someone had inserted a high-voltage plug up his bum. He started trembling. Then all his blood disappeared God knows where, leaving him pale as a corpse.

'Where do you get these ideas?' he managed to mutter awkwardly.

Montalbano reckoned he'd sufficiently avenged himself for the expropriation of his desk.

'Calm down, Mimì. That's not what I meant to say. What I meant was: it was you who set the mechanism in motion that led to my shooting.'

'Explain yourself,' said Augello, collapsing into the chair and dabbing all around his mouth and forehead with his handkerchief.

'You, my good friend, without consulting me, without asking if I agreed or not, put two officers on Ingrassia's tail. Did you really think he was so stupid he wouldn't notice? It took him maybe half a day to find out he was being shadowed. And he understandably thought it was me who gave the order. He knew he'd fucked up a couple of times and that I had him in my sights, and so, to brush up his image for Brancato, who was planning to get rid of him – it was you who related their phone conversation to me – he hired two arseholes to eliminate me. Except that his scheme turned into a fiasco. By this time Brancato, or somebody else, had got fed up with Ingrassia and his brilliant ideas – don't forget the pointless little murder of poor Cavaliere Misuraca – and so they took matters in hand and made him vanish from the face of the earth. If you hadn't put Ingrassia on his guard, Gegè would still be alive and I wouldn't have this pain in my side. And there you have it.'

'If that's how things went . . . I guess you're right,' said Mimì, annihilated.

'That's how things went, you can bet your arse on it.'

*

The plane pulled up very near to the gate, so the passengers didn't need to be shuttled by bus to the terminal. Montalbano saw Livia descend the ramp and walk towards the entrance with her head down. Hiding in the crowd, he watched Livia as she waited interminably for her baggage, collected it, loaded it onto a cart, and then headed towards the taxi stand. They had agreed the night before that she would take the train from Palermo to Montelusa and that he would limit himself to picking her up at the station. At the last minute, however, he had decided to surprise her and show up at Punta Ràisi airport.

'Are you alone? Need a lift?'

Livia, who was making her way towards the first cab in line, stopped in her tracks and shouted.

'Salvo!'

They embraced happily.

'But you look fantastic!' she commented.

'So do you,' said Montalbano. 'I've been watching you for over half an hour, ever since you got off the plane.'

'Why didn't you say something sooner?'

'I like seeing how you exist without me.'

They got in the car and immediately Montalbano, instead of starting the ignition, hugged and kissed her, put a hand on her breast and lowered his head, caressing her knees and stomach with his cheek.

'Let's get out of here,' said Livia, breathing heavily, 'or we'll get arrested for lewd behaviour in public.'

On the road to Palermo, the inspector had an idea and made a suggestion.

'Shall we stop in town? I want to show you La Vuccirìa.'

'I've already seen it. In the Guttuso painting.'

'That's a shitty painting, believe me. We'll book a hotel room, hang out a little, walk around, go to La Vuccirìa, get some sleep, and head back to Vigàta tomorrow morning. I don't have any work to do, in any case, so I can consider myself a tourist.'

*

Once inside the hotel, they failed in their intention to freshen up quickly and go out. They did not go out. They made love and fell asleep. Then they woke up and made love again. When they finally left the hotel it was already getting dark.

They went to La Vuccirìa. Livia was shocked and overwhelmed by the shouts, the exhortations, the cries of the merchants calling out their wares, the speech, the arguments, the sudden brawls, the colours so bright they seemed unreal, painted. The smell of fresh fish mingled with that of tangerines, boiled lamb entrails sprinkled with caciocavallo cheese, a dish called *mèusa*, and fritters, all of them fusing into a unique, almost magical whole.

Montalbano stopped in front of a second-hand clothes shop.

'In my university days, when I used to come here to eat *mèusa* and bread, which today would only make my liver burst, this shop was the only one of its kind in the world. Now they sell second-hand clothes, but back then the shelves were empty, all of them. The owner, Don Cesarino, used to sit there behind the counter – which was also completely bare – and receive clients.'

'Clients? But the shelves were all empty.'

'They weren't exactly empty. They were, well, full of purpose, full of requests. The man sold stolen goods to order. You'd go to Don Cesarino and say: I need a certain kind of watch; or, I want a painting, say, a nineteenth-century dock scene; or, I need this or that sort of ring. He'd take your order, write it down on a piece of pasta paper, the rough, yellow kind we used to have, he'd negotiate the price and then tell you when to come back. On the appointed date, and not one day later, he would pull the requested merchandise out from under the counter and hand it over to you. All sales were final.'

'But what need was there for him to have a shop? I

mean, he could have done that sort of business anywhere, in a cafe, on a street corner . . .'

'You know what his friends in La Vuccirìa used to call him? Don Cesarino *u putiàru,* "the shop-owner". Because Don Cesarino didn't see himself as a front man, as they might call him today, nor as a "receiver of stolen goods". He was a shopkeeper like any other, and his shop — for which he paid rent and electricity — was proof of this. It wasn't a facade.'

'You're all insane.'

*

'Like a son! Let me hug you like a son!' said the head-master's wife, squeezing him to her breast and holding him there.

'You have no idea how worried you had us!' said her husband, echoing her sentiments.

Headmaster Burgio had phoned him that morning to invite him to dinner. Montalbano had declined, suggesting he drop by in the afternoon instead. They showed him into the living room.

'Let's get right to the point,' Burgio began, 'we don't want to take up too much of your time.'

'I have all the time in the world, being unemployed for the moment.'

'My wife told you, when you were here that time for dinner, that I call her a woman of fantasy. Well, right after you left, she started fantasizing again. We had wanted to call you sooner, but then what happened happened.'

'Suppose we let the inspector decide whether or not they're fantasies?' the signora said, slightly piqued, before continuing in a polemical tone: 'Shall you speak, or shall I?'

'Fantasies are your domain.'

'I don't know if you still remember, but when you asked my husband where you could find Lillo Rizzitano, he answered that he hadn't had any news of him since July 1943. Then something came back to me: that a girlfriend of mine also disappeared during that period. Except that I actually heard from her a while later, but in the strangest way . . .'

Montalbano felt a chill run down his spine. The two lovers of the Crasticeddru had been murdered very young.

'How old was this friend of yours?'

'Seventeen. But she was a lot more mature than me. I was still a little girl. We went to school together.'

She opened an envelope that was on the coffee table, took out a photograph, and showed it to Montalbano.

'This was taken on our last day of school, our final year. She's the first one on the left in the back row, and that's me next to her.'

All smiling and wearing the Fascist uniforms of the Giovani Italiane. The teacher was giving the Roman salute.

'Since the situation in Sicily was becoming too dangerous with all the bombing, schools closed on the last day in April, and we were spared the dreaded final exam. We passed or failed solely on the basis of our grades. Lisetta – that was my friend's name, Lisetta Moscato – moved to a little inland village with her family. She wrote to me every other day, and I still have all her letters, at least the ones that arrived. The mail in those days, you know ... My family also moved out; we went all the way to the mainland, to live with one of my father's brothers. When the war was over, I wrote to my friend at both addresses, the one in the inland village and the one in Vigàta. But she never wrote back, and this worried me. Finally, in late 1946, we returned to Vigàta, and I looked up Lisetta's parents. Her mother had died, and at first her father didn't want to see me. Then he was rude to me and said Lisetta had fallen in love with an American soldier and gone away with him, against her family's wishes. And he added that as far as he was concerned, his daughter might as well be dead.'

'That does seem plausible, frankly,' said Montalbano.

'What did I tell you?' the headmaster cut in triumphantly.

'But you see, Inspector, the whole thing was strange just the same, even without counting what happened later. It's strange because, first of all, if Lisetta had fallen in love with an American soldier, she would have let me know in any way possible. And second, because in the letters she sent me from Serradifalco — that was the name of the village where they'd taken refuge — she kept harping on the same theme: the torment she suffered being separated from a mysterious young man with whom she was terribly in love, whose name she would never tell me.'

'Are you sure this mysterious lover really existed? Might he not have been some girlish fantasy?'

'Lisetta wasn't the type to indulge in fantasies.'

'You know,' said Montalbano, 'at age seventeen, and even later, you can never swear by matters of the heart.'

'Put that in your pipe and smoke it,' said the head-master.

Without saying a word, the signora extracted another photo from the envelope. It showed a young woman in bridal dress, giving her arm to a good-looking boy in a US army uniform.

'This came to me from New York in early 1947, according to the postmark.'

'And this, in my opinion, dispels all doubt,' the head-master concluded.

'Not at all. If anything, it raises doubt.'

'In what sense, signora?'

'Because it was the only thing that came in the envelope – only this photograph of Lisetta and the soldier, nothing else, no note, nothing. Not even any writing on the back of the photo; you can see for yourself. So, can you explain to me why a true, intimate friend would send me only a photograph without writing a single word?'

'Did you recognize your friend's handwriting on the envelope?'

'The address was typed.'

'Ah,' said Montalbano.

'And one last thing: Lisetta Moscato and Lillo Rizzitano were first cousins. And Lillo really loved her, like a little sister.'

Montalbano looked at the headmaster.

'He adored her,' Burgio admitted.

NINETEEN

The more he mulled it over, circled round it, snuck up beside it, the more convinced he became that he was on the right track. He hadn't even needed his customary meditative walk to the end of the jetty. Upon leaving the Burgio house with the wedding photo in his pocket, he'd raced off directly to Montelusa.

'Is the doctor in?'

'Yes, but he's busy. I'll let him know you're here,' said the receptionist.

Pasquano and his two assistants were standing around the marble table, on top of which lay a naked corpse with eyes agape. And the dead man had good reason to look so wide-eyed, as if in surprise, since the three were drinking a toast with paper cups. The doctor had a bottle of spumante in his hand.

'Come on in, we're celebrating.'

Montalbano thanked the assistant, who handed him a cup, and Pasquano poured him a finger or two of the sparkling wine.

'To whose health?' asked the inspector.

'To mine. With this guy here, I've just performed my thousandth autopsy.'

Montalbano drank up, called the doctor aside, and showed him the photograph.

'Do you think the dead girl from the Crasticeddru could have had a face like this one?'

'Would you please go fuck yourself?' Pasquano gently asked.

'Sorry,' said the inspector.

He turned on his heels and left. He was the arsehole, not the doctor. He'd let himself get carried away by his enthusiasm and had gone and asked Pasquano the most idiotic question imaginable.

He had no better luck at the crime lab.

'Is Jacomuzzi in?'

'No, he's at the commissioner's office.'

'Who's in charge of the photography lab?'

'De Francesco, in the basement.'

De Francesco eyed the photo as if he hadn't yet learned that one could reproduce images on light-sensitive film.

'What do you want me to do?'

'Tell me if you think it's a photomontage.'

'Ah, that's not my game. I only know about taking pictures and developing them. The more difficult stuff we send to Palermo.'

*

Then the wheel turned in the right direction, and things started falling into place. Montalbano phoned the photographer of the magazine that had published the review of Maraventano's book, whose name he remembered.

'Sorry to trouble you. Is this Mr Contino?'

'Yes, it is. Who's speaking?'

'This is Inspector Montalbano. I need to talk to you about something.'

'Pleased to make your acquaintance. You can come right now, if you like.'

The photographer lived in the old part of Montelusa, in one of the few houses to survive a landslide that had done away with an entire quarter, one that bore an Arab name.

'Actually, I'm not a photographer by profession. I teach history at the lyceum, and I love it. How can I be of help to you?'

'Do you think you could tell me if this photograph is a montage?'

'I could try,' said Contino, examining the photo. 'When was it taken, do you know?'

'Around 1946, I'm told.'

'Come by again tomorrow.'

Montalbano hung his head and said nothing.

'Is it very urgent? I'll tell you what, I can give you a preliminary answer in, say, two hours, but I'll need more time to confirm it.'

'It's a deal.'

✳

The inspector spent the two hours in an art gallery that was featuring a show by a seventy-year-old Sicilian painter still caught up in a sort of populist rhetoric, but felicitous in his intense and lively use of colour. Yet he lent only a distracted eye to the paintings, as he was impatient for Contino's answer. Every five minutes he looked at his watch.

'So, what did you find?'

'I've just finished. In my opinion, it is definitely a photomontage. Rather well done.'

'What makes you think so?'

'The background shadows. The girl's head has been mounted in place of the real bride's head.'

Montalbano had not told him this. In no way had Contino been alerted to this fact or been led to this conclusion by the inspector.

'I'll say even more: the girl's face has been retouched.'

'In what way?'

'She's been, well, made to look a little older.'

'Could I have it back?'

'Sure, I don't have any more use for it. I thought it was going to be more difficult, but there's no need for any further confirmation.'

'You've been extremely helpful.'

'Listen, Inspector, the opinion I gave you is just between us, okay? It has no legal value whatsoever.'

*

The commissioner greeted him at once, with arms joyfully open.

'What a wonderful surprise! Do you have a little time? Come along with me, we'll go to my house. I'm expecting a phone call from my son. My wife will be so happy to see you.'

The commissioner's son, Massimo, was a doctor who belonged to a volunteer organization that defined itself as 'without borders'. Its members went to work in war-torn countries, lending their skills as best they could.

'My son's a pediatrician, you know. He's in Rwanda at the moment. I'm very worried about him.'

'Is there still fighting?'

'I wasn't referring to the fighting. Every time he manages to call us, he sounds more and more overwhelmed by the horror and anguish.'

The commissioner fell silent. To distract him from his preoccupations, Montalbano told him the news.

'I'm ninety-nine per cent certain I know the first and last name of the dead girl we found in the Crasticeddru.'

The commissioner said nothing, but only gaped at him.

'Her name was Lisetta Moscato, aged seventeen.'

'How the devil did you find that out?'

Montalbano recounted the whole story.

The commissioner's wife took his hand as if he were a little boy, and had him sit down on the sofa. They spoke for a short while, and then the inspector stood up and said he had an engagement and had to go. It wasn't true, but he didn't want to be there when the call came. The commissioner and his wife should be allowed to enjoy their faraway son's voice in peace and by themselves, however full of sorrow and pain his words might be. As he was leaving the house, he heard the telephone ring.

*

'I've kept my word, as you can see. I brought you back the photograph.'

'Come in, come in.'

Signora Burgio stepped aside to let him in.

'Who is it?' her husband called loudly from the dining room.

'It's the inspector.'

'Well, invite him inside!' the headmaster roared as if his wife had somehow refused to let him in.

They were eating supper.

'Shall I set a place for you?' the signora asked pleasantly. And without waiting for an answer, she put a soup dish on the table for him. Montalbano sat down, and the signora served him some fish broth, reduced to a divine density and enlivened with parsley.

'Were you able to find anything out about the photo?' she asked, without noticing the disapproving look her husband was giving her for being, in his opinion, too forward.

'Unfortunately, yes, signora. I think it's a photo-montage.'

'My God! So whoever sent it to me wanted me to believe something that wasn't true!'

'Yes, I do think that was the purpose. To try to put an end to your enquiries about Lisetta.'

'See? I was right!' the woman practically yelled at her husband, and then she started to weep.

'Come on, why are you crying?' Burgio asked.

'Because Lisetta is dead, and they wanted me to think she was alive and happily married!'

'Well, it might have been Lisetta herself who—'

'Don't be ridiculous!' said the signora, throwing her napkin on the table.

There was an awkward silence. Then Mrs Burgio spoke again.

'She's dead, isn't she, Inspector?'

'I'm afraid she is.'

The headmaster's wife got up and left the dining room, covering her face with her hands. As soon as she was out of the room they heard her give in to a kind of plaintive whimpering.

'I'm sorry,' said the inspector.

'She got what she was looking for,' Burgio said without pity, keeping to the logic of his own side of the marital quarrel.

'Let me ask you one question. Are you sure that the feelings Lillo and Lisetta had for each other were only the kind that you and your wife mentioned?'

'What do you mean?'

Montalbano decided to speak plainly.

THE TERRACOTTA DOG

'Couldn't Lillo and Lisetta have been lovers?'

The headmaster started laughing, swatting the idea away with a swipe of the hand.

'Look, Lillo was madly in love with a Montelusa girl he'd stopped hearing from after July 1943. Besides, the corpse in the Crasticeddru couldn't be him, for the simple reason that the farmer who saw him bleeding and being loaded onto the truck by the soldiers, and then carried away who knows where, was a sensible, serious person.'

'Then,' said Montalbano, 'this can mean only one thing: that it's not true that Lisetta ran away with an American soldier. Therefore Lisetta's father told your wife a big fat lie. Who was Lisetta's father, anyway?'

'I vaguely remember his name was Stefano.'

'Is he still alive?'

'No, he died at least five years ago.'

'What did he do for a living?'

'I think he dealt in timber. But Stefano Moscato was not someone we talked about in my house.'

'Why not?'

'Because he, too, wasn't our kind of person. He was in cahoots with his relatives, the Rizzitanos, need I say more? He'd had trouble with the law, I don't know exactly what sort. In those days, in good, respectable families, you simply didn't talk about people like that. It was like talking about shit, if you'll excuse my language.'

Signora Burgio came back, eyes red, an old letter in her hand.

'This is the last letter I received from Lisetta when I

243

was staying in Acquapendente, where I'd moved with my family.'

Serradifalco, June 10, 1943

My dear Angelina,

    How are you? How is everyone in your family? You have no idea how much I envy you, since your life in a northern town can't be even remotely comparable to the prison in which I spend my days. And don't think I'm exaggerating by using the word 'prison'. Aside from Papa's asphyxiating surveillance, there's also the monotonous, stupid life of a village with only a handful of houses. Just imagine, last Sunday, as we were coming out of church, a local boy whom I don't even know said hi to me. Papa noticed, called him aside, and started slapping him. Sheer madness! My only recreation is reading. And I have a friend: Andreuccio, a ten-year-old boy, my cousins' son. He's very smart. Have you ever noticed that little children are sometimes more clever than we are?

    For several days now, Angelina, I've been living in despair. I received — by means so adventurous it would take me too long to explain here — a little note, four lines, from Him Him Him. He says he's desperate, he can no longer stand not seeing me, and now, after staying put all this time in Vigàta, they've just received orders to leave in the next few days. I feel like I'm dying without him. Before he leaves, before he goes away, I must must must spend a few hours with him, even if it means doing something crazy. I'll keep you informed. Meanwhile I send you a great big hug. Yours truly,

Lisetta

'So you never did find out who this "Him" was,' said the inspector.

'No. She never wanted to tell me.'

'Did you receive any other letters after this one?'

'Are you joking? It was already a miracle I got this

244

one. At the time you couldn't cross the Strait of Messina; they were bombing it non-stop. Then, on July 9, the Americans landed and all communications were cut.'

'Excuse me, signora, but do you remember your friend's address at Serradifalco?'

'Of course. It was care of the Sorrentino family, Via Crispi 18.'

＊

He was about to put the key in the lock, but stopped in alarm. Voices and noises were coming from inside the house. He thought of going back to the car and getting his pistol, but did nothing. He opened the door cautiously, without making the slightest noise.

Then all at once he remembered that he'd completely forgotten about Livia, who had been waiting for him for God knows how long.

It took him half the night to make peace.

＊

At seven in the morning he tiptoed out of bed and dialled a phone number.

'Fazio?' he said very softly. 'I need you to do me a favour. You have to call in sick.'

'No problem.'

'By this evening, I want to know everything – from the cradle to the grave – about a certain Stefano Moscato, who died here in Vigàta about five years ago. Ask around town, check the records office and anywhere else you can think of. It's very important.'

'Don't worry, I'll take care of it.'

He hung up the phone, grabbed a pen and a sheet of paper, and wrote:

> *Darling, I have to run out for something urgent and didn't want to wake you. I'll be back by early afternoon, promise. Why don't you get a cab and go to see the temples again? They're as splendid as ever. All my love.*

He stole out of the house like a thief. Had Livia opened her eyes, there would have been hell to pay.

*

It took him an hour and a half to get to Serradifalco. It was a clear day, and he even started whistling. He felt happy. It made him think of Caifas, his father's dog, who used to mope about the house, lethargic and melancholy, until he saw his master start getting his cartridges ready, and immediately he would turn frisky and spry, before transforming into a mass of sheer energy when he was finally out in the fields for the hunt.

Montalbano found Via Crispi right away; number 18 was a small nineteenth-century building of two storeys. There was one doorbell, with the name SORRENTINO inscribed beside it. A pleasant girl of about twenty asked him what he wanted.

'I'd like to speak with Andrea Sorrentino.'

'That's my father. He's not at home. You can find him at the town hall.'

'Does he work there?'

'Sort of. He's the mayor.'

*

'Of course I remember Lisetta,' said Andrea Sorrentino. He wore his sixty-odd years quite well, only a few white hairs. A handsome man. 'But why do you ask?'

'I'm conducting a rather confidential investigation. I'm sorry I can't tell you more. But you must believe me: it's very important that I get some information about her.'

'All right, Inspector. I have very beautiful memories of Lisetta, you know. We used to take long walks in the country. With her at my side, I felt so proud, like a grown-up man. She used to treat me as if we were the same age. But after her family left Serradifalco and she returned to Vigàta, I never heard from her again.'

'Why's that?'

The mayor hesitated a moment.

'Well, I'll tell you because it's all in the past now. I think my father and Lisetta's father had a terrible row. Around the end of August 1943, my father came home in an awful state. He'd been to Vigàta, to see Uncle Stefano – *u zu Stefano*, as I called him – I don't remember what for. He was pale and had a fever. I remember my mother got very scared, and so I, too, got scared. I don't know what transpired between the two of them, but the next day, at the dinner table, my father said that in our house, the Moscatos' name must never be mentioned again. I obeyed, even though I really wished I could ask him about Lisetta. You know how it is, with these horrible feuds between relatives . . .'

'Do you remember the American soldier Lisetta met here?'

'Here? An American soldier?'

'Yes. Or so I've been led to believe. She met an American soldier in Serradifalco, they fell in love, she followed him, and a little while later they got married in the United States.'

'I heard some vague talk of this marriage business, when an aunt of mine, my father's sister, was sent a photo of Lisetta in bridal dress with an American soldier.'

'So why were you surprised when I mentioned it?'

'I was surprised that you said Lisetta met the American here. You see, Lisetta disappeared from our house at least ten days before the Americans occupied Serradifalco.'

'What?'

'Oh, yes. One afternoon, it must have been around three or four o'clock, I saw Lisetta getting ready to leave. I asked her where we were going on our walk that day, and she told me I shouldn't feel hurt, but she wanted to take her walk by herself. Of course I felt deeply hurt. That evening, at supper time, Lisetta still hadn't returned. Uncle Stefano, my father and some local peasants went out looking for her but never found her. Those were terrible hours for us. There were Italian and German soldiers about, and the grown-ups were worried she'd come to harm... The following afternoon, Uncle Stefano said goodbye, telling us he wouldn't be back until he found his daughter. Lisetta's mother stayed behind with us; poor thing, she was devastated. Then the Americans landed, and we were cut off by the front. The very day the front moved on, Stefano Moscato came back to get his wife and said he'd found Lisetta in Vigàta and that her escape had been a childish prank. Now, if you've been following me, you will have understood why Lisetta could not have met her future husband here in Serradifalco, but must have met him in her own town, in Vigàta.'

TWENTY

I know the temples are splendid. Since I've known you I've been forced to see them about fifty times. You can therefore stick them, column by column, you know where. I'm going off by myself and don't know when I'll be back.

Livia's note oozed with rage, and Montalbano took it in. But since a wolf-like hunger had seized hold of him on his way back from Serradifalco, he opened the fridge: nothing. He opened the oven: nothing. Livia, who didn't want the housekeeper about for the time of her stay in Vigàta, had taken her sadism to the point of cleaning everything utterly. Not the tiniest piece of bread was to be found. He got back in his car and drove to the Trattoria San Calogero, where they were already rolling down their shutters.

'We're always open for you, Inspector.'

To quell his hunger and to spite Livia, he ate so much he nearly had to call the doctor.

✻

'There's one statement here that's got me thinking,' said Montalbano.

'You mean where she says she might do something crazy?'

They were sitting in the living room having coffee, the inspector, the headmaster and Signora Angelina.

Montalbano was holding young Lisetta's letter, which he'd just finished rereading aloud.

'No, signora, we know she eventually did that. Mr Sorrentino told me so, and he would have no reason to lie to me. A few days before the landing, therefore, Lisetta got it in her head to flee Serradifalco and come here, to Vigàta, to see the one she loved.'

'But how would she have done that?'

'She probably asked some military vehicle for a lift. In those days the German and Italian troops must have been constantly on the move. A pretty girl like her, she wouldn't have had to try very hard,' interjected Headmaster Burgio, who'd decided to cooperate, having resigned himself to the fact that once in a while, his wife's fantasies might have some connection to reality.

'But what about the bombing? And the machine-gun fire? My God, what courage,' said the signora.

'So, which statement do you mean?' the headmaster asked impatiently.

'The one where Lisetta writes that her lover has told her that, after all this time in Vigàta, they've now received the order to leave.'

'I don't understand.'

'You see, signora, that statement tells us he'd been in Vigàta for a long time, which implies that he was not from the town. Second, it also informs Lisetta that he was about to be compelled, forced, to leave town. Third, she says "they", and therefore he's not the only one who has to leave Vigàta; it's a whole group of people. All this leads me to think he's a soldier. I could be wrong, but it seems like the most logical conclusion.'

'Yes, logical,' echoed the headmaster.

'Tell me, signora, when did Lisetta first tell you she was in love? Do you remember?'

'Yes, because in the last few days I've done nothing but try to recall every last detail of my meetings with Lisetta. It was definitely around May or June 1942. I refreshed my memory with an old diary I dug up.'

'She turned the whole house upside down,' grumbled her husband.

'We need to find out what troops were stationed here between early 1942, or even earlier, and July 1943.'

'You think that's easy, Inspector?' Burgio commented. 'I, for example, can remember a whole slew of different troops. There were the anti-aircraft batteries, the naval batteries, there was a train armed with cannon that remained hidden inside a tunnel, there were soldiers in barracks, soldiers in bunkers . . . Sailors, no; they would come and go. It'd be practically impossible to find out.'

They became discouraged. Then the headmaster stood up.

'I'm going to phone Burruano. He stayed in Vigàta the whole time, before, during and after the war. Whereas I was evacuated at a certain point.'

His wife resumed speaking.

'It was probably an infatuation – at that age it's hard to distinguish, you know – but it certainly was something serious, serious enough to make her run away from home, to make her go against her father, who was like her jailer, or so she used to tell me, at least.'

A question came to Montalbano's lips. He didn't want to ask it, but the hunter's instinct got the better of him.

'Excuse me for interrupting, but could you be more precise – I mean, could you tell me exactly what Lisetta meant by that word, "jailer"? Was it a Sicilian father's jealousy of the female child? Was it obsessive?'

Signora Angelina looked at him a moment, then lowered her eyes.

'Well, as I said, Lisetta was much more mature than me; I was still a little girl. Since my father forbade me to go to the Moscatos' house, we used to meet up at school or in church, where we would spend a few quiet hours together. And we would talk. Lately, I've been going over and over in my mind what she said or hinted at back then. I think there were a lot of things I didn't understand at the time . . .'

'Such as?'

'For example, up until a certain point, Lisetta referred to her father as "my father"; after that, however, she always called him "that man". But this might not mean anything. Another time she said to me, "One day that man's going to hurt me, he's going to hurt me very badly." And at the time I imagined a beating, a whipping. Now I'm starting to have a terrible feeling about the true meaning of that statement.'

She stopped, took a sip of coffee, and continued.

'She was brave, very brave. In the shelter, when the bombs were falling and we were trembling and crying with fear, it was she who gave us courage and consoled us. But to do what she did, she needed twice that much courage, to defy her father and run out under a hail of bullets, to come all the way here and make love to someone who wasn't even her official lover. Back then we were different from today's seventeen-year-olds.'

Signora Angelina's monologue was interrupted by the return of her husband, who seemed restless.

'I couldn't find Burruano, he wasn't home. Come, Inspector, let's go.'

'To look for Burruano?'

'No, no, I've just had an idea. If we're lucky, and I've guessed right, I'll donate fifty thousand lire to San Calogero on his next feast day.'

San Calogero was a black saint revered by the townsfolk.

'If you've guessed right, I'll throw in another fifty myself,' said Montalbano, caught up in the old man's enthusiasm.

'Think you could tell me where you're going?'

'I'll tell you later,' the headmaster said to his wife.

'And leave me here in the lurch?' the woman insisted.

Burgio, frantic, was already out of the door. Montalbano bent down to her. 'I'll keep you informed of everything.'

*

'How the hell did I forget *La Pacinotti*?' the headmaster muttered to himself as soon as they were in the street.

'Who's she?' Montalbano asked. He imagined her fiftyish and stubby. Burgio didn't answer. Montalbano asked another question.

'Should we take the car? Are we going far?'

'Far? It's right round the corner.'

'Would you explain to me who this Pacinotti woman is?'

'Woman? She was a ship, a mother ship that would repair any damage the warships sustained. She anchored in the port towards the end of 1940 and never moved. Her crew was made up of sailors who were also mechanics, carpenters, electricians, plumbers . . . They were all kids. And because the ship was there for so long, many of them became like family and ended up seeming like towns folk. They made friends, and they also took girlfriends. Two of them married local girls. One of them has since died, name was Tripcovich; the other's name is Marin and he owns the repair garage in Piazza Garibaldi. You know him?'

'He's my mechanic,' the inspector said, bitterly thinking he was about to resume his journey through the old people's memories.

*

A fiftyish-year-old man in filthy overalls, fat and surly, said nothing to the inspector and attacked Headmaster Burgio.

'Why are you wasting your time coming here? It's not ready yet. I told you the work would take a long time.'

'I didn't come for the car. Is your father here?'

'Of course he's here. Where else would he be? He's here busting my balls, telling me I don't know how to work, that the mechanical geniuses in his family are him and his grandson.'

A lad of twenty or so, also in overalls, who'd been looking under a car bonnet, stood up and greeted the two men with a smile. Montalbano and Burgio walked across the garage, which must have originally been a warehouse, and came to a kind of partition made of wooden boards.

Inside, behind a desk, was Antonio Marin.

'I overheard everything,' he said. 'And if arthritis hadn't messed me up, I could teach that one a thing or two.'

'We need some information.'

'What do you need to know, Inspector?'

'It's better if I let Headmaster Burgio tell you.'

'Do you remember how many crew members of the *Pacinotti* were killed or wounded or declared missing in combat?'

'We were lucky,' the old man said, growing animated. Apparently he liked talking about that heroic time; at home they probably told him to shut up whenever he started in on the subject. 'We had one dead from bomb shrapnel, name was Arturo Rebellato; and one wounded, also from shrapnel, and his name was Silvio Destefano; and one missing, Mario Cunich. We were all very close, you know; most of us hailed from up north, Venice, Trieste . . .'

'Missing at sea?' asked the inspector.

'What sea? We were moored in the harbour the whole time. We practically became an extension of the wharf.'

'Then why was he declared missing?'

'Because on the evening of July the seventh, 1943, he never returned to ship. The bombing had been heavy that afternoon, and he was out on a pass. Cunich was from Monfalcone, and he had a friend from the same town who was also my friend, Stefano Premuda. Well, the next morning Premuda forced the whole crew to go looking for Cunich. We spent the entire day going from house to house asking after him, to no avail. We went to the military hospital, the civilian hospital, we went to the place where they collected all the dead bodies found under the rubble . . . Nothing. Even the officers joined in the search, since some time before that they'd been given advance notice, a kind of warning, that in the coming days we were going to have to weigh anchor . . . We never did, though; the Americans arrived first.'

'Couldn't he have simply deserted?'

'Cunich? Never! He believed in the war. He was a Fascist. A good kid, but a Fascist. And he was smitten.'

'What do you mean?'

'Smitten, in love. With a girl from here. Like me, actually. He said that as soon as the war was over, he was going to get married.'

'And you never had any news of him again?'

'Well, when the Americans landed, they decided that a repair ship like ours, which was a jewel, suited them just fine. So they kept us in service, in Italian uniform, but they gave us an armband to wear on our sleeves to avoid any misunderstandings. So Cunich had all the time in the world to return to the ship, but he never did. He just disappeared. I stayed in touch with Premuda afterward, and now and then I'd ask him if he'd heard from Cunich or had any news of him . . . Nothing, not a word.'

'You said you knew Cunich had a girlfriend here. Did you ever meet her?'

'Never.'

One more thing needed to be asked, but Montalbano stopped, and with a glance he let Burgio have the honour.

'Did he at least tell you her name?' the headmaster asked, accepting Montalbano's generous offer.

'Well, Cunich was very reserved. But he did tell me once that her name was Lisetta.'

What happened? Did an angel pass, did time stop? Montalbano and Burgio froze, and the inspector grabbed his side. He felt a violent pain, while the headmaster brought his hand to his heart and leaned against a car to keep from falling. Marin became terrified.

'What did I say? My God, what did I say?'

*

Immediately outside the garage, the headmaster started shouting cheerfully, 'We guessed right!'

And he traced a few dance steps. Two passers-by, who knew him as a pensive, sombre man, stopped in shock. Having got it out of his system, Burgio turned serious again.

'Don't forget we promised San Calogero fifty thousand lire a head.'

'I won't forget.'

'Do you know San Calogero?'

'I haven't missed the annual celebration since I moved to Vigàta.'

'That doesn't mean you know him. San Calogero is someone who — how shall I say? — who doesn't let things slide. I'm telling you this for your own good.'

'Are you joking?'

'Absolutely not. He's a vengeful saint, and it doesn't take much to get his dander up. If you make him a promise, you have to keep it. If you, for example, get in a car crash and narrowly escape with your life, and you make a promise to the saint which you don't keep, you can bet your last lira you're going to get in another accident and lose your legs at the very least. Get the idea?'

'Perfectly.'

'Let's go home now, so you can tell my wife the whole story.'

'So *I* can tell her?'

'Yes, because I don't want to give her the satisfaction of hearing me say she was right.'

*

'To summarize,' said Montalbano, 'things may have gone as follows.'

He was enjoying this investigation in slippers, in a home from another age, over a cup of coffee.

'The sailor Mario Cunich, who became a kind of local boy around Vigàta, fell in love with Lisetta Moscato, who loved him too. How they managed to meet and talk to each other, God only knows.'

'I've given it a lot of thought,' said Signora Angelina. 'There was a period – I think it was from 1942 until March or April 1943 – when her father had to go far away from Vigàta on business. They could have fallen in love then, and they would certainly have had plenty of opportunities to spend time together in secret.'

'They did fall in love, that much we know,' resumed Montalbano. 'Then her father's return again prevented them from seeing each other. Soon the evacuation also came between them. So when news came of his imminent departure ... Lisetta escaped, she came here, she met Cunich, but we don't know where. The sailor, so he could have as much time as possible with Lisetta, didn't return to ship. And at some point, they were murdered in their sleep. So far, everything clicks.'

'Clicks?' asked Angelina, taken aback.

'I'm sorry, I merely meant that thus far, our reconstruction makes sense. The person who killed them may have been a jilted lover, or even Lisetta's father, who may have caught them together and felt dishonoured. We may never know.'

'What do you mean, we may never know?' said Angelina. 'Aren't you interested in finding out who murdered those two poor kids?'

He didn't have the heart to tell her that he didn't care that much about the killer himself. What really intrigued him was why someone, perhaps even the killer, had taken it upon himself to move the bodies into the cave and set up that scene with the bowl, the jug and the terracotta dog.

*

Before going back home he stopped at a grocery store and bought two hundred grammes of peppered cheese and a loaf of durum-wheat bread. He got these provisions because he was sure he wouldn't find Livia at the house. And indeed she wasn't there; everything was the same as when he'd left to see the Burgios.

He didn't have time to set the bag of groceries on the table when the phone rang. It was the commissioner.

'Montalbano, I thought I should tell you that Under Secretary Licalzi called me today, wanting to know why I hadn't yet put in a request for your promotion.'

'But what the hell does that man want from me, anyway?'

'I took the liberty of inventing a story of love, something mysterious, I said, left unstated, between the lines . . . He took the bait; apparently he's a passionate reader of pulp romances. But he did settle the matter. He told me to write to him and ask that you be given a substantial bonus. So I wrote the request and sent it. You want to hear it?'

'Spare me.'

'Too bad. I thought I'd written a little masterpiece.'

Montalbano set the table and cut a thick slice of bread before the telephone rang again. It wasn't Livia, as he had hoped, but Fazio.

'Chief, I've been working all bleeding day for you. This Stefano Moscato wasn't the kind of guy you'd want to sit down to dinner with.'

'A mafioso?'

'Really and truly mafioso, I don't think so. But he was certainly violent. Various convictions for brawling, violence and assault. They don't seem like Mafia offences to me; a mafioso doesn't get himself convicted for stupid shit.'

'What's the date of the last conviction?'

'Nineteen eighty-one, if I'm not mistaken. With one foot in the grave he still busted some guy's head with a chair.'

'Do you know if he did any time in jail in 1942 and 1943?'

'Sure did. Assault and battery. From March 1942 to April 1943 he was in Palermo, at Ucciardone prison.'

The news from Fazio greatly enhanced the flavour of the peppered cheese, which was already no joking matter all by itself.

TWENTY-ONE

Galluzzo's brother-in-law opened his news programme with the story of a grisly bombing, clearly bearing the Mafia's signature, on the outskirts of Catania. A well-known and respected businessman from that city, Corrado Brancato, owner of a large warehouse that supplied supermarkets around the island, had decided to treat himself to an afternoon of rest in a small house he owned just outside town. After turning the key in the lock, he had, for all intents and purposes, opened the door onto nothingness: a horrific explosion, triggered by an ingenious device linking the door to an explosive charge, literally pulverized the house, the businessman and his wife, Giuseppa née Tagliafico. Investigations, the newsman added, were proving difficult, since Mr Brancato had a clean record and did not appear to be in any way involved with the Mafia.

Montalbano turned off the television and started whistling Schubert's Eighth, the 'Unfinished'. It came out splendidly, he didn't miss a note.

He dialed Mimì Augello's number. Surely his second-in-command would know more about this most recent development. There was no answer.

When he'd finally finished eating, Montalbano made every trace of the meal disappear, carefully washing even the glass from which he'd drunk three gulps of wine. He undressed and was about to get into bed when he heard a vehicle pull up, followed by some voices, a car door shutting, and the car driving away. Very quickly, he slipped under the covers, turned off the light, and pretended to be sleeping deeply. He heard the front door open and close, then Livia's footsteps, which came to a sudden halt. Montalbano realized she'd stopped in the bedroom doorway and was staring at him.

'Stop clowning around.'

Montalbano gave in and turned on the light.

'How did you know I was faking?'

'From your breathing. Do you know how you breathe when you're asleep? No. I do.'

'Where've you been?'

'To Eraclea Minoa and Selinunte.'

'By yourself?'

'Mr Inspector, I'll tell you everything, I'll confess, just drop this third degree, for Christ's sake! I went with Mimì Augello.'

Montalbano's face turned ugly, and he pointed a threatening finger.

'I'm warning you, Livia; Augello already moved into my desk once. I don't want him moving into anything else of mine.'

Livia stiffened.

'I'm pretending I don't understand. It's better for both of us. But, in any case, I'm not some piece of property of yours, you arsehole of a Sicilian.'

'All right, I'm sorry.'

They kept arguing a good while, even after Livia got undressed and came to bed. As for Mimì, however, Montalbano was determined not to let him get away with this. He got up.

'Now where are you going?'

'To give Mimì a ring.'

'Leave the guy in peace. He would never dream of doing anything that might offend you.'

'Hello, Mimì? Montalbano here. Oh, you just got in? Good. No, no, don't worry, Livia's just fine. She thanks you for the wonderful time she had with you today. And I, too, want to thank you. Oh, by the way, Mimì, did you know that Corrado Brancato was blown up today in Catania? No, I'm not kidding, they said so on TV. You haven't heard anything? What do you mean, you haven't heard anything? Oh, of course, you were out all day. And our colleagues in Catania were probably looking for you over land and sea. And no doubt the commissioner, too, was wondering what had become of you. Well, what can you do? Try to patch it up, I guess. Good night, Mimì. Sleep tight.'

'To say you're a real piece of shit is putting it mildly,' said Livia.

*

'All right,' said Montalbano. It was three o'clock in the morning. 'I admit it's all my fault, that when I'm here I get all wrapped up in my thoughts and act as if you didn't exist. I'm too accustomed to being alone. Let's go away.'

'And where will you leave your head?' asked Livia.

'What does that mean?'

'It means you're going to have to bring your head with you, along with everything inside it. And therefore, inevitably, you'll keep thinking about your own concerns even if we're a thousand miles away.'

'I promise I'll empty my head out before we leave.'

'And where will we go?'

Since Livia had clearly caught the archaeological-touristic bug, he thought it wise to play along.

'You've never seen the island of Mozia, have you? Tell you what: this very morning, around eleven, we'll leave for Mazara del Vallo. I've got a friend there, Assistant Commissioner Valente, whom I haven't seen in a long time. From there we'll head on to Marsala and eventually to Mozia. Then, when we get back to Vigàta, we'll plan another tour.'

They made peace.

*

Giulia, Assistant Commissioner Valente's wife, was not only the same age as Livia, but also a native of the Genoa suburb of Sestri. The two women took an immediate liking to each other. Montalbano took a bit less of a liking to Giulia, owing to the shamefully overcooked pasta, a beef stew conceived by an obviously deranged mind, and dishwater coffee of a sort that even airline crews wouldn't foist on anyone. At the end of this so-called lunch, Giulia suggested to Livia that the two of them stay at home and go out later; Montalbano accompanied his friend to the office. There, awaiting the assistant commissioner, was a man of about forty with long sideburns and a sun-baked Sicilian face.

'Every day, it's something else! I'm sorry, Mr Commissioner, but I need to talk to you. It's very important.'

'Inspector, let me introduce Farid Rahman, a friend of mine from Tunis,' said Valente. Then, turning to Rahman, 'Will it take long?'

'Fifteen minutes at the most.'

'I'll go and visit the Arab quarter,' said Montalbano.

'If you'll wait for me,' Farid Rahman interjected, 'I'd be delighted to be your guide.'

'I have an idea,' suggested Valente. 'I know my wife doesn't know how to make coffee. Piazza Mokarta is three blocks from here. Go and sit in the cafe there and have yourself a decent cup. Farid will come and pick you up.'

*

He didn't order the coffee immediately. First he went to work on a hefty, fragrant dish of *pasta al forno* that lifted him out of the gloom into which the culinary art of Signora Giulia had plunged him. By the time Rahman arrived,

Montalbano had already done away with all trace of the pasta and had only an innocent, empty demitasse of coffee in front of him. They headed off to the Arab quarter.

'How many of you are there in Mazara?'

'We're now more than a third of the local population.'

'Have there been many incidents between the Arabs and the Mazarese?'

'No, very few, practically nothing compared to other cities. I think we're sort of a historical memory for the Mazarese, almost a genetic fact. We're family. Al-Imam al-Mazari, the founder of the Maghrebin juridical school, was born in Mazara, as was the philologist Ibn al-Birr, who was expelled from the city in 1068 because he liked wine too much. But the basic fact is that the Mazarese are seafaring people. And the man of the sea has a great deal of common sense; he understands what it means to have one's feet on the ground. And speaking of the sea – did you know that the motor trawlers around here have mixed crews, half Sicilian, half Tunisian?'

'Do you have an official position here?'

'No, God save us from officialdom. Here everything works out for the best because it's all done unofficially. I'm an elementary-school teacher, but I also act as a liaison between my people and the local authorities. Here's another example of good, common sense: when a school principal gave our community some classrooms to use, we instructors came over from Tunis and created our school. But the superintendency is officially unaware of this situation.'

✻

The Arab quarter was a piece of Tunis that had been picked up and carried, unaltered, to Sicily. The shops were closed because it was Friday, the day of rest, but life in the narrow little streets was still colourful and animated. First, Rahman showed Montalbano the large public baths, the social meeting place for Arabs from time immemorial; then he took him to a smoking den, a cafe with hookahs. They passed by a sort of empty storefront, inside of which an old man with a grave expression sat on the floor, legs folded under him, reading from a book and offering commentary. In front of him, sitting the same way, were some twenty boys listening attentively.

'That's one of our imams, explaining the Koran,' said Rahman, who made as if to keep walking.

Montalbano stopped him, resting a hand on his arm. He was struck by the truly religious absorption of those kids, who once outside of the empty store would again let loose, shouting and scuffling as always.

'What's he reading to them?'

'The eighteenth sura, the one about the cave.'

Montalbano, without knowing the cause, felt a slight tremor in his backbone.

'The cave?'

'Yes, *al-kahf*, the cave. The sura says that when some young people prayed to God not to let them be corrupted and led astray from the path of the true religion, He made them fall into a deep sleep inside a cave. And so that there would always be total darkness inside the cave, God reversed the course of the sun. They slept for about three hundred and nine years. Also with them was a dog, who slept in front of the entrance, but on guard, with his front legs extended—'

He broke off, having noticed that Montalbano had turned very pale and was opening and closing his mouth as if gasping for air.

'What's wrong, signore? Do you feel ill, signore? Do you want me to call a doctor? Signore!'

Frightened by his own reaction, Montalbano felt faint, his head spinning, legs buckling. Apparently he was still feeling the effects of the wound and the operation. A small crowd, meanwhile, had gathered around Rahman and the inspector. The teacher gave a few orders, and an Arab ran off and quickly returned with a glass of water. Another arrived with a wicker chair in which he forced Montalbano, who felt ridiculous, to sit. The water revived him.

'How do you say in your language: God is great and merciful?'

Rahman told him, and Montalbano did his best to imitate the sounds of the words. The small crowd laughed at his pronunciation, but repeated them in chorus.

*

Rahman shared an apartment with an older colleague named El Madani, who was at home at that moment. Rahman made tea while Montalbano explained the reasons for his malaise. Rahman was entirely unaware of the discovery of the two young murder victims in the Crasticeddru, whereas El Madani had heard mention of it.

'What I'd like to know, if you'd be so kind,' said the inspector, 'is to what extent the objects placed inside the cave correspond to what the sura says. As far as the dog is concerned, there's no doubt whatsoever.'

'The dog's name is Kytmyr,' said El Madani, 'but he's also called Quotmour. Among the Persians, you know, that dog, the one in the cave, became the guardian of written communication.'

'Does the sura say anything about a bowl with money inside?'

'No, there's no bowl, for the simple reason that the sleepers have money in their pockets. When they awake, one of them will be given money to go and buy the best food there is. They're hungry. But the one sent on this mission is betrayed by the fact that the coins are not only no longer current, but are now worth a fortune. People follow him back to the cave, hoping to find a treasure, and that is how the sleepers come to be discovered.'

'But in the case that concerns me,' Montalbano said to Rahman, 'the bowl can be explained by the fact that the boy and girl were naked when placed inside the cave, and therefore the money had to be put somewhere.'

'Agreed,' said El Madani, 'but it is not written in the Koran that they were thirsty. The water receptacle has no connection to the sura.'

'I know many legends about sleepers,' Rahman added, 'but none of them says anything about water.'

'How many sleepers were there in the cave?'

'The sura is vague about this – the number is probably

not important – three, four, five, six, not counting the dog. But it has become common belief that there were seven sleepers, eight with the dog.'

'If it's of any use to you,' said El Madani, 'you should know that the sura is a retelling of an old Christian legend, the Seven Sleepers of Ephesus.'

'There's also a modern Egyptian drama, *Ahl al-kahf*, which means "The People of the Cave", by the writer Taufik al-Hakim. In it the young Christians, persecuted by the emperor Decius, fall into a deep sleep and reawaken in the time of Theodosius the Second. There are three of them, as well as the dog.'

'Therefore,' Montalbano concluded, 'whoever put the bodies in the cave must have known the Koran, and perhaps even the play by this Egyptian.'

*

'Mr Burgio? Montalbano here. I'm calling you from Mazara del Vallo. I'm about to leave for Marsala. Sorry to be in such a rush, but I have to ask you something very important. Did Lillo Rizzitano know Arabic?'

'Lillo? Not a chance.'

'He couldn't perhaps have studied it at university?'

'Impossible.'

'What was his degree in?'

'In Italian, with Professor Aurelio Cotroneo. He may have even told me what his thesis was about, but I can't remember.'

'Did he have any Arab friends?'

'Not that I know of.'

'Were there any Arabs in Vigàta around 1942 to 1943?'

'Inspector, the Arabs were here at the time of their domination, and now they've returned, poor things, but not as dominators. No, during that period there weren't any. But what are the Arabs to you?'

*

It was already dark outside when they left for Marsala. Livia was cheerful and animated. She was very happy to have met Valente's wife. At the first intersection, instead of turning right, Montalbano turned left. Livia noticed immediately, and the inspector was forced to make a difficult U-turn. At the second intersection, Montalbano did the exact opposite: instead of going left, he turned right, and this time Livia was too engrossed in what she was saying to realize it. To their great astonishment, they found themselves back in Mazara. Livia exploded.

'You really try a woman's patience!'

'But you could have kept an eye out yourself!'

'Your word is worth nothing! You promised me before leaving Vigàta that you'd empty your head of all your concerns, and instead you keep getting lost in your own thoughts.'

'I'm sorry, I'm sorry.'

He paid very close attention for the first half hour of road, but then, treacherously, the thought returned: the dog made sense, as did the bowl with the money, but not the jug. Why?

He hadn't even begun to venture a hypothesis when he was blinded by a truck's headlights and realized he had drifted left of centre and was heading straight into what would have been a ghastly collision. He jerked the wheel wildly, deafened by Livia's scream and the angry blast of the truck's horn, and they bounced their way across a newly ploughed field before the car came to a halt, stuck in a furrow. Neither of them said a word; there was nothing to say. Livia was panting heavily. Montalbano dreaded what lay in store for him the moment the woman he loved caught her breath. Like a coward he took cover and sought her compassion.

'You know, I didn't tell you earlier because I didn't want to alarm you, but this afternoon, after lunch, I was unwell . . .'

*

Then the whole incident turned into something between tragedy and a Laurel and Hardy film. The car would not budge, were they even to fire cannons at it. Livia withdrew into a scornful silence. At a certain point, Montalbano abandoned his efforts to get out of the rut, for fear of overheating the engine. He slung their bags over his shoulder, Livia following a few steps behind. A passing motorist took pity on the wretched pair at the edge of the road and drove them to Marsala. After leaving Livia at a hotel, Montalbano went to the local police station, identified himself, and with the help of an officer woke up someone with a tow truck. Between one thing and the next, when he lay down beside Livia, who was tossing in her sleep, it was four o'clock in the morning.

TWENTY-TWO

To win forgiveness, Montalbano made up his mind to be affectionate, patient, pleasant and obedient. It worked, and Livia soon cheered up. She was enchanted by Mozia, amazed by the road just under the water's surface, which linked the island with the coast, and charmed by the mosaic flooring of white and black river pebbles in an ancient villa.

'This is the *tophet*,' said their guide, 'the sacred area of the Phoenicians. There were no buildings; the rites were performed out in the open.'

'The usual sacrifices to the gods?' asked Livia.

'To god,' the guide corrected her, 'the god Baal Hammon. They would sacrifice a first-born son, strangle him, burn him, and put his remains in a vase that they would bury in the ground, and beside it they would erect a stela. Over seven hundred of these stelae have been found here.'

'Good God!' exclaimed Livia.

'It was not a very nice place for children, signora. When Dionysius of Syracuse sent the admiral Leptines to conquer the island, the Mozians, before surrendering, slit their children's throats. However you roll the dice, fate was never kind to the little ones of Mozia.'

'Let's get out of here,' said Livia. 'I don't want to hear any more about these people.'

*

They decided to leave for the island of Pantelleria. They stayed there for six days, finally without quarrels or arguments. It was the right place for Livia to ask one night, 'Why don't we get married?'

'Why not?'

They wisely decided to think it over calmly. The one who stood to lose the most was Livia, since she would have to move far from her home in Boccadasse and adapt to a new rhythm of life.

*

As soon as the aircraft took off, carrying Livia away with it, Montalbano rushed to the nearest public telephone and called his friend Zito in Montelusa. He asked him for a name and got his answer, along with a Palermo phone number, which he dialled at once.

'Professor Riccardo Lovecchio?'

'That's me.'

'A mutual friend, Nicolò Zito, gave me your name.'

'How is the old carrot top? I haven't heard from him for a long time.'

The loudspeaker requested that passengers for the

Rome flight go to the gate. This gave him an idea as to how he might see the man immediately.

'Nicolò's doing well and sends his regards. Listen, Professor, my name's Montalbano. I'm here at Punta Ràisi airport and have roughly four hours before I have to catch another flight. I need to speak with you.' The loud-speaker repeated the request on cue, as if in cahoots with the inspector, who needed answers, and fast.

'Listen, are you Inspector Montalbano of Vigàta, the one who found the two young murder victims in the cave? Yes? What a coincidence! You know, I was going to look you up one of these days! Come see me at home, I'll wait for you. Here's the address.'

*

'I, for example, once slept for four days and four nights in a row, without eating or drinking. Of course, contributing to my sleep were some twenty-odd joints, five rounds of sex, and a billy club to the head from the police. It was 1968. My mother got very worried and wanted to call a doctor. She thought I was in a deep coma.'

Professor Lovecchio had the look of a bank clerk. He didn't show his age of forty-five; a faint glint of madness sparkled in his eye. He was fuelling himself on straight whisky at eleven in the morning.

'There was nothing miraculous about my sleep,' Lovecchio went on. 'To achieve a miracle you have to be out for at least twenty years. In the Koran, again – I think it's in the second sura – it's written that a man, whom the commentators identify as Ezra, slept for a hundred years. The prophet Salih, on the other hand, slept for twenty years, he, too, in a cave, which isn't the most comfortable place for getting a good sleep. Not to be outdone, the Jews, in the Jerusalem Talmud, boast of a certain Hammaagel, who, in the inevitable cave, slept for seventy years. And let's not forget the Greeks. Epimenides woke up after fifty years — in a cave. In those days, in short, all you needed was a cave and somebody who was dead tired, and you had a miracle. The two youngsters you found had been sleeping for how long?'

'From 1943 to 1994. Fifty years.'

'The perfect time to be woken up. Would it complicate your deductions if I told you that in Arabic one uses the same verb for sleeping and dying? And that a single verb is also used for waking up and coming back to life?'

'What you're saying is absolutely spellbinding, but I've got a flight to catch and have very little time. Why were you thinking of contacting me?'

'To tell you not to be fooled by the dog. And that the dog seems to contradict the jug and vice versa. Do you understand why?'

'Not a bit.'

'You see, the legend of the sleepers is not oriental in origin, but Christian. In Europe, it was Gregory of Tours who first introduced it. It tells of seven youths of Ephesus who, to escape the anti-Christian persecutions of Decius, took refuge in a cave, where the Lord put them to sleep. The cave of Ephesus exists; you can even find it in the *Italian Encyclopedia*. They built a sanctuary over it, which was later destroyed. The Christian legend says there's a spring inside the cave. Thus the sleepers, as soon as they awoke, drank first, then sent one of their own in search of food. But at no time in the Christian legend, or in any of its endless European variants, is there any mention of a dog. The dog, whose name is Kytmyr, is purely and simply the poetic invention of Mohammed, who loved animals so much he once cut off a sleeve so as not to wake up the cat that was sleeping on it.'

'You're losing me.'

'But there's no reason to get lost, Inspector. I was merely trying to say that the jug was put there as a symbol of the spring that was in the Ephesian cave. So, to conclude: the jug, which thus belongs to the Christian legend, can only co-exist with the dog, which is a poetic invention of the Koran, if one has an overview of all the variants that the different cultures have contributed to the story . . . In my opinion, the person who staged that scene in the cave can only be someone who, in his studies . . .'

As in a comic book, Montalbano saw the lightbulb flash in his brain.

*

He screeched to a halt in front of the Anti-Mafia Commission offices. The guard on duty raised his sub-machine gun in alarm.

'I'm Inspector Montalbano!' he shouted, holding up his driver's licence, the first thing he'd happened to grab. Short of breath, he ran past another officer acting as usher and yelled, 'Please inform Mr De Dominicis that Inspector Montalbano's on his way up, quick!'

In the lift, taking advantage of being alone, Montalbano mussed up his hair, loosened his tie, and unbuttoned his top button. He thought of pulling his shirt a bit out of his trousers, but decided that would be excessive.

'De Dominicis, I've got it!' he said, panting slightly, closing the door behind him.

'You've got what?' asked De Dominicis, alarmed by the inspector's appearance and rising from his gilded armchair in his gilded office.

'If you're willing to give me a hand, I'll let you in on an investigation that—'

He stopped, putting a hand over his mouth as if to prevent himself from saying anything more.

'What's it about? Give me a hint, at least.'

'I can't, believe me, I really can't.'

'What am I supposed to do?'

'By this evening at the latest, I want to know what the subject of the university thesis of someone named Calogero Rizzitano was. His academic adviser was a certain Professor Cotroneo, I think. He must have graduated in late 1942. The subject of this thesis is the key to everything. We could deal a mortal blow to—'

Again he interrupted himself, became bug-eyed, and said to himself dementedly, 'I haven't said anything, you know.'

Montalbano's agitation infected De Dominicis.

'What can we do? The students . . . at the time . . . why, there must have been thousands! Assuming the records still exist.'

'What are you saying? A few dozen, not thousands. At the time, all the young men were in the service. It should be easy to find out.'

'Then why don't you look into it yourself?'

'They would be sure to waste a great deal of my time with their red tape, whereas for you they would open every door.'

'Where can I reach you?'

'I'm heading back to Vigàta in a hurry; I don't want to lose track of certain developments. Phone me as soon as you've got any news. Call me at home, don't forget. Not at the office; there may be a mole there.'

He waited until evening for De Dominicis's call, which never came. This did not worry him, however; he was sure that De Domenicis had swallowed the bait. Apparently, even for him, the going had not been easy.

*

The next morning he had the pleasure of seeing Adelina the housekeeper again.

'Why haven't you been around these days?'

'Whattaya mean, why? 'Cause the young lady don't like seein' me 'bout the house when she's here, that's why.'

'How did you know Livia was gone?'

'I found out in town.'

Everybody, in Vigàta, knew everything about everyone.

'What'd you buy for me?'

'I'm gonna make you *pasta con le sarde*, and *purpi alla carrettera* for after.'

Exquisite, but deadly. Montalbano gave her a hug.

*

Around midday the telephone rang and Adelina, who was cleaning the house top to bottom to get rid of every trace of Livia's presence, went to answer.

'Signuri, Dr Didumminici wants you.'

Montalbano, who'd been sitting on the veranda re-reading Faulkner's *Pylon* for the fifth time, rushed inside. Before picking up the receiver, however, he quickly established a plan of action for getting De Dominicis out of his hair once he'd obtained the information.

'Yes? Hello? Who's this?' he said in a tired voice full of disappointment.

'You were right, it was easy. Calogero Rizzitano graduated on November 13, 1942. You'd better write this down, because the title is a long one.'

'Wait while I look for a pen. For what it's worth . . .'

De Dominicis noticed the flatness in Montalbano's voice.

'Are you all right?'

Complicity had made De Dominicis more concerned and personal.

'Am I all right? Need you ask? I told you I needed an

answer by last night! I'm no longer interested! You're too late. Everything's fucked now, fizzled out.'

'I couldn't have done it any sooner, believe me.'

'All right, all right. Let's have the title.'

'*The Use of Macaronic Latin in the Mystery Play of the Seven Sleepers by an Anonymous Sixteenth-Century Author.* Now you tell me what the Mafia could have to do with a title—'

'It has a lot to do with it! It has everything to do with it! Except that now, because of you, I don't need it any more and I certainly can't thank you for it.'

He hung up and burst into a high-pitched whinny of joy. Immediately a sound of breaking glass could be heard in the kitchen: in terror, Adelina must have dropped something. Taking a running start, he leapt from the veranda onto the sand, executed a somersault, then a cartwheel, then a second somersault and a second cartwheel. The third somersault failed, and he collapsed on the sand, out of breath. Adelina ran towards him from the veranda screaming:

'*Madunnuzza beddra!* He's gone crazy! He's broke 'is neck!'

*

To set his own mind at rest, Montalbano got in his car and drove to the Montelusa public library.

'I'm looking for a mystery play,' he said to the chief librarian.

The chief librarian, who knew him as a police inspector, was mildly astonished but said nothing.

'All we've got,' she said, 'are the two volumes of D'Ancona and two more by De Bartholomaeis. But these books can't be taken out. You'll have to consult them here.'

He found the *Mystery Play of the Seven Sleepers* in the second tome of the D'Ancona anthology. It was a short, very naive text. Lillo's thesis must have centred around the dialogue between two heretical scholars who expressed themselves in an amusing macaronic Latin. But what most interested the inspector was the long preface by D'Ancona. It contained everything: the quotation from the Koranic sura, the legend's itinerary through various European and African countries, in all its different variants and mutations. Professor Lovecchio had been correct: sura number eighteen of the Koran, taken by itself, would have proved a very tough nut to crack. It had to be complemented with the contributions of other cultures.

*

'I'm going to venture a hypothesis, and I'd like to have your approval,' said Montalbano, who had brought the Burgios up to date on his latest discoveries. 'You both told me, with a great deal of conviction, that Lillo saw Lisetta as a little sister and was crazy about her. Right?'

'Yes,' the two said in chorus.

'Good. Now, let me ask you a question. Do you think Lillo would have been capable of killing Lisetta and her young lover?'

'No,' said the old couple without a moment's hesitation.

'I'm of the same opinion,' said Montalbano, 'precisely because it was Lillo who put the two bodies in a position — so to speak — to be hypothetically resurrected. No killer wants his victims to come back to life.'

'And so?' asked the headmaster.

'If, in an emergency, Lisetta had asked him to put them up, she and her boyfriend, at the Rizzitano house on the Crasto, how do you think Lillo would have responded?'

Signora Angelina didn't pause to think twice.

'He would have done whatever Lisetta asked of him.'

'Let's try, then, to imagine what happened during those days in July. Lisetta runs away from Serradifalco, with luck she makes it to Vigàta, meets up with Mario Cunich, and the boyfriend deserts his post — or strays from his ship, let's say. The two now have nowhere to hide. Going to Lisetta's house would be like walking into the wolf's den; it's the first place her father would look. So she asks Lillo Rizzitano for help; she knows he won't say no. Lillo puts the couple up at his house at the foot of the Crasto, where he's been living alone since the rest of his family was evacuated. Who killed the two lovers, and why, we don't know, and perhaps we never will. But there can be no doubt that it was Lillo who buried them in the cave, because he followed, step by step, both the Christian and the Koranic versions of the story. In both cases, the sleepers will one day awake. But what did he mean, what was he trying to say by staging that scene? Was he trying to tell us that the two lovers are asleep and will one day awake or be awakened? Or was he hoping, in fact, that someone in the future would find them and wake them up? Purely by chance, it was I who found them and woke them up. But, believe me, I really wish I had never discovered that cave.'

He was telling the truth, and the old couple realized this.

'I could stop here,' he continued. 'I've managed to satisfy my own personal curiosity. I'm still missing some answers, it's true, but the ones I've found are probably enough for me. As I said, I could stop here.'

'They may be enough for you,' said Signora Angelina, 'but I would like to see Lisetta's killer before me.'

'If you see him, it'll be in a photograph,' her husband said wryly, 'because by now it's ninety-nine per cent certain that the killer is dead and buried.'

'I'll leave it up to you two,' said Montalbano. 'You tell me: what should I do? Should I continue? Should I stop? It's your decision, since these murders are no longer of any interest to anyone. You are perhaps the only link the two dead lovers still have to this world.'

'I say you should go ahead,' said Mrs Burgio, bold as ever.

'Me too,' said the headmaster, seconding her after a pause.

*

When he arrived at the exit for Marinella, instead of turning and heading home, he let the car continue along the coastal highway as if of its own will. There was little traffic, and in just a few minutes he was at the foot of the

Crasto mountain. He got out of the car and climbed up the slope that led to the Crasticeddru. A stone's throw from the weapons cave, he sat down on the grass and lit a cigarette. He remained seated, watching the sunset while his brain was whirring: he had an obscure feeling that Lillo was still alive. But how would he ever flush him out? As darkness began to fall, he headed back to the car, and at that moment his eye fell on the gaping hole in the side of the mountain, the entrance to the unused tunnel, boarded up since time immemorial. Right near the mouth, there was a pile of sheet metal and, beside it, a sign on two stakes. His legs took off in that direction before his brain had even given the order. He arrived out of breath, his side smarting from the dash. The sign said: GAETANO NICOLOSI & SON CONSTRUCTION CO. — PALERMO — VIA LAMARMORA, 33 — PROJECT FOR THE EXCAVATION OF A HIGHWAY TUNNEL — WORKS MANAGER, COSIMO ZIRRETTA, ENG. — ASST. MANAGER, SALVATORE PERRICONE. This was followed by some other information of no interest to Montalbano.

He made another dash to his car and sped like a bullet back to Vigàta.

TWENTY-THREE

At the Gaetano Nicolosi & Son Construction Co. of Palermo, whose number Montalbano had got from directory enquiries, nobody was answering the phone. It was too late in the day; the company's offices must have been deserted. Montalbano tried and tried again, eventually losing hope. Having cursed a few times to let off steam, he then requested the number of the engineer Cosimo Zirretta, assuming that he, too, was from Palermo. He'd guessed right.

'Hello, this is Inspector Montalbano from Vigàta. How did you manage the expropriation?'

'What expropriation?'

'The land that the road and tunnel you were building cuts through, outside of Vigàta.'

'Look, that's not my domain, I'm only responsible for the construction. That is, I *was* responsible until an ordinance put a halt to the whole project.'

'So who should I talk to?'

'Somebody from the company.'

'I phoned there but nobody answered.'

'Then try Commendatore Gaetano or his son Arturo. When they get out of Ucciardone.'

'Oh, really?'

'Yes. Extortion and bribery.'

'So there's no hope?'

'Well, you can hope that the judges will be lenient and let them out in five years. Just kidding. Actually, you could try the company's lawyer, Di Bartolomeo.'

*

'Listen, Inspector, it's not the company's job to deal with expropriation procedures. That's up to the city council of the district in which the expropriated land is located.'

'Then what are you people doing there?'

'That's none of your business.'

And the lawyer hung up. A little touchy, this Di Bartolomeo. Maybe his job was to cover the arses of Nicolosi father and son from the repercussions of their frauds, except that this time he hadn't succeeded.

*

The office hadn't been open five minutes before the company land surveyor Tumminello saw Inspector Montalbano standing in front of him, looking somewhat agitated. And, in fact, it had been a restless night for Montalbano; he'd been unable to fall asleep and so had stayed up reading Faulkner. The surveyor, whose troubled son – who was mixed up with hoodlums, brawls, and motorcycles – once again hadn't come home that night, turned pale, and his hands began to shake. Montalbano, noticing the other's reaction upon seeing him, imagined the worst.

This guy's trying to hide something.

He was still a cop, no matter how well read.

'Is anything wrong?' asked Tumminello, expecting to hear that his son had been arrested. Which, in fact, would have been a stroke of luck, or the least of all evils, since he might as easily have had his throat slit by his little friends.

'I need some information. About an expropriation.'

Tumminello visibly relaxed.

'You over your scare now?' Montalbano couldn't resist asking him.

'Yes,' the surveyor admitted frankly. 'I'm worried about my son. He didn't come home last night.'

'Does he do that often?'

'Yes, actually. You see, he's mixed up with—'

'Then you shouldn't worry,' Montalbano cut him off. He didn't have time for the problems of youth. 'I need to see the bill of sale or expropriation for the land used to build the Crasto tunnel. That's your area, isn't it?'

'Yes, it is. But there's no point in taking out the documents; I know all the information. Tell me specifically what it is you want to know.'

'I want to know about the land that belonged to the Rizzitano family.'

'As I expected,' said the surveyor. 'When I heard about the weapons being discovered, and then about the two dead bodies, I thought: didn't those places belong to the Rizzitanos? And so I went and looked at the documents.'

'And what do the documents say?'

'First, there's something you should know. There were a lot of proprietors whose land stood to be damaged, so to speak, by the construction of the road and tunnel. Forty-five, to be exact.'

'Jesus!'

'There's even a little postage stamp of land, two thousand square metres, which, because it was divided up in an inheritance, has five owners. The note of transfer can't be made out collectively to the heirs; it must be made out individually to each one. Once our order was granted by the prefect, we offered the proprietors a modest sum, since most of the land in question was farmland. For Calogero Rizzitano, who was a presumed proprietor, since there's no piece of paper confirming his ownership – I mean there's no deed of inheritance, since his father died without leaving a will – for Calogero Rizzitano we had to resort to Article 143 of the Code of Civil Procedure, which concerns rightful claimants who cannot be found. As you probably know, Article 143 states—'

'I'm not interested. How long ago did you make out this note of transfer?'

'Ten years ago?'

'Therefore, ten years ago, Calogero Rizzitano could not be found.'

'Nor after that, either. Because out of the forty-five

landowners, forty-four appealed for a higher figure than the sum we were offering. And they got it.'

'And the forty-fifth, the one who did not, was Calogero Rizzitano.'

'Exactly. And we put the money due to him in escrow. Since for us, to all intents and purposes, he's still alive. Nobody asked for a declaration of presumed death. So when he reappears, he can pick up his money.'

*

When he reappears, the land surveyor had said. But every-thing pointed to the conclusion that Lillo Rizzitano was in no mood to reappear. Or, more likely, was no longer in any condition to reappear. Headmaster Burgio and Montal-bano had taken for granted that the wounded Lillo, carried on board a military truck and driven who knows where on the night of July 9, had survived. But they had no idea how serious his wounds might have been. He could well have died in transit or in hospital, if they'd even brought him to a hospital. Why keep conjuring visions out of nothing? It was very possible that, at the moment of their discovery, the two corpses in the Crasticeddru were in better shape than Lillo Rizzitano had been in for some time. For fifty years and more, not a word, not a line. Nothing. Not even when they requisitioned his land and demolished the remains of his house and everything else that belonged to him. The meanders of the labyrinth the inspector had willingly entered led him straight into a wall. But perhaps the labyrinth was being kind to him by preventing him from going any further, stopping him in front of the most logical, most natural solution.

*

Supper was light, yet cooked, in every regard, with a touch the Lord grants only very rarely to the Chosen. But Montalbano did not thank the commissioner's wife; he merely looked at her with the eyes of a stray dog awarded a caress. The two men then retired to the study to chat. For Montalbano the commissioner's dinner invitation had been like a life preserver thrown to a man drowning not in a stormy sea, but in the flat, unrippled calm of boredom.

The first thing they discussed was Catania, and they concurred that informing the Catania police of their investigation of Brancato had led, as its first result, to the elimination of the very same Brancato.

'We're like a sieve,' the commissioner said bitterly. 'We can't take one step without our enemies' knowing about it. Brancato had Ingrassia killed because he was getting too nervous, but when the people pulling the strings learned that we had Brancato in our sights, they took care of him as well. And so the trail we were so painstakingly following was conveniently obliterated.'

He was gloomy. The idea that moles were planted everywhere offended him; it embittered him more than a betrayal by a family member.

Then, after a long pause during which Montalbano

did not open his mouth, the commissioner asked 'How's your investigation of the Crasticeddru murders coming along?'

From the commissioner's tone of voice, Montalbano could tell that his superior viewed this investigation as mere recreation for the inspector, a pastime he was being allowed to pursue before he returned to more serious matters.

'I've managed to find out the man's name, too,' he said, feeling vindicated in the eyes of the commissioner, who gave a start, astonished and now interested.

'You are extraordinary! Tell me how.'

Montalbano told him everything, even mentioning the theatricals he'd performed for De Dominicis, and the commissioner was quite amused. The inspector concluded with an admission of failure of sorts. It made no sense to continue the search, he said, since, among other things, nobody could prove that Lillo Rizzitano wasn't dead.

'All the same,' the commissioner said after a moment's reflection, 'if somebody really wants to disappear, it can be done. How many cases have we seen where people apparently vanish into thin air and then, suddenly, there they are? I don't want to cite Pirandello, but let's take Sciascia at least. Have you read the little book about the disappearance of Majorana, the physicist?'

'Of course.'

'I am convinced, as was Sciascia himself, that in the end Majorana wanted to disappear, and succeeded. He did not commit suicide. He was too religious.'

'I agree.'

'And what about that very recent case of the Roman university professor who stepped out of his home one day and was never seen again? Everybody looked for him – police, carabinieri, even his students, who loved him. It was a planned disappearance, and he also succeeded.'

'True,' Montalbano concurred. Then he thought about what they were saying and looked at his superior. 'It sounds to me as if you're encouraging me to continue the investigation, though on another occasion you reproached me for getting too involved in this case.'

'So what? Now you're convalescing, whereas the other time you were on the job. There's quite a difference, I think,' the commissioner replied.

*

Montalbano returned home and paced from room to room. After his meeting with the surveyor, he had decided to screw the whole investigation, convinced that Rizzitano was good and dead. Now the commissioner had gone and resurrected him, so to speak. Didn't the early Christians use the word *dormitio* to mean death? It was quite possible Rizzitano had put himself 'in sleep', as the Freemasons used to say. Fine, but if that was the case, Montalbano would have to find a way to bring him out of the deep well in which he was hiding. That would require something big, something that would make a lot of noise, something the newspapers and television stations all over Italy would talk about. He had to unleash a bombshell. But what? He needed to forget about logic and dream up something fantastic.

It was eleven o'clock, too early to turn in. He lay down on the bed, fully dressed, and read *Pylon*.

'At midnight last night the search for the body of Roger Shumann, racing pilot who plunged into the lake on Saturday p.m., was finally abandoned by a three-seater biplane of about eighty horsepower which managed to fly out over the water and return without falling to pieces and dropping a wreath of flowers into the water approximately three quarters of a mile away from the spot where Shumann's body is generally supposed to be . . .'

There were only a few lines left until the end of the novel, but the inspector sat up in bed with a wild look in his eyes.

'It's insane,' he said, 'but I'm going to do it.'

*

'Is Signora Ingrid there? I know it's late, but I need to speak to her.'

'Signora no home. You say, I write.'

The Cardamones specialized in finding housekeepers in places where not even Tristão da Cunha would have dared set foot.

'*Manau tupapau*,' said the inspector.

'No understand.'

He'd cited the title of a Gauguin painting. That eliminated Polynesia and environs from the housekeeper's possible land of origin.

'You ready write? Signora Ingrid phone Signor Montalbano when she come home.'

*

When Ingrid got to Marinella, wearing an evening dress with a slit all the way up to her arse, it was already past two in the morning. She hadn't batted an eyelash at the inspector's request to see her right away.

'Sorry, but I didn't have time to change. I was at the most boring party.'

'What's wrong? You don't look right to me. Is it simply because you were bored at the party?'

'No, your intuition's right. It's my father-in-law. He's started pestering me again. The other morning he pounced on me when I was still in bed. He wanted me right away. I convinced him to leave by threatening to scream.'

'Then we'll have to take care of it.'

'How?'

'We'll give him another massive dose.'

At Ingrid's questioning glance, he opened a desk drawer that had been locked, took out an envelope, and handed it to her. Ingrid, seeing the photos portraying her getting fucked by her father-in-law, first turned pale, then blushed.

'Did you take these?'

Montalbano weighed the pros and cons; if he told her

it was a woman who took them, Ingrid might knife him then and there.

'Yeah, it was me.'

The Swedish woman's mighty slap thundered in his skull, but he was expecting it.

'I'd already sent three to your father-in-law. He got scared and stopped bothering you for a while. Now I'll send him another three.'

Ingrid sprang forward, her body pressing against Montalbano's, her lips forcing his open, her tongue seeking and caressing his. Montalbano felt his legs giving out, and luckily Ingrid withdrew.

'Calm down,' she said, 'it's over. It was just to say thank you.'

On the backs of three photos personally chosen by Ingrid, Montalbano wrote: RESIGN FROM ALL YOUR POSTS, OR NEXT TIME YOU'LL BE ON TV.

'I'm going to keep the rest here,' said the inspector. 'When you need them, let me know.'

'I hope it won't be for a long time.'

'I'll send them tomorrow morning, and then I'll make an anonymous phone call that'll give him a heart attack. Now listen, because I have a long story to tell you. And when I'm done, I'm going to ask you to lend me a hand.'

*

He got up at the crack of dawn, having been unable to sleep even a wink after Ingrid had left. He looked in the mirror: his face was a wreck, maybe even worse than after he'd been shot. He went to the hospital for a check-up, and they pronounced him perfect. The five medicines they'd been giving him were reduced to just one. Then he went to the Montelusa Savings Bank, where he kept the little money he was able to put aside. He asked to meet privately with the manager.

'I need ten million lire.'

'Do you need a loan, or have you got enough in your account?'

'I've got it.'

'I don't understand, then. What's the problem?'

'The problem is that it's for a police operation I want to pay for myself, without risking the State's money. If I go to the cashier now and ask for ten million in bills of one hundred thousand, it'll seem strange. That's why I need your help.'

Understanding, and proud to take part in a police operation, the manager bent over backwards for Montalbano.

*

Ingrid pulled her car up alongside the inspector's, right in front of the road sign indicating the superhighway for Palermo, just outside of Montelusa. Montalbano gave her a bulging envelope with the ten million lire inside, and she put it in her shoulder bag.

'Call me at home as soon as you're done. And be careful not to get your purse snatched.'

She smiled, waved him a kiss from her fingertips, and put her car in gear.

*

In Vigàta he got a new supply of cigarettes. On his way out of the tobacco shop, he noticed a big green poster with black lettering, freshly pasted up, inviting the townspeople to attend a cross-country motorbike race the following Sunday, starting at three in the afternoon, in the place called the 'Crasticeddru flats'.

He could never have hoped for such a coincidence. Perhaps the labyrinth had been moved to pity and was opening another path for him?

TWENTY-FOUR

The 'Crasticeddru flats', which stretched out behind the rocky spur, weren't close to being flat, not even in dreams. But the vales, jags and marshes made it an ideal place for a cross-country motorcycle race. The weather that day was a definite foretaste of summer, and people didn't wait for three o'clock to go out to the flats. Actually, they began to gather in the morning – grandmothers, grandfathers, tots and teens and everyone else determined not so much to watch a race, as to enjoy a day in the country.

That morning, Montalbano phoned Nicolò Zito.

'Are you coming to the cross-country motorbike race this afternoon?'

'Me? Why should I? We've sent one of our sports reporters and a cameraman over there.'

'Actually, I was suggesting that we go together, the two of us, just for fun.'

*

They got to the flats at about 3.30, but there was no sign the race would be starting any time soon. There already was, however, a deafening racket, produced mostly by fifty or so motorcycles being tested and revved up, and by loud-speakers blasting raucous music.

'Since when are you interested in sport?' Zito asked in amazement.

'Now and then I get the urge.'

Although they were outside, they had to shout to converse. As a result, when a little touring plane trailing its publicity banner appeared high in the sky over the ridge of the Crasticeddru, few in the crowd noticed, since the noise of the plane – which is what usually makes people look up – couldn't reach their ears. The pilot must have noticed he would never get their attention in this fashion since, after flying three tight circles round the crest of the Crasticeddru, he headed straight for the flats and the crowd, going into an elegant dive and flying extremely low over everyone's head. He practically forced people to read his banner and then to follow it with their eyes as he pulled up slightly, flew over the ridge three more times, descended to the point of almost touching the ground in front of the cave's gaping entrance, and then dropped a shower of rose petals from the aircraft. The crowd fell silent. They were all thinking of the two young lovers found dead in the Crasticeddru as the small plane turned round and came back, skimming the ground, this time dropping countless little strips of paper. It then headed westward toward the horizon and disappeared. And while the banner had aroused a lot of curiosity

0

— since it wasn't advertising a soft drink or a furniture factory, but displayed only the two names Lisetta and Mario — and the rain of rose petals had given the crowd a kind of thrill, the words on the strips of paper, all identical, set them all guessing, sending them on a lively merry-go-round of speculation and conjecture. What indeed was the meaning of: LISETTA AND MARIO ANNOUNCE THEIR REAWAKENING? It couldn't be a wedding or christening announcement. So what was it? Among the swirl of questions, only one thing seemed certain: that the plane, the petals, the pieces of paper and the banner had something to do with the dead lovers found in the Crasticeddru.

Then the races began, and the people watched and amused themselves. Nicolò Zito, upon seeing the rose petals fall from the plane, had told Montalbano not to move from where he stood and had then disappeared into the crowd.

He returned fifteen minutes later, followed by a Free Channel cameraman.

'Will you grant me an interview?'

'Of course.'

This unexpected compliance on Montalbano's part convinced the newsman of his suspicion, which was that the inspector was involved up to his neck in this business with the aircraft.

'Just a few minutes ago, during the preliminaries for the cross-country motorcycle race currently taking place here in Vigàta, we were all witness to an extraordinary event. A small advertising plane . . .' And here he followed with a description of what had just occurred. 'Since, by a fortunate coincidence, we have Inspector Salvo Montalbano here with us among the crowd, we would like to ask him a few questions. In your opinion, Inspector, who are Lisetta and Mario?'

'I could dodge the question,' the inspector said bluntly, 'and say I don't know anything about this and that it might be the work of some newly-weds who wished to celebrate their marriage in an original way. But I would be contradicted by what is written on that piece of paper, which speaks not of marriage but of reawakening. I shall therefore answer honestly and say that Lisetta and Mario were the names of the two young people found murdered inside the cave of the Crasticeddru, that spur of rock right here in front of us.'

'But what does all this mean?'

'I can't really say. You'd have to ask whoever it was that organized the plane stunt.'

'How were you able to identify the two?'

'By chance.'

'Could you tell us their last names?'

'No. I could, but I won't. I can disclose that she was a young woman from these parts, and he was a sailor from the North. I should add that the person who wanted, in such manifest fashion, to remind us of their rediscovery — which this person calls "reawakening" — forgot about the dog, which, poor thing, also had a name: he was called Kytmyr, and was an Arab dog.'

'But why would the murderer have wanted to stage such a scene?'

'Wait a second. Who said that the murderer and the person behind this spectacle are one and the same? I, for one, don't believe they are.'

'I've got to run and edit the report,' said Nicolò Zito, giving Montalbano a strange look.

Soon the crews from TeleVigàta, the RAI regional news and the other private stations arrived. Montalbano answered all their questions politely and with, for him, unnatural ease.

✳

Prey to violent hunger pangs, he stuffed himself with seafood appetizers at the Trattoria San Calogero and then raced home, turned on the television, and tuned into the Free Channel. In his report on the mysterious aeroplane, Nicolò Zito piled it on thick, pumping up the story in every way possible. What crowned it all, however, was not his own interview, which was aired in its entirety, but another interview – which Montalbano hadn't expected – with the manager of the Publi-2000 agency of Palermo, which Zito had tracked down easily, since it was the only advertising agency in western Sicily that had an aeroplane available for publicity.

The manager, still visibly excited, recounted that a beautiful young woman – 'Jesus, what a woman! She looked unreal, she really did, like a model in a magazine. Jesus, was she beautiful!' – an obvious foreigner because she spoke bad Italian – 'Did I say bad? I'm wrong, actually, on her lips our words were like honey' – no, he couldn't be sure as to her nationality, maybe German or English – had come to the agency four days earlier – 'God! An apparition!' – and had asked about the plane. She'd explained in great detail what she wanted written on the banner and the strips of paper. Yes, the rose petals were also her doing. And, oh yes, as for the place, was she ever particular! Very precise. Then the pilot, on his own, the manager explained, had a brilliant idea: instead of releasing the pieces of paper at random along the coastal road, he thought it would be better to drop them on a large crowd that had gathered to watch a race. The lady – 'For the love of God, let's stop talking about her or my wife will kill me!' – paid in advance, cash, and had the invoice made out to a certain Rosemarie Antwerpen at a Brussels address. He had asked nothing more of the lovely stranger – 'God!' – but then, why should he have? She certainly wasn't asking them to drop a bomb! And she was so beautiful! And refined! And polite! And what a smile! A dream.

Montalbano relished it all. He had advised Ingrid: 'You must make yourself even more beautiful than usual. That way, when they see you, they won't know what's what any more.'

TeleVigàta went wild with the story of the mysterious beauty, calling her 'Nefertiti resurrected' and cooking up a fanciful story intertwining the pyramids with the Crasti-ceddru; but it was clear they were following the lead set by

Nicolò Zito's story on their competitor's news programme. Even the regional RAI news gave the matter extensive coverage.

Montalbano was getting the uproar, the commotion, the resonance he had sought. His idea had turned out to be right.

✲

'Montalbano? It's the commissioner. I just heard about the plane. Congratulations. A stroke of genius.'

'The credit goes to you. It was you who told me to carry on, remember? I'm trying to flush our man out. If he doesn't turn up reasonably soon, it means he's no longer among us.'

'Good luck. Keep me posted. Oh, it was you, of course, who paid for the plane?'

'Of course. I'm counting on my promised bonus.'

✲

'Inspector? This is Headmaster Burgio. My wife and I are speechless with admiration. What an idea.'

'Let's hope for the best.'

'Don't forget, Inspector: if Lillo should turn up, please let us know.'

✲

On the midnight edition of the news, Nicolò Zito devoted more time to the story and showed photos of the two corpses in the Crasticeddru, zooming in on the images in detail.

Provided courtesy of the ever-eager Jacomuzzi, thought Montalbano.

Zito isolated the body of the young man, whom he called Mario, then that of the young woman, whom he called Lisetta. Then he showed the aeroplane dropping rose petals and gave a close-up of the words on the strips of paper. From here he went on to weave a tale that was part mystery, part tear-jerker, and decidedly not in the Free Channel style, but rather more like TeleVigàta fare. Why were the two young lovers killed? What sad fate led them to that end? Who was it that took pity on them and set them up in the cave? Had the beautiful woman who showed up at the advertising agency perhaps returned from the past to demand revenge on the victims' behalf? And what connection was there between this beauty and the two kids from fifty years ago? How were we to understand the word 'reawakened'? And how did Inspector Montalbano happen to know even the name of the terracotta dog? How much did he know about this mystery?

*

'Salvo? Hi, it's Ingrid. I hope you didn't think I ran off with your money.'

'Come on! Why, was there some left?'

'Yes. The whole thing cost less than half the amount you gave me. I've got the rest with me. I'll give it back to you as soon as I return to Montelusa.'

'Where are you calling from?'

'Taormina. I met someone. I'll be back in four or five days. Did I do a good job? Did it go they way you wanted?'

'You did a fantastic job. Have fun.'

*

'Montalbano? It's Nicolò. Did you like the reports? I think I deserve some thanks, no?'

'For what?'

'For doing exactly what you wanted.'

'But I didn't ask you to do anything.'

'That's true – not directly, at least. Except that I'm not stupid, and so I gathered that you wanted the story to get as much publicity as possible and to be presented in a way that would touch people's hearts. I said things I will never live down for the rest of my life.'

'Well, thanks – even though, I repeat, I still don't know why you want me to thank you.'

'You know, our switchboard has been overwhelmed with phone calls. The RAI, Fininvest, Ansa and all the national newspapers have asked for a videotape of the report. You've made quite a splash. Can I ask you a question?'

'Sure.'

'How much did the aeroplane cost you?'

*

He slept splendidly, as gods pleased with their handiwork are said to sleep. He'd done everything possible, and even something impossible. Now there was nothing to do but wait for an answer. The message had been sent out, in such a way as to allow somebody to decipher the code, as Alcide Maraventano would say. The first phone call came in at seven in the morning. It was Luciano Acquasanta of *Il Mezzogiorno*, who wanted to corroborate one of his opinions. Was it not possible the two young people were sacrificed in the course of some Satanic rite?

'Why not?' said Montalbano, polite and open to anything.

The second call came fifteen minutes later. It was Stefania Quattrini, from the magazine *Essere Donna*. Her theory was that Mario was caught making love to Lisetta by another, jealous woman – we know what sailors are like – who did away with both of them. She probably then skipped the country, but on her deathbed confided in her daughter, who in turn told her own daughter of the grandmother's crime. This girl, to make good in some way, had gone to Palermo – she spoke with a foreign accent, didn't she? – and arranged the whole business with the aeroplane.

'Why not?' said Montalbano, polite and open to anything.

Cosimo Zappalà of the weekly magazine *Vivere!* communicated his hypothesis to Montalbano at 7.25. Lisetta and Mario, drunk on love and youth, were in the habit of strolling through the countryside hand in hand, naked as Adam and Eve. Surprised one unlucky day by a contingent of retreating German soldiers, also drunk, but on fear and ferocity, they were raped and murdered. On his deathbed, one of the Germans ... And here this version linked up curiously with Stefania Quattrini's.

'Why not?' said Montalbano, polite and open to anything.

At eight, Fazio knocked on the door and brought him all the dailies available in Vigàta, as he'd been ordered to do the night before. The inspector leafed through them while repeatedly answering the phone. All of them, with greater or lesser degrees of emphasis, reported the story. The headline that most amused him was the one in the *Corriere*, which read: POLICE INSPECTOR IDENTIFIES TERRA-COTTA DOG DEAD FOR FIFTY YEARS. All of it, even the irony, was grist for his mill.

✻

Adelina was amazed to find him at home and not out, as was usually the case.

'Adelina, I'm going to be staying home for a few days. I'm waiting for an important phone call, so I want you to make my siege comfortable.'

'I din't unnastand a word you said.'

Montalbano then explained that her task was to alleviate his voluntary seclusion by putting a little extra imagination in her lunch and dinner dishes.

✻

Around ten, Livia called.

'What's going on? Your phone is always busy!'

312

'I'm sorry. It's just that I've been getting all these calls in reference to—'

'I know what they're in reference to. I saw you on TV. You were so unselfconscious and glib, you didn't seem yourself. It's obvious you're better off when I'm not around.'

*

He rang Fazio at headquarters and asked him to bring all mail home to him and to buy an extension cord for the phone. The mail, he added, should be brought to him at home each day, as soon as it arrived. And Fazio should pass the word on: anyone who asked for him at the office must be given his private number by the switchboard operator, with no questions asked.

Less than an hour passed before Fazio arrived with two unimportant postcards and the extension cord.

'What's new at the office?'

'What's new? Nothing. You're the one who attracts the big stuff. Inspector Augello only gets the little shit: purse snatchings, petty theft, a mugging here and there.'

'I attract the big stuff? What's that supposed to mean?'

'It means what I said. My wife, for instance, is scared of rats. Well, I swear, she draws them to her like a magnet. Wherever she goes, the rats soon arrive.'

For forty-eight hours he'd been like a dog on a chain. His field of action was only as large as the extension cord would allow, and therefore he could neither walk on the beach nor go out for a run. He carried the phone with him everywhere, even when he went to the bathroom, and every now and then — the mania took hold of him after twenty-four hours — he would pick up the receiver and bring it to his ear to see if it was working. On the morning of the third day a thought came into his mind, *Why bother to wash if you can't go outside?* This was followed by another, closely related thought, *So what need is there to shave?*

On the morning of the fourth day, filthy and bristly, wearing slippers and the same shirt since the first day, he gave Adelina a fright.

'*Maria santissima, signuri!* Whata happen to you? Are you sick?'

'Yes.'

'Why don' you call a doctor?'

'It's not the sort of thing for a doctor.'

*

He was a very great tenor, acclaimed in all the world. That evening he was to sing at the Cairo Opera, at the old theatre which hadn't yet burned down, though he knew well that it would soon be devoured by flames. He'd asked an attendant to inform him the moment Signor Gegè sat down in his box, the fifth from the right on the second level. He was in costume, the last touches having been applied to his make-up. He heard the call, 'Who's on next?' He didn't move. The attendant arrived, out of breath, and told him that Signor Gegè — who hadn't died, this was well known, he'd escaped to Egypt — hadn't shown up yet. He dashed onto the stage, looking out into the theatre through a small opening in the curtain: it was full. The only empty box was the fifth from the right, second level. He made a split-second decision: he returned to his dressing room, took off his costume and put his regular clothes back on, leaving the make-up, including the long, grey beard and thick, white eyebrows, untouched. Nobody would ever recognize him again, and therefore he would never sing again. He well understood that his career was over and he would have to scramble to survive, but he didn't know what to do about it. Without Gegè he couldn't sing.

He woke up bathed in sweat. In his own fashion, he had produced a classic Freudian dream, that of the empty theatre box. What did it mean? That the pointless wait for Lillo Rizzitano would ruin his life?

✷

'Inspector? It's Headmaster Burgio. It's been a while since we last spoke. Have you any news of our mutual friend?'

'No.'

Monosyllabic, hasty, at the risk of seeming impolite, he had to discourage long or pointless phone conversations. If Rizzitano were to make up his mind, he might think twice if he found the line busy.

'I'm afraid the only way we'll ever get to talk to Lillo, if you'll forgive my saying so, is to hire a medium.'

✷

He had a big squabble with Adelina. The housekeeper had just gone into the kitchen when he heard her start yelling. Then she appeared in the bedroom.

'Signuri, you din't eat nothin yesterday for lunch or dinner!'

'I wasn't hungry, Adelì.'

'I work m'self to death cookin' d'licious things and you jes turn up ya nose at 'em.'

'I don't turn up my nose at them, I'm just not hungry, as I said.'

'An' this house's become a pigsty! You don' want me to wash the floor, you don' want me to wash ya clothes! For five days you been wearin the same shirt anna same shorts! You stink, signuri!'

'I'm sorry, Adelina. I'll snap out of it, you'll see.'

'Well, lemme know when you snap out of it, and I'll come back. 'Cause I ain't settin' foot back in 'ere. Call me when ya feelin' better.'

*

He went out onto the veranda, sat down on the bench, put the telephone beside him, and stared at the sea. He couldn't do anything else – read, think, write – nothing. Only stare at the sea. He was losing himself in the bottomless well of an obsession, and he knew it. He remembered a film he'd seen, perhaps based on a novel by Dürrenmatt, in which a police inspector stubbornly kept waiting for a killer who was supposed to pass through a certain place in the mountains, when in fact the guy would never come through there again. But the inspector didn't know this, and so he waited and waited, and meanwhile days, months, years went by . . .

*

Around eleven o'clock that same morning, the telephone rang. Nobody had called since Headmaster Burgio, several hours before. Montalbano didn't pick up the receiver; he froze as though paralysed. He knew, with utter certainty – though he couldn't have explained why – who would be there at the other end.

He made an effort, and picked up.

'Hello? Inspector Montalbano?'

A fine, deep voice, even though it belonged to an old man.

'Yes, this is he,' said Montalbano. And he couldn't refrain from adding 'Finally!'

'Finally,' the other repeated.

They both remained silent a moment, listening to their breathing.

'I've just landed at Palermo. I could be at your place in Vigàta by one-thirty this afternoon at the latest. If that's all right with you, perhaps you could tell me exactly how to find you. I've been away a long time. Fifty-one years.'

TWENTY-FIVE

He dusted, swept and scrubbed the floors with the speed of a slapstick silent movie. Then he went into the bathroom and washed as he had done only once before in his life, when, at age sixteen, he'd gone on his first date. He took an interminable shower, sniffing his armpits and the skin on his arms, then doused himself, for good measure, with eau de cologne. He knew he was being ridiculous, but he chose his best suit, his most serious tie, and polished his shoes until they looked as if they had their own internal light source. Then he got the idea to set the table, but only for one. He was, it was true, in the throes of a canine hunger, but he was sure he would not be able to swallow.

He waited, endlessly. One-thirty came and went, and he felt sick and had something like a fainting spell. He poured himself a double shot of whisky and gulped it down. Finally, liberation: the sound of a car coming up the driveway. He quickly threw the front door wide open. There was a taxi with a Palermo licence plate, and a very well-dressed old man got out, holding a cane in one hand

and an overnight bag in the other. The man paid the driver, and while the car was manoeuvring to leave, he looked around. He stood erect, head high, and cut an impressive figure. Immediately Montalbano felt he had seen him somewhere before. He went out to meet him.

'Is it all houses around here?' the old man asked.

'Yes.'

'There used to be nothing, only brush and sand and sea.'

They hadn't greeted each other or introduced themselves. They already knew one another.

*

'I'm almost blind, I see very poorly,' said the old man, seated on the bench on the veranda. 'But it seems very beautiful here, very peaceful.'

Only then did the inspector realize where he had seen the old man. Actually, it wasn't exactly him, but a perfect double, a jacket-flap photo of Jorge Luis Borges.

'Would you like something to eat?'

'You're very kind,' said the old man after a moment's hesitation. 'But just a small salad, perhaps some lean cheese, and a glass of wine.'

'Let's go inside, I've set the table.'

'Will you eat with me?'

Montalbano had a knot in the pit of his stomach, but above all he felt strangely moved.

'I've already eaten,' he lied.

'Then, if you don't mind, could you set me a place out here?'

Rizzitano had used the Sicilian verb *conzare*, meaning 'to set the table' – like an outsider trying his best to speak the local language.

'What made me realize you'd figured almost everything out,' Rizzitano said while eating slowly, 'was an article in the *Corriere*. I can't watch television any more, you know; all I see are shadows that hurt my eyes.'

'TV hurts my eyes, too, and my vision is excellent,' said Montalbano.

'But I already knew you had found Lisetta and Mario. I have two sons; one's an engineer, the other's a teacher like me, both married. One of my daughters-in-law is a rabid *leghista*, an insufferable imbecile. Actually, she's very fond of me, but she considers me an exception, since she thinks all southerners are criminals or, in the best of cases, lazy. She never misses an opportunity to say to me, "You know, Papa, down in your parts" – for her, "my parts" extend from Sicily up to and including Rome – "in your parts so-and-so was murdered, so-and-so was kidnapped, so-and-so was arrested, so-and-so planted a bomb . . ." Well, one day she said, "In your own town, inside a cave, they found two young people murdered fifty years ago . . ."'

'How's that?' Montalbano interjected. 'Does your family know you're from Vigàta?'

'Of course they know. However, I never told anyone, not even my wife, rest her soul, that I still owned property in Vigàta. I said my parents and most of my relatives had been wiped out during the bombing. In no way could anybody connect me with the corpses in the Crasticeddru; they didn't know that it was on a piece of my land. But when I heard the news, I got sick, with a high fever. Everything started coming violently back to me. But I was telling you about the article in the *Corriere*. It said that a police inspector in Vigàta, the same one who'd found the bodies, had not only succeeded in identifying the two young victims, but had also learned that the terracotta dog's name was Kytmyr. Well, that made me certain you'd managed to find my university thesis. And so I knew you were sending me a message. I lost some time persuading my sons to let me come here alone; I told them I wanted to revisit, one last time before I die, the place where I was born and lived as a boy.'

Montalbano was still not convinced on this point, so he went back to it.

'So everybody, in your home, knew that you were from Vigàta?'

'Why should I have hidden it? I never changed my name, either, and have never had false documents.'

'You mean you were able to disappear without ever wanting to disappear?'

'Exactly. A person is found when somebody really needs to find him, or really sets his mind to it . . . In any case, you must believe me when I say that I've lived my life with my real first and last names; I entered competitions and even won, I taught, I got married, had children, and I have grandchildren who bear my name. Now I'm retired, and my pension is made out to Calogero Rizzitano, birthplace Vigàta.'

'But you must at least have written to, say, the town hall, or the university, to request the necessary documents?'

'Of course. I did write to them, and they sent me what I needed. You mustn't make a mistake of historical perspective, Inspector. At the time, nobody was looking for me.'

'But you didn't even claim the money the city government owed you for the expropriation of your land.'

'That was precisely the point. I'd had no contact with Vigàta for thirty years, since the older you get, the less you need documents from your birthplace. But the documents required for the expropriation money, those were a little risky. Somebody might have remembered me then. Whereas I had turned my back on Sicily long before that. I didn't want – I still don't want – to have anything to do with it. If there existed some kind of special device that could remove the blood circulating in my veins, I'd be happy.'

'Would you like to go for a walk along the beach?' Montalbano asked when his guest had finished eating.

They'd been walking for five minutes, the old man leaning on his cane but holding onto Montalbano with his other he arm, when he asked, 'Would you tell me how you were able to identify Lisetta and Mario? And how did you figure out that I was involved? Forgive me, but walking and talking at the same time is very taxing for me.'

As Montalbano was telling him the whole story, now

and then the old man would twist his mouth as if to say that was not how it went.

Montalbano then felt Rizzitano's arm weighing heavier on his. Wrapped up in his own words, he hadn't noticed that the old man was tired from the walk.

'Shall we go back?'

They sat down again on the bench on the veranda.

'Well,' said Montalbano. 'Why don't you tell me how things really went?'

'Yes, of course, that's why I'm here. But it costs me a great deal of effort.'

'I'll try to spare you the effort. Tell you what: I'll say what I think happened, and you correct me if I'm wrong.'

'All right.'

'Well, one day in early July, 1943, Lisetta and Mario came to your house at the foot of the Crasto, where at that moment you were living alone. Lisetta had run away from Serradifalco to rejoin her boyfriend, Mario Cunich, a sailor from the *Pacinotti*, a mother ship that was supposed to leave a few days later—'

The old man raised his hand and the inspector stopped.

'Excuse me, but that's not what happened. And I remember everything, down to the smallest details. The memory of the aged becomes clearer and clearer with time. It has no pity. On the evening of the sixth of July, around nine o'clock, I heard someone knocking desperately at the door. I went to see who it was, and there was Lisetta, who had run away. She'd been raped.'

'On her way from Serradifalco to Vigàta?'

'No. By her father, the night before.'

Montalbano didn't feel like opening his mouth.

'And that was only the beginning,' said the old man. 'The worst was yet to come. Lisetta had confided to me that, now and then, her father – Uncle Stefano, as I used to call him, since we were related – used to take certain liberties with her. One day, Stefano Moscato, who, not long before, had come out of prison and been evacuated to Serradifalco with the rest of the family, discovered the letters that Mario had sent to his daughter. He told her he wanted to talk to her about something important, then took her out to the country, threw the letters in her face, beat her and raped her. Lisetta was . . . she'd never been with a man before. But she didn't create a scandal; she had very strong nerves. The next day she simply ran away and came to see me. I was like a brother to her, more than a brother. The following morning I went into town to tell Mario that Lisetta had come. Mario showed up early that afternoon. I left them alone and went for a walk in the country. When I got back home around seven that evening, Lisetta was alone. Mario had returned to his ship. We made some supper, and then we went to the window to watch the fireworks – that's what they looked like – of the Allied strike on Vigàta. Lisetta finally went upstairs to sleep, in my bedroom. I stayed downstairs and read a book by the light of an oil lamp. That was when . . .'

Rizzitano broke off, exhausted, and heaved a long sigh.

'Would you like a glass of water?'

The old man seemed not to have heard him.

'... that was when I heard someone shouting in the distance. Actually, at first it sounded to me like a wailing animal, a howling dog. But in fact it was Uncle Stefano, calling his daughter. The sound of that voice made my hair stand on end, because it was the agonized, agonizing cry of a cruelly abandoned lover who was suffering and screaming out his pain like an animal; it was not the voice of a father looking for his daughter. It upset me terribly. I opened the door. Outside was total darkness. I shouted that I was alone in the house. I said, "Why come looking for your daughter at my house?" Then suddenly there he was in front of me, as though catapulted. He ran inside like a madman, trembling, insulting me and Lisetta. I tried to calm him and approached him. He punched me in the face and I fell backward, stunned. Finally I noticed he had a pistol in his hand. He said he was going to kill me. Then I made a mistake. I retorted that he only wanted his daughter so he could rape her again. He shot at me but missed; he was too agitated. Then he took better aim, but another shot exploded in the room. I used to keep a loaded shotgun in my room, near the bed. Lisetta had taken it and fired at her father from the top of the stairs. Struck in the shoulder, Uncle Stefano staggered, and his weapon fell from his hand. Coldly, Lisetta ordered him to get out or she would finish him off. I have no doubt she would have done so without hesitation. Uncle Stefano looked his daughter long in the eye, then began to whimper with his mouth closed, and not only, I suspect, because of his wound. Then he turned his back and left. I bolted all the doors and windows. I was terrified, and it was Lisetta who gave me back my courage and strength. We remained barricaded inside the next morning as well. Around three o'clock Mario arrived, we told him what had happened, and he decided to spend the night with us. He didn't want to leave us alone there, since Lisetta's father would surely be back. Around midnight a horrific bombing raid was launched over Vigàta, but Lisetta remained calm because her Mario was with her. On the morning of July ninth, I went to Vigàta to see if the house we owned in town was still standing. I strongly advised Mario not to open the door for anyone and to keep the shotgun within reach.'

He stopped.

'My throat is dry.'

Montalbano ran into the kitchen and returned with a glass and a pitcher of cold water. The old man took the glass in both hands; his whole body was shaking. The inspector felt keenly sorry.

'If you'd like to rest awhile, we can resume later.'

The old man shook his head.

'If I stop now, I'll never resume. I stayed in Vigàta until late afternoon. The house hadn't been destroyed, but it was a tremendous mess: doors and windows blown out by the shock waves, upended furniture, broken glass. I cleaned up as best I could, and that kept me busy till evening. My bicycle was gone from the entrance hall, stolen. So I headed back to the Crasto on foot. It was an hour's walk. Actually I had to walk by the side of the main road because there were so many military vehicles, Italian and German, moving in both directions. The moment I arrived at the top of the dirt road that led to my house, two American fighter-bombers appeared overhead and started machine-gunning and dropping fragmentation bombs. The planes were flying very low to the ground and roaring like thunder. I threw myself into a ditch and almost immediately was struck very hard in the back by something that I first thought was a large stone sent flying by an exploding bomb. In fact it was a military boot, with the foot still inside, severed just above the ankle. I sprang to my feet and started running up the driveway, but I had to stop to vomit. My legs were giving out, and I fell two or three times, as behind me the noise of the aircraft began to fade and I could hear the cries and screams and prayers more clearly, and the orders being shouted between the burning trucks. The instant I set foot in my house, I heard two shots ring out upstairs, quickly, one right after the other. Uncle Stefano, I thought, had managed to get inside the house and carry out his revenge. Near the door there was a big iron bar that was used to bolt it shut. I grabbed it and went upstairs without a sound. My bedroom door was open; a man was standing just inside with his back to me, still holding the revolver in his hand.'

The old man, who until this point hadn't once looked up at the inspector, now stared him straight in the eye.

'In your opinion, do I have the face of a murderer?'

'No,' said Montalbano. 'And if you're referring to the man in the room with the gun in his hand, you can set your mind at rest. You acted out of necessity, in self-defence.'

'Someone who kills a man is still someone who kills a man. The legal formulas come later. What counts is the will of the moment. And I wanted to kill that man, no matter what he had done to Lisetta and Mario. So I raised the rod and dealt him a blow to the nape of the neck with all my might, hoping to shatter his skull. He fell forward, revealing the scene on the bed. There were Mario and Lisetta, naked, clutching one another, in a sea of blood. They must have been making love when they were surprised by the bombs falling so close to the house, and then embraced each other like that out of fear. There was nothing more to be done for them. Something perhaps could still have been done for the man on the floor behind me, who was gasping his last. With a kick I turned him face up. He was some flunky of Uncle Stefano's, a cheap thug. Systematically, with the iron bar, I began to beat his head to a pulp. And then I went crazy. I started running from room to room, singing. Have you ever killed anyone?'

'Yes, unfortunately.'

'You say "unfortunately", which means you felt no satisfaction. What I felt was not so much satisfaction as joy. I felt happy; I sang, as I said. Then I collapsed in a chair, overwhelmed by the horror, horrified with myself. I hated myself. They had managed to turn me into a murderer, and I hadn't been able to resist. On the contrary, I was pleased to have done it. The blood inside me was infected, no matter how hard I might try to cleanse it with reason, education, culture, and whatever else you want. It was the blood of the Rizzitanos, of my grandfather and my father, of men the honest people in town preferred not to mention. Men like them, even worse than them. Then, in my delirium, a possible solution appeared. If Mario and Lisetta were to go on sleeping, then all this horror had never happened. It was a nightmare, a bad dream. And so . . .'

The old man couldn't go on. Montalbano was afraid he would pass out.

'Let me tell the rest. You took the two kids' bodies, transported them to the cave, and set them up there.'

'Yes, but that's easy to say. I had to carry them inside one by one. I was exhausted, and literally soaked with blood.'

'The second cave, the one you put the bodies in, was it also used to store black-market goods?'

'No. My father had closed up the entrance to it with a dry wall of stones. I removed the stones and later put them back in place when I was done. I used flashlights to help me see; we had quite a few at our country house. Now I had to find the symbols of sleep, the ones from the legend. The jug and the bowl with coins were easy enough, but what about the dog? Well, the previous Christmas in Vigàta—'

'I know the whole story,' said Montalbano. 'When the dog was sold at auction, somebody in your family bought it.'

'My father did. But since Mama didn't like it, we put it in a storeroom in the cellar. I remembered it. When I had done everything and closed up the cave with the great hinged boulder, it was pitch dark outside and I felt almost at peace. Lisetta and Mario really were asleep. Nothing had happened. And so the corpse I found upstairs on my return no longer frightened me. It didn't exist; it was the fruit of my war-ravaged imagination. Then utter pandemonium broke out. The house began to shake from bombs exploding just a few yards away, but I couldn't hear any aeroplanes. They were shelling from the ships at sea. I raced outside, afraid I might get buried under the rubble if the house were hit. On the horizon it looked as if day were breaking. What was all that light? I wondered. Suddenly, behind me the house exploded, literally, and I was struck on the head with a piece of debris and passed out. When I opened my eyes, the light on the horizon was even brighter, and I could hear a continuous, distant rumble. I managed to drag myself to the road and started waving and gesturing, but none of the passing vehicles would stop. They were all fleeing. I was in danger of being run over by a truck. Finally, one stopped, and an Italian soldier hoisted me aboard. From what they were saying, I gathered that the American invasion had begun. I begged them to take me with them, wherever they were going. And they did. What happened to me after that I doubt is of any interest to you. I'm very tired.'

'Would you like to lie down awhile?'

Montalbano had to carry him bodily, then helped him to undress.

'Please forgive me,' he said, 'for awakening the sleepers and bringing you back to reality.'

'It had to happen.'

'Your friend Burgio, who was a big help to me, would love to see you again.'

'No, not me. And if you have no objection, you should act as if I never came.'

'No, of course not, I've no objection.'

'Do you want anything else from me?'

'Nothing. Only to say that I'm deeply grateful to you for answering my call.'

They had nothing more to say to each other. The old man looked at his watch so closely he appeared to be sticking it in his eye.

'Let's do this. Let me sleep for an hour or so, then wake me up, call me a taxi, and I'll go back to Punta Ràisi.'

Montalbano drew the blinds over the window and headed for the door.

'Just a minute, Inspector.'

From the wallet he had laid on the night table the old man took out a photograph and handed it to Montalbano.

'This is my youngest granddaughter, seventeen years old. Her name's Lisetta.'

Montalbano went over to a shaft of light. Except for the jeans she was wearing and the motor scooter she was leaning against, this Lisetta was identical to the other, a perfect likeness. He handed the photo back to Rizzitano.

'Excuse me again, but could you bring me another glass of water?'

*

Seated on the veranda, Montalbano answered the questions his policeman's mind was asking. The assassin's body, assuming they'd found it under the rubble, certainly could never have been identified. Lillo's parents had either believed that those remains belonged to their son, or that, according to the peasant's story, he'd been picked up by the soldiers as he was dying. And since they never heard from him again, he must surely have died somewhere. For Stefano Moscato, however, those remains belonged to his triggerman, who after finishing his work – that is, after killing Lisetta, Mario and Lillo and disposing of their bodies – had returned to the house to steal a few things but was crushed under the bombs. Assured that Lisetta was dead, he had come out with the story of the American soldier. But a relative of his from Serradifalco, when he came to Vigàta, had refused to believe it and severed relations with him. The photomontage recalled to mind the photograph the old man had shown him. Montalbano smiled. Elective affinities were a clumsy game compared to the unfathomable convolutions of the blood, which could give weight, form and breath to memory. He glanced at his watch and gave a start. Well over an hour had passed. He went into the bedroom. The old man was enjoying a peaceful sleep, his breathing untroubled, his expression calm and relaxed. He was travelling through the land of dreams, no longer burdened with baggage. He could sleep a long time, since he had a wallet with money and a glass of water on the night table. Montalbano remembered the stuffed dog he'd bought for Livia in Pantelleria. He found it on top of the dresser, hidden behind a box. He put it on the floor, at the foot of the bed, then closed the door softly behind him.

Author's Note

The idea for writing this story came to me when, as a courtesy to two Egyptian student stage directors, we studied *The People of the Cave*, by Taufik al-Hakim, in a class of mine.

It seems therefore appropriate to dedicate this book to my students at the Silvio d'Amico National Academy of the Dramatic Arts, where I have been teaching stage direction for over twenty-three years.

It is boring to repeat, with each new published book, that the events, characters and situations are purely fictional. Still, it is necessary. So while I'm at it, I would like to add that the names of my characters come to me by virtue of their amusing assonances, with no malice intended.

Notes

page 5 – **four large Saracen olive trees** – Very ancient olive trees with gnarled trunks, tangling branches, and very long roots. The name suggests that they date from the time of the Arab conquest of Sicily, which began in earnest in the late ninth century, after more than a century of isolated raids, and lasted until the Norman conquest, which began in 1060.

page 20 – **'a man of honour'** – An epithet that stands for 'mafioso', used mostly by the mafiosi themselves. Tano the Greek's regret for the decline of honour among them is a common refrain among mobsters of the older generation, such as the 'repentant' Tommaso Buscetta.

page 23 – **to speak in what he called Talian** – Many uneducated Sicilians, even in this day of mass media and standardized speech, can only speak the local dialect and tend to struggle with proper Italian. Often what comes out when they attempt to use the national language is a linguistic jumble that is neither fish nor fowl. In such speech the first syllable of the word 'italiano' is often dropped to 'taliano', especially when the preceding word ends in a vowel, as in *'parlare taliano'*.

page 25 – **notify the carabinieri** – The Italian carabinieri are a

337

national police force, bureaucratically separate from local police forces and actually a branch of the military.

page 25 – **'like I'm running a chicken farm here'** – Gallo and Galluzzo both mean 'rooster', the second being a diminutive of the first.

page 34 – **'they think *omertà* is on the decline'** – *Omertà* is the traditional Sicilian 'law of silence', in force particularly among members of the Mafia.

page 36 – **'*madunnuzza biniditta!*'** – 'Blessèd little Madonna!' (Sicilian dialect).

page 36 – **caught in the net, the chamber of death** – A reference to traditional Sicilian tuna- and sword-fishing and the *mattanza*, when the fish are slaughtered. Schools of the fish are caught in nets which are then gradually closed until the space holding them, the *cammara della morte*, becomes very small, like a death chamber.

page 42 – **'the testimony of Cavaliere Misuraca'** – The honorific title of *cavaliere*, bestowed on members of various orders of knighthood (e.g. Cavaliere di Malta, Cavaliere della Repubblica) and often awarded in the modern age to successful men in different areas of business and industry (such as *il cavaliere* Silvio Berlusconi), was given out wholesale during the Fascist period. Cavaliere Misuraca, as the unfolding episode implies, was probably a beneficiary of this Fascist largesse or earned his title for his efforts in war.

page 45 – **government was red, black, or sky blue** – Red refers to the Communist and Socialist parties, black to the Fascist (or now 'Post-Fascist') Party, sky blue to the now-defunct Christian Democratic Party.

page 50 – 'the *repubblichini*?' – These were the members and supporters of the so-called Republic of Salò, the puppet government instituted in 1943 under the Nazi occupation in the North Italian town of the same name, after German parachutists boldly snatched Mussolini away from the anti-Fascist partisans who had captured him. The 'government' was made up of die-hard Fascists under the recently deposed and now resurrected Duce.

page 51 – **the first Fascist militias** – These were the *fasci di combattimento*, an association of private militias that engaged in strike-breaking, street violence and other forms of political action and intimidation. The Fascist movement was born from these groups.

page 54 – '**Asinara**' – A high-security prison on the island of the same name.

page 60 – *càlia e simenza* – A mix of roasted chickpeas and pumpkin seeds; sometimes peanuts are added.

page 78 – '*Il Mezzogiorno*' – This is an actual newspaper. Its name means 'The South' (or, literally, 'Midday').

page 79 – '*Essere Donna*' – The magazine is purely fictional; its name means 'To Be a Woman'.

page 108 – '**a traitor or repenter**' – In Italy, Mafia turncoats who turn state's witness are called *pentiti*, or 'repenters'.

page 125 – '*L'è el dì di mort, alegher!*' – 'It's the Day of the Dead, oh joy!' (Milanese dialect). Delio Tessa (1886–1939) is a well-known Milanese dialect poet. The Day of the Dead, November 2, is commonly called All Souls' Day in English.

page 128 – **Customs Police** – This is the Guardia di Finanza, a police force subordinate to the Ministry of Finance and responsible for overseeing customs, state monopolies and taxes. Their duties include serving as the national coastguard.

page 141 – *pasta 'ncasciata* – A casserole of *pasta corta* – that is, elbow macaroni, penne, ziti, mezzi ziti, or something similar – tomato sauce, minced beef, Parmesan cheese and béchamel.

page 141 – **'Give land to those who work!'** – In Italian, *'La terra a chi lavora!'* This was the rallying cry of the land-reform movement that, in the late 1940s, demanded the break-up of the large landed estates, much of whose vast territories (*latifondi*) lay fallow while the peasantry went hungry.

page 163 – **'*podestà*'** – The head of the municipal government, equivalent to the mayor, in the Fascist period. It was an appointed, not elected, office.

page 171 – **Sex standing up . . . to a bad end.** – *'Fùttiri addritta e caminari na rina / portanu l'omu a la ruvina'* (Sicilian proverb).

page 173 – **National Police** – The carabinieri.

page 173 – **'outstanding corpse'** – The term *cadavere eccellente* – is Italian jargon for the dead body of an important personage, especially when the death has occurred in shady circumstances.

page 174 – **'Falcone and Borsellino!'** – Giovanni Falcone and Paolo Borsellino were prominent investigating magistrates in the struggle against the Mafia in Sicily, both murdered by the mob in 1992.

page 180 – **'Epiphany of 1943'** – In Italy the Christmas holiday lasts until the first day after the Epiphany (January 6).

page 181 – **'Gentile'** – Giovanni Gentile (1875–1944) was a prominent Italian philosopher and politician of Sicilian birth (Castelvetrano, province of Trapani), author of many important works of philosophy from the turn of the century onwards and editor and organizer of the *Enciclopedia Italiana* – (1925–1943). As minister of education under the Fascist government from 1922 to 1924, he instituted sweeping reforms of the national educational system; as president of two commissions for the reform of the Italian constitution, he also contributed to laying the institutional foundations of the Fascist corporate state in 1925. Though his political influence steadily declined thereafter, he remained loyal to the regime until the bitter end, even serving as president of the Accademia d'Italia under the Nazi collaborationist Republic of Salò, established after the armistice of September 8, 1943. He was killed by anti-Fascist partisans in Florence on April 15, 1944.

page 181 – '**lyceums**' – The Italian word is *liceo* (sing.), which, like the French *lycée*, harks back to the ancient Greek *Lykeion*, the Gymnasium near Athens where Aristotle taught.

page 200 – **fresh anchovies** *all'agretto* – Baked in a sauce of lemon juice.

page 230 – **La Vuccirìa** – The large, old market district in Palermo.

page 231 – *mèusa* – Calf's spleen sliced into thin strips and cooked in fat.

page 233 – **Giovani Italiane** – This was the compulsory Fascist youth organization (the 'Young Italians') for adolescents aged sixteen and seventeen. The groups for younger children were the Figli della Lupa (Children of the She-Wolf) and the Balilla (named after the boy who incited the Genoese to rebel against the Austrian occupation in 1746). The girls' uniform of the Giovani Italiane consisted of a black pleated skirt, a white blouse with an M (for Mussolini) on the front, and a black beret.

page 267 – **pasta al forno** – A casserole of pasta and a variety of other ingredients that may include meat, eggs, vegetables, tomato, or cream sauces, and so on. It is a typically southern Italian dish.

page 276 – **sacred area of the Phoenicians** – Early Phoenician settlements existed in coastal Sicily and its surrounding islands before the Greek era. The most important Phoenician centres were Panormos (modern Palermo), Soloeis and Motya (modern Mozia). Later Carthaginian settlement (fifth and fourth centuries BC) in the southern and western regions of the island reinforced this Sicilian link to Phoenician civilization, opposing these regions to the Greek culture fast gaining prominence in much of the rest of the island. Following the Punic Wars, when Rome defeated Carthage, all of Sicily became Roman (after 210 BC). In the Middle Ages, the Arab rule of the island from the late ninth to the mid-eleventh century again revived Sicily's historic links to the cultures of North Africa and the Middle East.

page 283 – **'pasta con le sarde, and purpi alla carrettera'** – *Pasta con le sarde* is a classic Sicilian dish served usually with bucatini, broad spaghetti-like strings that are hollow in the middle. The sauce consists of fresh sardines, tops of wild fennel, pine nuts, raisins, garlic and saffron. *Purpi alla carrettera* is octopus served in a sauce of olive oil, lemon and a great deal of hot pepper.

page 306 – **RAI regional news** – The RAI (Radiotelevisione Italiana) is the government-owned national television network, which also has regional news broadcasts.

page 310 – **'Fininvest, Ansa'** – Fininvest is the financial and media conglomerate owned by Silvio Berlusconi; Ansa is an acronym for Azienda Nazionale Stampa Associata, the national news agency.

NOTES

page 312 — ***Corriere*** — *Corriere della Sera*, the Milan daily and the premier newspaper of Italy.

page 320 — **'leghista'** — A member or supporter of the formerly secessionist Northern League (Lega Nord), a right-wing political party known for its prejudice against foreign immigrants and southern Italians.

Notes compiled by Stephen Sartarelli

picador.com

blog
videos
interviews
extracts

Praise for the Montalbano series

'The novels of Andrea Camilleri breathe out
the sense of place, the sense of humour, and the sense
of despair that fill the air of Sicily. To read him is
to be taken to that glorious, tortured island'
Donna Leon

'Both farcical and endearing, Montalbano is a cross between
Columbo and Chandler's Philip Marlowe, with the added
culinary idiosyncrasies of an Italian Maigret . . . The smells,
colours and landscapes of Sicily come to life'
Guardian

'Sly and witty . . . Montalbano must pick his way through a
labyrinth of corruption, false clues, vendettas – and delicious
meals. The result is funny and intriguing with a fluent
translation by New York poet Stephen Sartarelli'
Observer

'Delightful . . . funny and ebulliently atmospheric'
The Times

'This savagely funny police procedural proves that
sardonic laughter is a sound that translates ever so smoothly
into English'
New York Times Book Review

'Camilleri is as crafty and charming a writer as
his protagonist is an investigator'
Washington Post